Peaches on the Pine

TWD Hughes

Cover image: detail of Inume Pass, Utagawa Hiroshige (歌川広重)

Public domain, via Wikimedia Commons

1

As I bit into the peach, the crisp, sour juice caused my head to reel. A moment later, the oozing, slightly blood-like liquid condensed to a bubbling sensation on the roof of my mouth.

You might think of a peach as all luscious sweetness. But for me, it is now forever balanced on the edge of a smarting acidity. Jarring my senses, it jolted back a distant thought into the current.

It was strange to think this was the first time that I had eaten a peach since that summer a decade before. I had certainly made no conscious effort to preserve the memory of that year since returning to England and setting about the business of work, real work, in a familiar environment.

Because I had thought my time in Japan was behind me. Now, I viewed it as the final act of childhood, to be put away as one folds neatly and shelves the clothes no longer fit to wear. When I first went there, I'd thought it would be an extended holiday. I was escaping change; desperately trying to keep things the same. The irony of moving to the other side of the world with no goal other than continuing on the same path as before was lost on me at that time.

Things didn't stay the same. In fact, I found the death of an old, tired life, and the birth of an entirely new one.

And so eating the peach, the symbol of Takada – of the mountain Peach Town – brought back those caustic, undeniable months; put into context all that followed. In that brief moment, I felt the waters lap against me, heard the whisper of complicity wash back once again.

2

The Matsugawa River flows through its namesake pines to the small mountain city of Takada. Its source lies high in the peaks of the Central Japanese Alps, parallel to the long, fertile Iizu valley, past the plains of rice fields and the rich foothills of orchards. In late summer, as I first found it, when the last of the snows have long since fed the course and the torrent abated, the Matsugawa runs lazily to join the broad wash of the Tenkyo, as it rolls back down the valley's length to the sea.

On its way to Takada, this Pine River gushes first in runnels and rivulets, pulsing through steep cut gorges, then pounds less playfully as the mass of water moves inexorably down. On this section, the flow moves less with its infant syncopation, but with a rhythmic certainty of purpose, still freighted with its wild origins. Even in this middle stage of the Matsugawa's course there are numerous cascades, small cataracts where bed rocks splinter the falling river into fragments.

Then, just above the city, tall ranks of pines clamour round, beyond the reaches of the neat rows of peach and pear trees. And here is the series of dams that channel the river, taming it. This intervention into the movement of the water allows farmers the consistent irrigation of the slopes, with their little allotments and allowances of land, even as it frustrates occasional kayakers, the solitary traffic at this altitude.

A road lopes alongside here, looping uphill as the waters plummet down. It crosses and re-crosses the course at a great height, the connective struts of bridges linking the two sides of the gorge. It is an endless dance of the magnetic and the attracted; the luminous intensity of the light, and the fervour of insect. And as the road and river play, flitting to and fro, now closer at hand, now further away, they are always drawn near by the gravity of their passions.

So it continues upstream, until the road grows bored with the sport and makes one last, incisive move, breaking free to cross the mountains to the next valley.

Anyone who has stood in dry summer, facing downwind, downstream, on one of the broad beds of bone-like rocks before a dam, bleached white to giddiness, and looked out across the lock gates to the peaceful city below, knows a feeling of simple satisfaction. You too would admire the engineer for his invention, and stand simply in the backwood stillness of the mountains, understanding for the first time the empty beauty of water.

3

Around the shoulders of the world the immeasurable bulk of Russia hung limply. Down in the blankness of space I imagined multitudes of villages, specks of humanity in a hostile landscape; the bravery of quiet toil in the wilds of the planet. The vastness of the terrain we flew over seemed to beckon to us, darkly, as we chased time down across the continents, to arrive a day late. First Europe, then Asia, until finally the grave wasteland gave out into another immensity, the Pacific Ocean, with the Far East standing as society's last post before this frontier.

Forged between these two unforgiving wildernesses, the narrow sliver of our destination seemed a paltry final station of the known world, a fallen eyelash in a sea of tears, floating at the extremity of civilisation. This collection of islands, buffeted by typhoons and rocked by earthquakes, was our objective, and would be our home for the foreseeable future.

Japan was not unlike where we had come from, really. Michael and I had flown in from London, leaving behind one proud, strictly insignificant collection of islands for another. Just as we are both part of Europe, but also stand alone and apart from it, so Japan is quintessentially Asian – yet bound by the siege mentality of its history, indebted and defiant to its closest relations.

Of course, we did not know any of this when we boarded the flight to Tokyo. A skim through the cultural notes in the guidebook and a familiarisation with 'please' and 'thank you' in a new language had been enough to placate our imaginations. We gleaned only a glib mix of the garish and the sombre, the dualistic Japanese consciousness.

The in-flight experience had been a thoroughly charming affair. Content to make a game show of the safety instructions, the pretty flight attendants bobbed and mewed their way through the procedure; the prize a life jacket under your seat. Later, when gamely trying the traditional Japanese airline lunch, I experienced for the first time the stumbling block of expectations in the pursuit of food.

"Is there any fish in the 'traditional lunch'?" I enquired, fully expecting the answer to be 'yes'.

"No" came the unequivocal answer. "No fish in the lunch. Vegetable, meat, chicken only."

Disliking all aquatic food, I welcomed this unexpected news, and crudely dug with chopsticks into the lunch. Indeed there were vegetables, after a fashion; the fashion being cold, crisp and looking uncomfortably like excised bunions. Indeed there was meat, though its provenance shall forever remain a mystery. First off, I reached an impasse at the chicken.

Lovingly coated in a crispy shell and looking deceptively like chicken nuggets, I bit into the chunk hungrily… to discover that, while it was indisputably chicken, it was also wrapped, lovingly, in a delicate layer of salmon paté. I removed the article from my mouth with as much oriental control as I could, and contented myself with having learnt a lesson.

"Excuse me," I ventured, when the attendant returned to collect the dishes. "But there *was* fish in the meal."

"Oh no," the lady replied. "No fish in the food."

"Look," I said, pointing to the orange mixture, oozing from the hunk of chicken, balancing it as decorously as I could between the two slender pieces of wood.

"Oh, maybe yes," she admitted, looking squarely at the morsel. "But no fish. Just fish sauce," she beamed, definitively satisfied.

"No, maybe not then," I sighed, probing the eviscerated salmon.

***

Michael and I had never met before we arrived at the airport to share a flight. Thankfully he shared the same gently enthusiastic, somewhat wry anticipation of the whole experience that I myself was nurturing. An easy going young man, seeking, as we all were in those days, to extend the university experience into our middle twenties, it became obvious why he had been employed to teach at the private school, where an outgoing personality was the number one requirement. With my more reserved manner, I was to be working in the public system in the same town.

Still – like myself – he was a product of that certain tier of British schooling, where the pastoral care instils a vague notion of superiority, while completely neglecting to inculcate the means to realise this beyond a code of massaging connections. And like myself, I felt he was unable to work with this.

Michael was out to protract the long summer of his youth by embarking on the 21st Century version of the Grand Tour; taking liberties in Asia on the meal ticket of the novelty of our Caucasian roots. This made me feel a little less like the joker in the pack – or the *gaijin* (the foreigner) in the pile of *hashi* (chopsticks) – but rather part of some strange rite of passage for a certain character type, compelled by unorthodoxy to escape, if only for a short time, and if only for show.

I watched everything with a detached, cool eye. Michael was a much more straightforward proposition – and all the more immediately likeable because of his enthusiasm and positivity. We were about to be transplanted into the heat of an Asian summer, but he was already brown from a season of surfing. Looking every inch the affable

8

handsome bum, with his shaggy dyed hair, goatee and slouchy dress, he was thankfully just English enough to avoid any stereotyping smothering his character.

Among the few non-orientals on the flight back to Tokyo's recently constructed Narita airport, we felt a pioneering spirit from the start – a buccaneering duo beyond the frontier. On board, the Japanese seemed to travel in streamlined matriarchal units, with an elderly lady in a sunhat and dark glasses wordlessly overseeing the enterprise, as if playing chaperone to the others in her cadre.

At once quietly cosmopolitan and also stolidly practical, these people were going home, temporary travellers in an unfamiliar landscape, now returning to the known. So, moving in reverse, lost in a sea of smooth faces and sleek, black hair, we laughed to each other and steeled ourselves for a future of ineluctable attention-seeking based on mere appearances and alien customs.

We flew through the night, skirting the edges of wild Kamchatka, the empty Russian peninsula of bears, marshes and mountains, the final marker of anything even tangentially European, emerging in the midday of another world, on the shores of Asia. We relaxed and gave ourselves over to the sinking feeling, nestling down into the bulk of the plane as it descended, sometimes in parallel with our stomachs, sometimes not. Apprehensive, excited, we collected our baggage, left the airport and headed out into the bright sunshine of Japan.

4

It would be nice to think that the arrival, the triumphant and cinematic sweep out into the fresh light and the alluring smells of another continent was a cool, measured affair. It was not. The summer we had left behind in England was slowly winding down to a gentle close. It was the first breath of the hot months' segue into autumn, the seamless merge of season with season that we were used to. But here the blast of hot, murky air that hit us when we stepped outside before taking the train into central Tokyo came like the winnowing discharge from a furnace.

I sat down immediately, crowding my bags around me in the shade of the platform. Michael smoked a cigarette, both of us gasping for air. I wondered quite how much of this I could stand – whether I would fight it, or be melted down and remoulded into some form I could not yet imagine. Michael looked down at me, pityingly, oblivious that his sweatbands had now been upgraded from lifestyle accessory to survival tool.

The platform was at once familiar – the clean symmetry of the track laid everything out before us. But the voice over the tannoy, indecipherable.

Once on the train back into Tokyo we could relax again. The cooled interior with its tinted glass and revolving rows of seats sped us through a landscape that was shocking in its vividness. The greens of the fields, parcelled here and there into a jigsaw of quadrilaterals, had a deep, submarine lustre. At a short remove from the tracks the hills rose up sharply, even here, only a little inland from the sea. The distances between these components of the land was minimal. Hills rose perpendicularly out of agricultural land, fields of crops were growing right up to the edge of a river bank; scattered houses seemed to burst out of the earth they were rooted upon. But regardless of the jumble, each module vibrantly occupied its own space.

Then there were the pylons. Immediately obvious, and so incongruous in the rich gloss of greens and earthy chthonic tones that washed over the scenery, lines of cables towed the sky along, surmounting the hills at a right angle to the railway, running parallel to the embankment of the canal; dashing off at high speed in every direction. They lent the air a disingenuous quality, bisecting the sky and carving up a portion of the light, holding back its moiety, letting the rest pass.

Having been awake for nearly 24 hours, we were both now tiring, sitting in the eye of a storm of images. As we moved into the outer suburbs of the vast sandpit of the capital city it began to drizzle, a light shower casting a grey patina on the views passing the windows.

In every direction the city rumbled on; identical signs, the same shops and the same mad little houses crammed in. Rather than fitting into the precisely composed space between field and tree as earlier in the journey, now they were squeezed in next to two other identically sized, microscopic detached houses, though each with their peculiar details. Some had traditional roofs with elaborate tiles and vast eaves, some featured apologetic bushes, bunched in a garden scarcely bigger than a sofa. All had the same air of maintaining privacy despite the overcrowding, with dense net curtains defending the windows.

Everything grew together in a wild patch of mixed bedfellows. Car garages, bowling alleys, restaurants, chemists and bakers stood shoulder to shoulder with houses, apartment blocks and what appeared to be uniformly white, low security institutions.

"What are all those little prisons," Michael asked, just at the moment the same thought occurred to me.

"I don't know. I mean, you don't expect the most salubrious view of a city from the railway tracks. But surely these can't *all* be for locking people up," I said.

"Maybe that's why they have such safe streets; zero tolerance. You get the angle of your bow wrong when you say 'good morning' to the people next door, and you're thrown in the neighbourhood chokey for the night."

Michael made this last comment through closed eyes, so he didn't see the answer to our puzzle come wandering out of the next of these buildings, wearing a cap, clutching his multi-coloured umbrella and swinging his schoolbag from his arm. They were schools.

Without time to wonder at the implications, I too closed my eyes. The next thing we knew, we were in Shinjuku station. We had been warned this was a lively place.

Specifically, it was the world's busiest train station. And as I would later conclude, it makes little difference what time you pass through; Shinjuku is always an infernal experience, but lunch time on a working day seemed a peculiarly astringent trial by fire.

Whereas main stations in other world cities may be painful affairs in their own right, this feeling is usually tempered by a nostalgic drama fostered by the surroundings. Shinjuku has nothing of a Grand Central. Housed in a gargantuan modern building that is linked in an enfilade of insidious concourses, there is nothing spectacular until you escape the immediate vicinity and are assaulted by the skyscrapers of the district. To do this, though, you must first do battle with legions of people, streaming through low-ceilinged corridors and harshly lit lobbies, passing maps of apocryphal origin and indecipherable expression.

This environment is the natural habitat of the common Japanese white collar worker. You might imagine a suited salaryman picking his way nervously through the assembled masses, watchful against soiling his briefcase. The reality is that he pushes and bolts, seemingly enjoying the sport, though rarely affected with the kind of ego that inflames at the crossing of swords on a daily commute in a London or Paris. The ticket machine is his armoury, a corner of a packed train his hunting ground; an unsuspecting woman's bottom the helpless prey to his pinch.

Along with this stoic demographic were many more strictly defined castes. The schoolchild, girls wearing loose legwarmer socks, or 'roossu sockussu', boys shod with Nike Air Force One basketball shoes or the ubiquitous Converse canvas sneakers, and crowned with fanciful manga hairstyles.

Then moving up the age range, the working class young man, with his ginger dyed hair and garage overalls, or the designer label-clad young lady about town.

However, while taking in these sights, we were also attempting to fight our way out of the station. The same sign in Japanese seemed to be worded differently in English ten times over in different locations; intricately creative versions leaving you wondering if you were still headed to your destination, or were simply lost in translation of the poetic renderings of Japanese compass points and the fanciful physical world.

But by which way must we leave the station of a thousand exits? Reduced to cartoonish simplicity, our emailed instructions suggested a modest affair, little more confusing than a double fronted shop.

Michael buttonholed a passing corporate footsoldier, then confidently set off, and I trailed my moaning suitcase behind, hurrying across the pedestrian crossings that lay in the mouth of subterranean carparks, deep in the guts of Shinjuku. Then suddenly we were out, looking up at the blank office windows and slabs of geodesic cladding. It was nothing like the small, orderly courtyard gardens I knew from pictures in my guidebook; the intensely still, interior spaces which were not even for sitting in, but contemplating at arms length.

The city hummed and the people came and went, in and out of the sixty gates of Shinjuku station, while we waited for our bus home. Taxis, laced with white doily headrests, drove up to the foot of tall buildings, where pairs of white-gloved stewards ran to and fro, halting pedestrians on the pavement.

There was an immaculate, almost fussy quality to the public transport, to the taxis and buses and trains, with the cleanliness of their floors; the faultless gleam of their crew. These three modes of transport shocked the traveller each in their own incongruous way: the trains through their alien futurism; the buses pulling up in their bulkily American swagger; the taxis with their odd mixture of asexual 1970s styling, automatic rear doors, and antimacassars. Everything was present to please the fare, but there remained the faintly menacing air that stepping on the grass was nevertheless strictly *verboten*.

Finally, rolling out of Tokyo, we counted the vertiginous golf ranges, baseball grounds and plumly perpendicular living arrangements. As afternoon ashened into evening, the bus climbed the beautiful highway. We went up into the hills, the road rising on stilts, running on cuttings alongside rivers, then banking around peaks. Soon, the clouds hung on the branches of the pines and we both drifted in and out of sleep, waking each other at intervals to point out a particularly astonishing view, or a road sign warning of possible monkey pedestrians. Michael began a conversation with three elderly ladies, remarkable for its sedulous good nature as much as its staggering lack of progression.

By the time we arrived in Takada, I knew that Michael was a funny, friendly guy. He could put anyone at their ease. He would flourish in a new setting.

But already, too, I felt sure that neither of us were the exciting characters here. Our arrival was not so important. I was sure I would be someone who could easily come and go. I was still hoping I could escape something, that by keeping life at a continent's distance, I could keep hold of my youth.

We got off the bus in the middle of the night, met our agent and she set us up in our apartments. I went to sleep tucked between an ageless tomorrow, and a yesterday which already seemed stretched across broad continents of time.

5

I woke up the next morning at dawn and was quite unable, despite being drained of energy and willpower, to get back to sleep. The heat was there already, waiting for me in the corners of my apartment, sitting in the far vertices of the ceiling with folded arms. Meanwhile, I had slept on the floor, on the thin mattress that was to be my bed. I was rather glad of this arrangement for the moment; stretched out on the cool matting, I lay beneath the miasma of warm air that floated in suspension at waist height. How it would feel in winter I had yet to imagine.

I dressed and walked out to the wide balcony running the breadth of the two modest rooms which made up my apartment. The sun was already coming up over the mountains. The view, above the tin roofs of the houses below, was spectacular. From this vantage point, half-way up the main route into town, I could look down to the south east, to the formidable, unbroken mass of hills that formed the Southern Alps National Park and lower wall of the Izu valley. If I turned 180 degrees and looked upslope, craning my neck around the partition between my balcony and that of next door, I could see the edge of the nearest mountain, the harbinger of the great Central Japanese Alps.

Standing directly behind the city centre with its municipal buildings and civic offices, Mt. Shuetsu loomed in the early morning haze. This north-west lining of mountains was closer by than those in the panorama downslope, and Shuetsu-san itself, though no taller than its brothers, was nevertheless rather more imposing, because of its more dramatically prominent features, its craggier peak; but mostly because of the audacious proximity it had wheedled from the town.

It was no longer afraid of humans, and now spent its time encroaching on the outskirts.

Before this edifice ran the stilted central Chuo Expressway from left to right, down the valley towards the flat, coastal areas, and up towards a break in the mountains and the long descent towards Tokyo.

My apartment was an economical affair; two 10 feet by 8 feet rooms with tatami matting on the floor. These would serve for living and sleeping, and could be configured separately using the sliding doors between them, or be made into one large room by removing them. The bathroom was tiny, with a cramped bath-tub, basin and western style toilet squeezed in beneath a roof that was barely higher than my head. With no window, it was a remarkably intimate business conducting one's ablutions, and the strange air venting meant that the rush of wind from passing lorries a floor below sent a draught down your back while you showered.

Nevertheless, along with the generous kitchen and hall (and ignoring the lack of furniture in general) it made a pleasant personal space from the inside.

From the outside it was a different matter. The night before, too tired to be critical, I had noticed the building's tired squalor. It was lucky that I had not allowed this to put me off, for by daylight, it was no worse than other homes around it, and in several cases it was somewhat smarter. It immediately became obvious that the Japanese were not obsessed with their houses in the way that the English were. The concept of making a show of care, let alone of competitive affluence, for the benefit of the neighbours was not known - at least not in this isolated mountain city. In confined gardens, pieces of junk metal lay in heaps with small bushes, building materials and recyclable waste. Rotting corpses of scooters were propped up next to front doors; ornamental trees were permanent stands for ancient bicycles. If there was not an immediate sense of purpose to each discarded part, there was at least the suggestion that everything was patiently waiting while its destiny slowly became clear.

I walked up the long, broad avenue in the direction of the Shuetsu-san. From its flanks descended a gravid wash of mist; not dense to the sight, but seemingly weighing heavily upon the air. At this time in the morning it was initially refreshing, but soon became tiring. It made the air thick, fleshy. On some mornings it would become an oppressive barrier, heated by the sun, close and cumbersome.

For now, the richness of this air was having an effect on me. The anaemic, polluted breaths of Tokyo were a distant memory as I took in drag after drag of the sky. I could almost imagine the vapour condensing in my lungs, churning around inside my body. There was a magic in this mountain-distilled mixture, intoxicating and powerful, perhaps dangerous in its heady strength.

When I had walked straight upwards a little way I stopped and turned around. My road stretched out as far as I could see in the haze, unforgivingly direct towards the valley floor. All around there was the lush bed of insect voices which I had half-heard in my sleep, topped by the irrepressible lead of what sounded like a cricket. It resonated on and on, in a remorseless chorus. The song never ended, and if one singer paused to take breath, his loss was immediately subsumed into the mass of the greater choir, the change in continuity suggested not so much by sound, but by a fluctuation in the pressure of the air itself.

After a few unproductive sallies to the left and right, trying to further acquaint myself with my immediate neighbourhood, I headed back down towards my apartment block, looking over the shimmering valley. The heaviness of the morning air was now dissolving, and I could see clearly the main road carving the plain beneath me. An out of town shopping strip reared itself up from a sea of arable land, lining the road as it disappeared north, an endlessly recurring liturgy of car park, supermarket, car park, supermarket, until the tongue of the road gave out into the distance, lost in the echo of the opposing walls of hills.

I had the rest of the day to myself. None of my future colleagues had yet arrived in Japan and Michael, having barely set his bags down, was already being pushed into the serious round of meeting and greeting at his private school, coerced by the owner.

***

Our agent, Mrs Masada, found employees like myself for the local city education department, but she also expertly sourced teachers for some of the private language schools in the area. She was the constant go-between; an eternal intermediary between two cultures and languages that did not truly understand each other. As such, she was in a position of some power in the little community. Her detractors suggested she used this position to her own advantage, playing both sides off against each other. Tales abounded of how she managed people and situations, conducting them shrewdly, then hiding the reasoning behind a shrug and an explanation that something was 'the Japanese way' – and she was as incapable of altering this as an outsider.

Could this be the whole story? I privately loved the idea of this insidious, calculating mind being ascribed to a middle-aged Japanese lady. Whatever the truth was, I began to see how she typified both the complementary and the contradictory aspects of our cultures: oriental bloody-mindedness clothed in formal reticence, and western motives, self-seeking and Byzantine, all hidden behind subtler charm.

I returned later that day from a trip to the convenience store to find her waiting for me in my apartment. As I opened the door I heard a rustling coming from my nominal bedroom, then Mrs Masada scooted out. The room was strewn with the eviscerated contents of my suitcase. It was immediately clear they we not merely lying where I had thrown them in my haste, hours before.

Strangely, I was quite relaxed and prepared for this kind of intrusion, knowing that as an intermediary of the landlord and general fixer, she had a set of keys. Besides, I had nothing to hide.

She was an interesting proposition. Short, painfully thin and immaculately well-dressed, presented in sombre navy and black, slyly flattering and friendly, with a face that was verging on caricature. Grave, hooded eyes framed by a pendulous fringe, with a pixie nose that was twitching now – possibly due to her being caught red-handed – and a wide, thin mouth. When she was thinking she looked vacant. Smiling transformed the lower part of her face only, all blankness above; prominent cheekbones, and those heavily cowled eyes untouched by anything breaking out below.

Was there something serpentine about the mouth? I struggled to read anything into it.

Chiemi Masada chose her words carefully, and the listener could imagine the workings taking place inside her head to select the best medium for her intentions; surreptitiously creative. We bowed towards each other, smiling, only me sweating in the closeness.

"I went out walking early this morning and I looked around. It's very beautiful here."

Mr Clifford Hughes
NHS Number: 4708508980
DoB: 29/11/1929
30 Ryebeck Court
Pickering
YO18 7FA

Kirkbymoorside Surgery
The Old School
Tinley Garth
Kirkbymoorside
York
YO62 6AR

=========Repeat Medication=========

- ☐ **Alendronic acid 70mg tablets**, 4 tablet, take one weekly with a full glass of water and do not lie down for 30mins after taking, Last Issued: Friday 24 Feb 2017, Next Issue Due: Fri 24 Mar 2017

- ✓☐ **Lisinopril 2.5mg tablets**, 28 tablet, . Stop if you have diarrhoea/vomiting and restart when you are well again, Last Issued: Friday 24 Feb 2017, Next Issue Due: Fri 24 Mar 2017

- ☐ **Natecal D3 600mg/400unit chewable tablets (Chiesi Ltd)**, 60 tablet, take one twice daily, Last Issued: Friday 24 Feb 2017, Next Issue Due: Sun 26 Mar 2017

- ☐ **Paracetamol 500mg tablets**, 200 tablet, take 1 or 2 4 times/day for for pain When Required, Last Issued: Thursday 01 Dec 2016, Next Issue Due: Thu 29 Dec 2016

- ✓☐ **Tamsulosin 400microgram modified-release capsules**, 30 capsule, take one daily at night for your prostate symptoms, Last Issued: Friday 24 Feb 2017, Next Issue Due: Sun 26 Mar 2017

- ☐ **Ultrabase cream (Derma UK Ltd)**, 500 gram, apply liberally to dry skin areas at least twice a day and after washing, Last Issued: Thursday 26 Mar 2015, Next Issue Due: Thu 23 Apr 2015

434916
Ordered 27/03/2017

PATIENTS – please read the notes overleaf

Should you pay prescription charges? Read all the statements in **Part 1** opposite. You don't have to pay a prescription charge if any of the statements apply to you (the patient) on the day you are asked to pay. (A valid War Pension exemption certificate only entitles you to free prescriptions for your accepted disablement.) Put a cross in the first box in **Part 1** that applies to you, read the declaration and complete and sign **Part 3**.

Benefits which DO NOT provide exemption. You are NOT entitled to exemption from prescription charges because you receive Pension Credit Savings Credit, Incapacity Benefit, Disability Living Allowance, Contribution based Jobseeker's Allowance or Contribution based Employment and Support Allowance. Only those benefits listed in **Part 1** provide exemption. An HC3 certificate does not entitle you to free prescriptions.

Evidence. You may be asked to provide evidence to show that you do not have to pay. You could show the relevant benefit award notice, or an exemption or pre-payment certificate. If you cannot show evidence at that time you can still get your prescription items free but NHS England may arrange to check your entitlement later if you do not show proof (see paragraph about Penalty Charges).

If you have to pay a prescription charge. You (or your representative) should put in **Part 2** the amount you have paid and then sign and complete **Part 3**.

Information about who must pay prescription charges and who is exempt can be found at www.nhs.uk/healthcosts. See leaflets HC11 (available online) or HC12 (available in hard copy - phone 0300 123 0849 to order). You can also ring 0300 330 1343 for information.

Not entitled to free prescriptions? A prescription pre-payment certificate (PPC) may reduce the cost of getting your prescription items dispensed. Call 0300 330 1341 for details of PPCs, the savings they offer and how to buy one. Buy on line at www.nhsbsa.nhs.uk or get an application form (FP95) from your pharmacy.'

Do you need a refund? If you are unsure if you are entitled to free prescriptions you should pay for the prescription item(s) and ask for a receipt form FP57. **You must get the FP57 form when you pay for the item(s), you cannot get the form later.** If you find you didn't have to pay, you can claim your money back up to 3 months after paying. The FP57 form tells you what to do.

Patient Representative. If you are unable to collect your prescription yourself, someone can take your completed form for you. If you claim exemption you must complete Part 1 or if you pay prescription charges your representative must complete Part 2. Your representative **must** complete Part 3. **Anyone who collects a schedule 2 or 3 controlled drug must sign the box in Part 1 when they collect the item(s)** and provide proof of identity if necessary.

Data collection. Information about the prescription items on this form will be processed centrally to pay monies due to the pharmacist, doctor or appliance contractor for the items they have supplied to you. The NHS will also use the information to analyse what has been prescribed and the cost. NHS England and the NHS Business Services Authority may use the information from this form to prevent and detect fraud and incorrectness in the NHS.

Penalty Charges. If it is found that you should have paid for your prescription items, you will face penalty charges and may be prosecuted under the powers introduced by the Health Act 1999. Routine checks are carried out on exemption claims including some where proof may have been shown. You may be contacted in the course of such checks.

"Ah yes, and you know, did you drink the water?" asked Chiemi.

"Why?" I enquired. "It's not poisonous, is it?"

"Yes. Of course not. It is very clean and healthy water. Mountain water," she said, eyeing me coolly. "It makes the fruit healthy."

Now warming to her job of settling me in, she seemed worried that there were aspects of the four small rooms that had escaped me. There were.

"Um, William-san you know, you must take off your outdoor shoes in the apartment, you know", admonished Chiemi. I looked down; my feet were shod in dusty walking boots. One of the chunky heels was trailing a dragnet consisting of three hairs and a fragment of sandwich from my 7-11 lunch.

"I'm terribly sorry," I said, as I laughingly took them off, placing them where instructed in the sunken stone area by the front door. Chiemi smiled, her eyes remained constant.

She then fixed me with the gravest of expressions, the eyes narrowing to murder holes of focus.

"William-san, you know, in Japan a teacher is a very good job. Maybe not like in your country. People will look up to you. You must behave in a good way."

"Yes. I understand," I answered, wondering where this would lead.

"You must behave in a good way for your school, because people know who you are," she said, a menace now creeping into her voice.

"I see," I replied, now genuinely worried. What was this building to? I knew there was an elaborate system of social dictums that needed to be navigated, but surely I could not have fallen foul of these already.

"The city education board are looking forward to meeting you to-morrow. But... " she trailed off. The corners of her mouth twitched downwards.

"William, you know," continued Chiemi, tellingly shearing my name of the honorific -san suffix. "We are a little worried about what the new teachers will wear tomorrow, when we meet the education board."

"Well, if you want me to put on a kimono, you'll have to get me drunk first," I ventured, trying to ease the tension. Once again the nerves at the sides of the wide mouth sank, in an unwittingly inverted smile.

"It is not so funny. I cannot see a suit. Did you bring a suit with you?" she asked. "You were told to bring a suit. If you do not have one we have time to go and buy a suit before tomorrow. We could lend you the money until your first pay."

"It's OK," I assured her, amused at the singular way they had been approaching what was, for them, clearly a difficult problem to discuss. "I have two suits with me, here in the wardrobe."

Indeed, she did want to check that I was telling the truth, and followed me back into the bedroom, with its large wardrobe running the length of one wall. Immediately her manner changed. "Ah yes! Nice. You will look very handsome in your suit. You must remember to wear it tomorrow."

"Yes, yes, I understand. I think I shall wear a suit tomorrow," I assured her as she scuttled out of the door, her fears allayed. I was a little taken aback by this, really, not by the fact that she had cast a cold eye upon my crumpled underwear, but rather that I came across to her as the sort of scruff who would need careful handling.

I had much to learn about the concerns of the Japanese, and their subtle ways of dealing with them. I switched on the light, then looked up at the dull glow ebbing though the room. A pair of pants clung to the lampshade, presumably flung there minutes before as someone dug into my possessions.

6

The next morning at 9:00am I was sitting in a cool room off the main courtyard at Takada City Hall. The sun was already fierce as I had made the 15 minute walk to the inauspicious looking building, past the small zoo which radiated its smells and sounds in the close morning air.

This took me through the centre of town, along the Ginza, or shopping arcade, then skirting the edge of the horseshoe ridge which separated the upper part of the city from the lower, mostly residential areas. Beneath this brow of the hill the land fell away sharply, with two main roads looping to the lower section, carved from the rock of the hillside. Once at the bottom, densely packed neighbourhoods crouched between the regularly spaced bridges which spanned the broad, shallow Matsugawa. Looking out from the ridge, across this flat area, the main shopping avenue curled away around Takada, hemming it in from the south and the east corners, before straightening again after this detour to run up and down the long valley.

In this flat land between the bright lights of the avenue's hypermarkets and gambling houses, and the beacon of the citadel, the centre of town, there was nothing. Old Japan decayed here, with its tiny, invisible family businesses, inconspicuous restaurants and incomprehensible services. Later, people would explain to me that its quiet decline had predated the unnatural bank-buoyed stagnation of the 1990s, where almost any business was too small to fail; it would simply not do for the sake of appearances. All was quiet in this bowl inside the bowl, fenced by the main road and the Parthenon of the municipal buildings, itself held in the infinite embrace of the mountains' basin. Nothing moved inside this levelled bell jar save the slow, stolid wash of the river.

However, up here upon the Acropolis, there was much action. Inside my air-conditioned room I watched with interest as countless men in grey or black trousers and short-sleeved shirts streamed back and forth across the quadrant of the car park. Dressed – as promised – in a new suit, I felt snug in this honeycomb of efficient activity, waiting in my corner for the others to arrive.

Past the tinted window walked men in twos and threes, carrying clipboards and files, most of them wearing glasses, all of them immaculately coiffed. Women too drifted past, smiling at colleagues, all wearing the regulation outfit of the 'Office Lady', prettily trussed up in tight skirt and fetching waistcoat. As the 'salaryman' is the dutiful male face of corporate Japan, working his way up the intricate ladders of business' social interaction, so his female counterpart is the office lady, or OL.

Her prospects are rather more limited, so her demeanour is all the more cheery, hoping to impress by good nature, as she cannot hope to compete on fair terms with her male colleagues. If she is pretty, then she shall be plucked from this obscurity to make someone a nice wife; if not her charms shall wither with her youth, and she shall move on, to work in a shop or to stack the shelves of one of the endless convenience stores, the window of opportunity growing smaller by the day.

While I was flattening my hair into a semblance of a side-parting, looking in the window's reflection and assuming an air of heroically selfless corporate subservience, Mrs Masada arrived with her henchmen. Jeremy and Jay were the old guard, the experienced teachers who had been here already for over a year. Both were dressed in a comfortable – yet distinctly preppy – manner. Clearly the suit was not required of them, this not being their formal introduction, but their attire was calculated and seemed smarmy enough to gain approval from those charged with upholding standards.

A brief 'hello' was all it took for each of us to size the other up. They were pleasant enough guys. Jeremy cast a sardonic look in Chiemi's direction as we shook hands, suggesting that he was not quite the stiff, weary ex-pat that he seemed, but hid a little British irony inside his otherwise stuffed polo shirt. He left me with a heads-up for my school; singing the praises of an English teacher there. Shimoida sensei, he promised, was the leading light of the Takada teachers, a forward thinking educator who did more to promote cross-cultural understanding through the shining example of his character and enthusiasm, than the entire syllabus contrived by the pedagogues at City Hall. I could not wait to meet him.

Meanwhile, Jay was a pleasant American, baby-faced, disconcertingly tall. His handshake was cold and distant; his greeting polite, but nothing more. There must be something more engaging than this, I thought, waiting for the other two new teachers, swapping like-for-like, one Englishman and one American.

If I had been waiting for something more amusing to walk through the door, then as it turned out, he walked right into it. This man, approaching the automatic slider to the room, arrived before my eyes as a rounded comic creation.

In this way, Brian Tchickenzpit, misjudging which of the plate glass doors would part way, chose unwisely, opting to walk into the immoveable pane. Thus he set out with the same fated steps upon his teaching career. The thud attracted everyone's attention. We all turned together to watch Brian pause, fully three or four seconds, take a step backwards, then approach once again, more slowly this time, to give the stationary door a second chance.

Still it did not budge; still he inched forward, until his nose again pressed up against the glass, though more gently this time. As he did so he was able to see the people in the room for the first time through the tinted glass, turned as one to view the proceedings. He forced a smile.

"I thought they had advanced technology here – this goddamn door won't open!" he mouthed through the window, stretching out his arms to implore the onlookers for help. Mrs Masada stood up briskly and made her way to the other half, standing in front of the motion sensor to open it.

"Good morning, Brian," she said coldly, turning immediately to sit down again.

He came and took his place next to me, awkwardly pulling the chair out so it shrieked in protest against the tiled floor, before collapsing into it. Then he remembered something and stood up again. He had forgotten to remove his suit jacket, which he then proceeded to do, by untying the arms which were knotted about his waist. Mrs Masada grimaced a little more than normal, while the rest of us stared in amazement.

He leaned back in his chair, puffing out gasps of hot breath into the air, and running a hand through straggly, shoulder-length hair.

"Whoa! Man, it's really hot out there. My apartment is only just around the corner, and I practically died getting here," he said, fanning himself with the introductory documents which were left in each of our places in anticipation of the meeting to follow. He turned to me. "Hi there," he said, "What's your name?"

"Hello," I said. "I'm William. You must be the new teacher from America then," comfortable in my hypothesis. I took in the undone top button beneath his tie and noted the performance sports sandals poking out from underneath the table where he slouched. I savoured the enduring look of discomfort on Chiemi's face.

After the initially uninspiring start, things were beginning to look up. It would not do, out here in Hicksville, to take things too seriously, and Brian looked like exactly the kind of chap who would tune the tense atmosphere down a note or two. Unintentionally, of course.

This was necessary with the air of proceedings so highly strung. There was one person left to meet, and with Chiemi visibly squirming in her chair in anticipation of the inauguration ceremony that she had planned, a strange, lanky figure strode through the door with an odd, incongruously swaggering gait.

Swinging nonchalantly across the threshold of the barrier that had outwitted Brian, one thumb crooked into his waistband, he stalked across the room on legs that seemed to terminate at nipple height, beaming a broad smile at the scene in general, like a venerable priest radiating his blessing. He stopped at the last place available, paused dramatically, and straightened his jacket, which was cut from a dismally formal grey flannel and matched to the trousers he wore. Combined with his round, thick framed glasses, the effect was of an overgrown schoolboy, the butt of the class joke.

He also looked like a singular character. Whereas Brian stood only five-eight or so, the new boy – resplendent in his trousers which failed pitifully to cover his ankles – was almost comically tall, the effect exacerbated by the insect-like stems of legs on which his meagre torso shook and rattled.

The beatific smile subsided, and he spoke to the room. Looking briskly at everyone in turn, he addressed us in a breakneck, staccato voice.

"Hello, my name's Neil. I come from Oxford, England. I've been studying Japanese for about three years. I've really been boning up on Japanese history before coming here, and I'm very excited to get to Japan at last. I'm really looking forward to teaching." He finished his patter, surveying the room with a paternalistic grin.

It seemed like a strange manner of speaking at first. Then, as the dignitaries filed in, and the full experience of a Japanese-style business meeting began to take hold, the style he had absorbed, with its compartmentalised units of sentences, started to make sense.

In a formidable relay, each taking up the slack when the previous speaker began to tire, the middle-aged man, and what I took to be his factotum, talked at us relentlessly in elaborate, politely formal Japanese. It was an intricate series of introductions, dedications and acknowledgements, addresses and appeals to the audience, all punctuated by little bows and asides to the other raconteur. All the while Mrs Masada tried to keep up a translation which was plainly beyond her, so sentences trailed off and ended in a slab-like look of perturbation. Where meaning did reveal itself, there was always the sense that she was not quite giving us the full gist of their words, and that this mediated speech was subject to so many levels of internal censorship that the best thing to do was to smile and nod without taking it too seriously.

And this is what we did for nearly two hours, the speakers pausing a moment here and there to allow our translator a moment's grace to put across a particularly muddled point. It became an endurance sport: who would flag first; the speakers relentlessly spitting out their platitudes; Mrs Masada creatively rewording every sentence that they spoke; or us, the listeners, heads turning back and forth between the two parties like we were watching a tennis match.

An extract from this strange linguistic casserole might read like this:
–

Japanese Dignitary, dressed perplexingly in a short-sleeved suit jacket: (speaks in Japanese, slowly, remorselessly, smiling now and then to emphasise an incomprehensible point).

Mrs Masada: Yes, and Mr Oni here wants to say that, ahh, he welcomes you for, uhhh (trails off, a look of engaged despair in her eye). You know Mr Oni is the deputy-vice chief of education in junior high schools in the city. He wants to say that Mr Okada, the deputy chief of education, who is a very important man, you know, is happy that you are here.

Assembled listeners: Thank you. Great. That's kind of him.

Japanese Dignitary #2: (takes centre stage deliberately, not exactly self-importantly, but proud in the knowledge that he is fulfilling a worthy task). (Talks in a softly cultured, but staccato Japanese, for all of five minutes; an edge of good-natured condescension in his voice?)

Mrs Masada: Um, he just wants to say that he is introducing aforementioned Mr Oni again. I know that Mr Oni has already talked, but it is Japanese way, you know.

Japanese Dignitary (almost leeringly self-satisfied): (In English – which in fairness was quite a shock at the time) Thank you!

Mrs Masada: He said 'Thank you'. In English, you understand? It is maybe a Japanese joke!

All of the assembled listeners laugh and await the next punchline. It had been some time in the making. The long day wears on.

The rest of the meeting proceeded in this manner. There were tentative forays into the labyrinthine matter of waste disposal, of which another seminar with guest speakers was promised, and we were given swatches of the five different kinds of rubbish bags to take away and contemplate. Much was said on the matter of school lunch. Directives given, as if the lunch is a medicine, upon how it is to be eaten. Dress loomed large in the instructions, though I think that we all understood each other by this time – although Brian had seemingly drifted in and out of sleep throughout the presentation, at whom most of the words were directed. Rotas were produced and handed out. Train etiquette, for travel to certain schools, was run through. Something was said, in the middle of all of this, about teaching, but what little it covered became subsumed in the general onslaught of do's and don'ts.

We were offered one final benediction, then the dignitaries removed themselves into some hierophantic ante-chamber. We collected together our pieces of paper, our charts and our garbage samplers and then we left. Mrs Masada stayed to talk with the eager Jeremy and Jay. We slunk off, me and Brian happy to be out of the formal atmosphere; Neil twitching at having left it a touch too soon.

7

Kicking our heels in the car park, comparing notes, Neil eventually motioned towards his brand new, somewhat ineffectual rental vehicle. Less a car, more a micro minivan; a vehicle so small its undercarriage could have been taken from a recumbent bicycle. Complete with a sliding side door and horrifically cheap grey vinyl interior, it was not built to impress.

Neil took this opportunity to introduce himself once again, this time on a more personal level. We had all noted, at least internally, Neil's unexpected seniority when he first swanned in. It turned out now that he was actually 30. Not such an advanced age, though most of the rest of us had graduated from university within the last three years. However, in Neil's case, he compounded his age with both a physique and a manner that suggested a far older man. I had myself taken him to be pushing 40. His black hair was swept back like a Brylcreemed latter-day Ronald Reagan, and along with the precocious wrinkles and thick glasses, it suggested a man rather older than was the case. No; Reagan was not the correct analogue. Neil's stiffness brought to mind more the avian, buttoned-down measure of a TS Eliot.

Still, he was definitely an engaging personality, and his fastidious ways complemented perfectly the easygoing goonery of Brian, who now fully awake, suggested that we hit the pool hall, having already sussed the lie of the land, American entertainment-wise.

We drove down from the citadel towards the main road that bypassed the town, pulling up at 'Strawberry Fields Forever Mega Pool', a convenient if baffling establishment. The Beatles connection was not immediately obvious, but the price was fair, and Neil put his Japanese to good effect to secure us a table.

Brian became enthusiastic in this distinctly American setting. "This is what I'm talking about! Look at these big, beautiful tables! I was raised on these babies back home."

"Where exactly is home?" I asked.

"Houston, Texas, sir," he said.

"Oh right. I don't know much about Houston," I admitted. "The Oilers used to be a good team before you lost them to another city, the energy and space industries are pretty big down there. Ah, and isn't it the fattest city in America?"

"Man, yeah there's a few problems like that. Really, it's just the middle of nowhere," he said apologetically.

"But where exactly are you from?" pushed Neil, whose geography of Houston perhaps meant further investigation would be revealing.

"Well, it's just a small town called, uh, Mission Bend," he said sheepishly.

"Mission Control, we have a Bender," I whispered to Neil.

We shot each other a satisfied look as Brian took a drag on his cigarette and then bent down to set the balls up, resting the burning stick on the edge of the table, ash falling like tiny leaves on the edge of the cloth.

"I used to play this game all the time back in college, and I used to be OK at it too. But it's been a while now, I guess. Who's up first?" he asked, retrieving the smoking cigarette and tapping the ash absentmindedly on the floor. Instantly a young man in black trousers, white shirt and waistcoat appeared, holding before him the offering of an ashtray.

"Oh, thanks. I mean *domo*," Brian managed.

The waistcoated chap produced a little brush and began to unobtrusively sweep up the mess left by the ash on the corner of the table, his fringe touching the baize, before departing. Brian had missed this tiny display, as he had been looking out of the window, transfixed by the neon glow to the strip outside. He turned around and unleashed a belch that first rolled around his mouth before doing the same in the echoing room. Two high school kids looked our way from the other end of the cavernous hall, but once again, Brian didn't seem to notice. Neil shook his head and gave a virulent little smile whose sarcasm cloaked its genuine annoyance. Brian didn't see this, either.

I sat out while Neil and Brian played the first game, sizing up the opposition. I didn't credit either of them initially with any skills, but it was possible, I suppose, that a misspent youth in the pool halls of Mission Bend had served Brian well, and thinking about it, Neil's stork-like demeanour could easily have been that of a keen, calculating amateur snooker player.

By the end of the first frame, however, which lasted an entire half hour, it was clear that I had been hopelessly generous in both of these suggestions. Brian belonged to that odd sect that lined up their shot for some considerable time before playing the balls in patently the opposite direction. This was always followed by an elaborate twirl, an arabesque of incompetence, and often as not by an unintentional dropping of his cue. Neil, for his part, simply put his head down, lined himself up, and gave a healthy crack to each shot, exclaiming, "Oh, I'd forgotten how much fun playing billiards can be!" after each visit to the table, like C-3PO cutting loose in his downtime.

Eventually enthusiasm won out over ineptitude, and I stepped up to play Neil, who was positively dancing with glee at possibly his first

34

ever sporting triumph. We contested a lazy frame, over drinks delivered by the attractive waitress, and talked.

"So what made you decide to come here?" I asked Neil.

"Well, I'd been living in Oxford ever since I went to university. After I graduated I worked in a few temporary jobs before I decided I had to make more of an effort to sort myself out and get a proper career." He studied the balls on the table.

"Oh yeah? What did you take at university?" I enquired.

"Linguistics and Modern Languages."

"So, how did you go about making a career out of that in the cutthroat business world?"

He smiled and laid into a cluster of balls by the cushion.

"I moved back to my parents in Hertfordshire, and worked in London for a couple of years, for a German management consultant. Yes – that is as bad as it sounds. I told myself that it made sense to work in the centre of things. I reasoned that a job in London in some vaguely financial field, even if it was a crap position and a crap company, was more positive than going round in circles ten minutes down the road from my front door in a job that was beneath me".

"And was it?" I asked. "I mean, was it worth it?"

"No, of course not. I hated it. The job. The people. The atmosphere. Any money that I made above what I could earn outside the capital was swallowed up by travelling, but travelling was cheaper than moving out of *chez parents*. So I ended up worse off in the long run, more tired and more frustrated. And still going round in circles.

"That's what my fine degree from a hallowed university was worth. That was the sum of all my learning."

"So what happened", I continued, sinking a few balls at the break in conversation. "Where have the last few years gone?"

Neil smiled once more. It was difficult to tell whether he enjoyed talking in this personal way or if it made him uncomfortable; whether he was someone who could discuss his mistakes, meeting them head on, or would rather disavow authorship of them.

He stopped for a moment, stretching his stringy frame as he craned his neck upwards, as if someone had scribbled the answer to this problem on the ceiling, and he was struggling to read it back to me.

"Now that you ask, that's a good question," he said in genuine puzzlement. "I finished the job in London when I was 25, and I'm 30 now. Thinking about it like that, it's a little depressing. Five years have passed" –

"*Five summers, with the length of five long winters,*" I added, with a mock solemnity.

"Well the simple, non-philosophising answer, is that I went back to the small job in the big, impersonal insurance company I'd worked for in Oxford while studying", Neil answered. "I stayed in the same house with the same landlords I had lived with during student days, and without realising it, I plotted my escape."

"That sounds a bit more exciting", I encouraged him, potting my last colour and finishing on a long black to win the frame. In his story-telling, Neil had only made one ball so far.

"Don't get carried away," he countered, "I was only joking. All I did was decide that I would learn about the things that interested me. I'd always found Japan an intriguing subject since I'd seen a couple of Japanese films. So I started to read about its history, culture, anything really. Later I began to learn the language and to practice

Kendo. But I never really gave any serious thought to coming out here until recently when I saw the advert for this job. I just realised that it was time to follow something that I was genuinely excited about, to go somewhere that I thought I knew something about."

Fair enough, I thought, this made sense. I certainly couldn't see Neil in any way connected with the business world. I tried to picture a slightly more youthful, dapper Neil arriving for work in the morning in a busy office, but it was a difficult imaginative leap. I had witnessed earlier the uncomfortable efforts to tidy himself up into a presentable state, and it stood to reason that he must have spent a few miserable, profoundly confused years before coming to this point in his life. I made up my mind about him – I'd warmed to Neil for his candour, his self-examination.

I was running through these ideas when suddenly Brian woke up from the stupor he had fallen into and joined the discussion.

"That's about the same with me," he said. "I mean I graduated five years ago, and I've been working in some pretty crappy jobs since then. I've been mostly working with computers, and it's a good job I know my way around them, because there's no way I'd be getting a job just based on my degree."

We looked at him expectantly. "Semiotics," he said in answer to our unspoken question.

Once again our eyes did not quite meet, but I felt that Neil and I were both enjoying this revelation from Brian. I'm sure that the concept of this nice, but slightly simian guy sitting in lecture halls for four years, studying how language had morphed into meaning from its grunting, primitive beginnings, amused Neil as much as it did me.

"So anyway, I knew some friends who took a year out to come and teach, and I just thought it would be a good idea at this point in my life," Brian continued. "I mean, it's not like I'm doing anything better, and besides, the pay's way better than I was getting back home."

"So I suppose it was really a career move, then," I said, looking around the laid-back pool hall, as Brian slouched against the table.

"What about you, William," he asked me, focusing his usually blank gaze in my direction. "What made you come all the way out here?"

It wasn't a malicious question, but it did, nevertheless, stop me in my tracks a little. It was a good question, no doubt. I was a little younger than these two, and felt pretty smug with my new masters degree tucked under my arm as I boarded the plane, but the reality was that I was no better off than either of them. In truth, I was probably rather less well prepared for the experience than either, not having escaped a sentence of working drudgery. These two had muddled by in their attempts to find their calling, maybe; I had flitted between one enterprise and the next, never sparing a thought for the future. It amounted to nothing more than a legacy of self-centred ennui. Brian had me snookered.

"Well, the truth is that someone found the advert for me and suggested that I ring it on the off-chance. So I did," I said, evasively, yet I hoped, matter-of-factly.

Again there were two pairs of expectant eyes, this time directed at me.

"Well, to tell the truth, it was my mother who suggested the idea to me," I admitted, imagining that I saw them, out of the corner of my eye, exchange a look that Neil and I had hitherto reserved for Brian's antics.

"In all honesty, I didn't know what I was going to do after my studies. I left it until right at the last moment, so that it would force my hand. And now here I am, my hand forced. But that's all part of the fun, surely?" I asked.

"You're right," said Brian. "I came here with the plan of simply earning a little scratch outside the States for a year or two. Beyond that, it's a trip into the unknown. But really, anything's better than being back home at the moment. The whole thing's going to shit, and I don't want to be up the creek when it hits the fan."

"You're mixing your faecal metaphors a little", Neil pointed out helpfully, "But we take your point."

Taking heart, Brian continued. "I mean, godammit, man, I'm almost embarrassed to be an American right now. Those guys are screwing up the country and giving us a bad name all over the world."

Neil nodded sagely. "The good news is, Brian, that you're in a country with zero understanding of the world at large. To them we are all the same. A lot of Japanese can't really discriminate between English and American, for example. You look at how much of their culture comes from American influences. Most of their limited understanding of the West comes from Yank imports, TV shows, movies and news, so the average person gets a fairly positive impression in general. This might be changing a little in the big cities, but out here in the country, where England is considered a small duchy in America ruled by the Fab Four, times have not changed. World events, for better or for worse, are largely ignored. I'm not saying it's a good thing or a bad thing, I'm just saying that for most people, this remains true. More than any other developed country, Japan is stuck in the past. Either ignoring the world, or seeing it through a cultural prism it knows is false, but can't look beyond. Historically – and I've read a lot about this – it comes from being an island nation, from having its identity slowly formed in this introspective way. It produces an insular mind, of the country in general, and of the individual person."

"And don't forget," I chipped in, wanting to keep up with Neil here in his expository manner of talking, "*insula* is the Latin word for 'island'."

"Is it really?" Neil said, in a way that from anyone else would have seemed patronising.

Brian was only a little better than Neil at remaining quiet when someone else was talking. Whereas Neil became so impassioned in any conversation that he would be beside himself ready to jump in, twitching and snorting in the traps, Brian drifted in and out, sudden trigger words bringing him to an ecstasy of anger. In this case, as no-one else was saying them for him, he had been mumbling quietly to himself, repeating like a mantra "Goddam Republicans, goddam Republicans"; pleasingly percussive, but devoid of wider reasoning. The conversation had turned a little conceptual for his tastes, and he was wanting to root it back in politics, and in the western, or as the Japanese would say, the American world.

But we were not rooted in the western world. And as we drove back in the amusing little van through the soft sunshine that had settled in like a tarpaulin over the frame of the mountains, I'm sure that all of us were feeling as exhilaratingly uneasy as I.

***

I grabbed a bubblegum flavoured drink from the vending machine at my doorstep; the ever-incongruous dispensers which sprung up, nurtured by odd patches of gravel, as if any old square metre of cracked tarmac was fertile soil for its mechanical roots.

As I looked out from my balcony, the mixture hissed and lurched about inside the metal bottle, an unstable concoction desperate for its freedom. I could cross off one more drink from a list of the unknown hundreds that still remained to be tried along the highways and staging posts of Japan.

I thought of these new people, brought together in this last place of the continents, each with their infinitely small reasons for leaving behind what they knew, and I was happy. With these odd characters as my witnesses, I felt sure that everything would amount to nothing less than a pleasant, ceaselessly amusing dream.

I waited one last moment in the stillness of the scene. In the distance, I could hear the whisper of water, as it trickled through the town.

And lustrous against the soft light, twinkling with welcome, my little rooms took me back in, laying me down under the gathering air of Takada.

8

Endless introduction followed endless introduction in my first week at school. It is enough to know that the greetings followed in the same vein as the formal presentations we had already experienced, but with generally younger and less grave faces – though not necessarily with any loss of the ceremonial or proscribed.

When these uncomfortable and disorientating first days were over, it seemed as if everyone understood that, while I was still an alien, at least I was a fixture of the perpetually unfamiliar. A daily intrigue to all whose path I crossed, I was able to reflect upon the position that I now found myself in. The set up was fairly sweet from where I was standing. And precisely where I was standing was, professionally and literally, a little to the left of centre in the classroom. In fact, I was almost out of the door at the side of the class, watching proceedings with an endlessly bemused and benign expression.

The school itself flowed straight from the architect's pen whose work Michael and I had observed on the journey from the airport. This same architect, stunningly fruitful in his endeavours, had seemingly built each school between Tokyo and this dead centre of the country, lining each suburb, valley and hill. Just like those which we had viewed with suspicion on that first day, it had something quintessentially Eastern about it. Eastern European. In fact 'Iron Curtain sanitorium' was the effect we all agreed upon (as everyone's school looked the same), though none of us could claim to have ever been further east than the Rhine until now.

Gleaming white, from the outside it was long, low and thoroughly uniform. The three storeys measured perhaps 150 yards down their longest side, and from this main façade budded two further vast parallel hallways, connected in series via two large courtyards.

This long main building sat high on a raised embankment, upon whose angled face were flower beds with the name of the school, Takamori, spelled out with flowers, written in the Roman alphabet. Alongside in Kanji, the Japanese pictorial characters, was 'spelled' their version of a school motto, which to my uncultured eye and dictionary appeared to be random words of exhortation, bursting with zeal from the prim flowerbeds.

This arrangement, with the school slunk like a leopard on a branch, overlooked a sports ground that can only be described as militaristic. It consisted of an enormous oval of gravel and clay – a plain with room to drill an army, with apparatus for baseball and football constellated around a running track. A fence ran around the edge of the ground, and this too was further defended by trees that stood tall behind it. Everything was built for durability. The football goals were moveable, enormously heavy and caked in rust. The open air changing rooms behind the baseball diamond, a little hut with shelter to three sides, were a solid little affair. In front were positively agricultural concrete water troughs with long metal tap heads.

But it was that uncompromising make up of the ground itself that was so unusual. A mixture of shale overlaying a type of clay, it seemed to have none of the benefits of grass. Abrasive in the dry, and no more usable in the wet than a grass and soil sports field, at first glance it was a curious choice. However, when one began to understand the volume of traffic that it must deal with in a week, it began to make sense, as anything less practical would simply be turned to dust within days of term commencing. Cunningly, the Japanese answer was to begin with a claggy dust and progress from there.

This fact, allied with the tall, industrial spotlights that hemmed in the perimeter, gave an effect that was somewhat custodial. Seeing the pupils trudging around its differently demarked zones on an early morning, all wearing identical tracksuits, did nothing to detract from this.

However, if you could never quite shake this impression, it offered at the same time a bleakly beautiful analogue. I could not push from my mind a certain concentration camp I had visited in France, high up in the mountains in Alsace, in the border lands between France and Germany. I remembered standing there in the thin, cold air, looking out across the terraced hills to the dark lands beyond, feeling the immaculate calm of the settled historical site, definitively entombed.

So it was with this prospect. When the pupils disappeared from their games, the white earth bled dry once more of the colour of flesh and of nylon, a pristine serenity came to the scene. Standing there, you couldn't see anything rolling away beneath the horizon of the sports ground, but looked out straight across the basin to the far walls of mountains which shimmered in the mist of heat, cloistering the known world of the valley.

Overhead kites circled, turning endlessly in the helix of their flight, never deigning to beat their wings, but rising on the thermals. They circled in small, silent groups, rising from the tops of the trees to the limits of sight, disappearing, reappearing, then entering again at a lower level, as if preparing for some feat of daring they had never yet built up the momentum to attempt. Daydreaming, I idly feared more than once that, emboldened by familiarity, one might bear away a child.

Inside the buildings however, all was functional austerity. Long corridors stretched off around quadrangles, disappearing into the gloomy darkness, victims of their own prodigious length. Each of the three school years had their own wing with a floor dedicated to the six carefully partitioned classes within it; every classroom was based on the same format, with two sliding door entrances, straight lines of individual, almost anachronistic desks, and a door leading to a communal balcony which ran the length of the wing.

***

The school day itself was a mass of tiny sections, each compartmentalised and inflexible, proscribing a range of activities from personal hygiene to civic integration. The seriousness with which some, seemingly peripheral, behaviours were pursued seemed quite peculiar to all of the foreigners, but were followed with a religious zeal by everyone else.

In between lessons I spent a good deal of time sitting alone in one of the upper floors of the main building, looking at that magnificent view, keeping in touch with people on the other side of the world by email. The English teachers' room was my base, containing my own compartmentalised world of my desk and drawer. Once I'd sat down and fetched out my possessions, everything had snicked back into place as neatly as the sliding doors between my bedroom and my living room. I had my own cloister, and when I shut myself away in the English room, I could dream away, gazing across the valley or reading.

The other Japanese teachers of English had their own base here too. And the lady who sat next to me was simply one of the most good-natured people I have ever been fortunate enough to know.

Kyoko Izumiyama was perhaps 50 years old. Her perfect little body measured barely five feet tall, and she carried herself with the most remarkably feminine softness, equal parts girlish and womanly. Never obsequious, but also never formal with me, she was a pleasure to be around. In fact, observing how the other teachers reacted to her,

Izumiyama brought joy wherever she went. As she entered a class-room or teacher's room, padding softly on gentle footfalls, I felt a certain type of happiness, without edge or irony, which I thought I'd made it my cynical lot in life to deny.

With her little bobbed hair, grown increasingly unruly around the crown of her head, she looked like an astonishingly sweet, off-kilter bunny. Her soft, dark eyes completed the effect, swimming with such a sparkling depth that you had to hold back from the edge.

Izumiyama sensei always had something interesting to say. Whereas some other teachers, perhaps understandably, had no interest in me – or any way to connect with me beyond shyly smiling – she would come and sit next to me, pressing a book to me with her dry little hands, always smothered in chalk dust, her full lips trembling.

"Do you know this book?" she would say. It could be a fairy tale, a classic novel, or a collection of poetry.

"Yes," I could usually reply. "This is very well known in England. I have read this before when I was at school."

"Me too," she replied earnestly, with her wide smile and her tiny, regular teeth. This time it was a collection of the great Romantic po-ets. I leafed through the book.

"I studied this when I was a college student. I thought it was very beautiful, but also very hard. I love the writing. It is so..." she strug-gled for the word in her enthusiastic but limited vocabulary... "beau-tiful."

Izumiyama sensei didn't have the words at hand to describe what she felt, but this was all the more touching.

She continued, her hands crossed upon her small breast, eyes staring at the far wall, bobbing her little head as she swallowed the words with muted gulps. "It makes me feel sad, but in my heart I have hope."

What would normally sound like a clumsy confession carried with it an immense power of unstructured emotion, capturing in this critique an essential truth, blamelessly without conceit. She laughed, her soft, girlish giggle, but it was not through embarrassment; it was in apology at her inability to express herself. Of course, it was not necessary.

I would then take whatever book it was, and leaf through it, desperate to show my genuine interest in as guileless a way as she had, terrified that I would not be able to give her the encouragement that I wanted to give. I would come across notes, written in a tiny hand, all in pencil. They littered the margins, the letters lovingly formed with soft, deliberate strokes. They clamoured all at once with a mewing, pitiable racket, each accosting the reader with their unformed ideas, products of a precocious, excited young mind. What was germinal then was now expressed but somehow arrested. It was the enthusiastic bloom of a woman at once perfectly rooted in her culture, and somehow broken by trying to communicate something just beyond herself. As I found out, this early passion, documented in these pages of her youth, was not something she could sow in the hearts of others in her class.

But I used to enjoy watching her gamine struggle between what she clearly loved, and the limits of what she could fulfil professionally. In her little grey fitted jacket and suede trainers she would call to take me to the lesson with her.

"Willu sensei!" she said as she bustled to her desk in the English teachers' room. "Excuse me, but we have a lesson to teach now."

"Oh right. Who is it this time?" I would always pretend that I was not following the schedule and was not in fact bothered about spending time with her.

"It is the very naughty second grade class. I am sorry that they are so bad!" she said.

"Oh I know," I said. "With the cheeky girl who sits at the side, next to the very quiet boy."

"Yes, yes!" she said, delighted that I appeared to know what she was talking about. "That is Okada-san. She is a very bad girl! Her parents are very worried about her. The boy who sits next to her is Sakamoto kun. I don't understand. He is a noisy boy outside class. When the lesson finishes, he is loud and talks with all his friends. But inside lessons, he does not speak. It is very strange!"

Only, it wasn't particularly strange. I would later see him walking home, the centre of attention in his group, or being collected in a car by a smart, doting mother. And in time I would learn to disassociate the classroom character of a child – the way they could look at me as if I was from another planet – with the balance of happiness they showed outside of it. After all, that was how I felt, out of my cosseted world, enduring the tribulation of a confusing lesson in a foreign language.

We made our way to the class, around the deep courtyard with its beautiful garden of carefully trimmed trees, its small vegetable patch in one corner, and pond with the large, restless goldfish in the middle. The tall pine near to the pond was the only tree whose top was touched by sunlight in the afternoon. Quiet had come to the garden. All was in shade.

With a couple of moments to go until the lesson officially began, the teacher was culturally obliged to tolerate any form of behaviour. It was the pupil's right, you see. In this interregnum of activity, in the five minutes of disputed succession between one approved pursuit and the next, the children enjoyed a bacchanal of freedom. Freedom from atavistic convention.

In this way, anything went. Today there was a group of boys outside on the balcony that stretched past all six of the classrooms on the wing, dangling the lunch serving utensils over the caretaker who was benignly looking at the garden, unaware of his personal sword of Damocles. A pencil case was being flung around the room in a cruel relay, as its hapless owner vainly attempted to recapture it. Like a test animal in a manufactured maze, the child made its unthinking, reflexive way from one side of the room to the other, automatically taunted by its classmates. She was not crying, but her face showed a misery which had gone beyond the demonstrable, and was instead a total blankness; the actions of her body conveyed the desperate paralysis of emotion, while the head was a blank tablet resting on the kinetic animal beneath.

As ever, I tried to catch the eye of the more spiteful of the kids, hoping to make them ashamed by employing mildly disapproving looks. When this didn't work, I simply adopted the tactics of the teacher. And so I tried to emulate Izumiyama sensei's beatific grin and serene thousand-yard stare.

She stood there rocking on her little heels, beaming her radiant smile, reflecting this store of goodness, the emotion that she could not hold within herself, out into the world. Occasionally she would quietly make a comment to the studious children in the first couple of rows who were already working on their English exercises, waiting for the lesson to begin. Then she turned, holding onto a tiny piece of chalk, and slowly wrote in her precise hand the date – immaculately formed – on the blackboard. When she had finished she turned around, her hands covered in chalk, the lines cracked into the dust, sides of her palms glistening like paper.

The bell went at that exact moment, the loudspeaker Big Ben chime ringing through the hallway outside, then dying, drifting out of the open windows. It was very hot still, as term had only been underway a few weeks. People slowly returned to their seats, grudgingly taking out their books from their desks. I knew how they felt. In early afternoon, when lunch had settled heavily in the stomach, a dense drowsiness fell upon you. Everything became heavy. You became very aware of the food sitting obstinately in your belly, weighing down your movements. I sympathised with them.

Izumiyama sensei, however, was seemingly not bound by these recurring realities of diet and weather. Bouncing back and forth, she would direct the apathetic class through its inexorable regime at the beginning of every lesson.

"Good afternoon class!" she trilled, lovingly in her high, soft voice. No audible response. She frowned, the expression looking clownish and misplaced on her hopelessly good-natured face.

"Once again!" she said, her head pathetically tilted to the side. "Good morning class!"

This time the startling lilt she injected into her greeting woke up anybody who was teetering on the verge of sleep and she achieved a grudging reply from the majority of the children. Those who were feigning sleep, of course, were not to be moved by this. They would not raise their heads for anyone.

"Will you please say a greeting to the class, Willu sensei," she asked me.

It was the beautiful beginning to every lesson, to be followed with an autistic devotion. We would not deviate from this at any cost.

There followed the painful and surprisingly difficult task of posing a brisk question to each member of the 40-strong class. It was difficult for several reasons. Firstly, the question must not be complicated. Specifically, it must be formulated in the fashion that the given wording had been learned in the prescriptive textbook. In other words it was no use saying "Did you do anything good after school yesterday?" or "What happened after school?" when the prescribed question, was "What did you do yesterday after school?" As for a casual version of this such as "What did you get up to last night?" quite apart from sounding a little inappropriate: forget about it.

The second problem was the existence of an unwritten rule that dictated the ideal as being as factual an answer as possible. So one then progressed to the enervating realisation that you could not legitimately ask a question which involved any personal response. By this I do not of course mean "What is your take on Japanese aid involvement in the Middle East?" but even fairly chaste enquiries such as "What is your favourite music?" Anything that required of the subject to give of themselves was gently discouraged, if not by the expression of distaste on the face of the teacher, then certainly by the lack of engagement from the pupil.

This segues neatly into the third stumbling block; the solipsism practiced by the object of the teacher's art. This could manifest itself in two ways. The recalcitrant interviewee would first stand up, arousing an undue expectation in the questioner, and then proceed to stare dumbly at an imaginary aperture in the floor, just in front of the teacher's feet. Alternatively, the pupil would be wracked internally with the most irrepressible mirth, lost in a world of hilarity to which only they were admitted. The end result in both of these variants, however, was that very few actually answered a question.

Occasionally there were good days, where a spirit of cooperation existed between student and teacher in order to get through the importunate questioning as efficiently as possible, to focus on lunch or baseball practice. But not today.

Today Izumiyama sensei, for all of her merits as a teacher and a person in general, was not sensitive to the ebbs and flows of the spirit of the classroom. It is possible to force through a point on a disengaged body of pupils simply through the vigour and passion of the address. I applaud this attitude, recognising in it a devotion and ardour that I know I could never summon myself. However, while the teacher bobbed and weaved delightfully, I stood there; an ever-expectant idiot. My eyes roved over the weary faces, trying to spark a confederacy of the redundant with someone. Not everyone was awake, I noticed, as I shifted awkwardly from one tired leg to the other.

***

On the walk back to the English teacher's room I asked her why the children were allowed to sleep in lessons. It seemed strange; the height of bad manners to the teacher in a western culture. Izumiyama sensei was unmoved.

"No, it is not rude," she said, with a small laugh, as if it was the most peculiar concept. "In Japan we think that the student must decide for themselves if they want to learn. If they do not, then they can sleep. If they do not want to learn it is better for the teacher that they sleep, than make noise."

She was right, of course. It was a good deal easier for the teacher, but it perhaps wasn't the attitude that educationalists would hold elsewhere, I felt. I explained to her that falling asleep in class was the rudest thing a child could do back home, but she remained un-convinced.

"Willu sensei," she explained, "Most of the students do exercise from seven o'clock each morning. Most will again play sport or go to their club activities for maybe two hours after school. If they want to sleep in a lesson I can understand. It is their right."

"But these are their lessons. Surely they should not be doing so much before school or after school? Then they will not be so tired during working time."

"We think that work is important, but students must take part in dif-ferent activities. Work is not enough. That is why the school day is so long. That is why many come to school on Saturday. It is very difficult for some children and they are unhappy at school. Some children do not like school. But Japanese people think that there can be only one way, and that this way is right for everyone."

It was a beautifully succinct piece of cultural doublethink and it made perfect sense to her. Trying to overcome tiredness by throwing themselves harder into the inflexible schedules, I'm sure that even the children on whom it cast its less helpful shadow logic perfectly understood the reason involved. I took my place at my desk, mental-ly checked out, and fired up my email to talk to people on the other side of the world.

9

In lessons, I felt like a spare part. I'd resigned myself to this. But back in the English teachers' room I was in my element, fielding cultural queries.

And when not breezily clearing up elements of etiquette (do you have to send the Queen two birthday presents each year; must umbrellas be constantly carried due to the perpetual blanket of fog), I was keeping in touch with people back home on email.

I'd exchanged a couple of messages with a university friend. Martin McQueen was one of those people who are, quite unknowingly, both an island of mystique and an invention constructed by others.

He was aware of the fact that he was an entertaining person. He was dry and sarcastically funny, and in the big old gloomy student house that six of us shared we would talk endlessly into the night, watching nonsense on TV, critiquing music; each new subject a fresh point to explore what we enjoyed, and more often what we disliked, about the world as we perceived it then.

We would sit in our safe communal living room, discussing the latest CD we had bought, trying to outdo each other in our recherché tastes, playing computer games or reading magazines, littering the floor with the filth of living several men deep in a small family sitting room. Unwashed plates lay scattered; papers and discarded academic work formed a matted mosaic. Sour beer cans on the windowsill reflected shards of light onto sardonic faces in the early afternoon.

But while he was part of this, Martin was unaware of the amusement he afforded his housemates behind his back. His mannerisms were legendary, the verbal tics, the physical peccadilloes; the intrigue of so paltry a little body generating so much mess.

For he indeed was on the small side. Barely five and a half feet tall, with an adolescent's physique still, and a childishly spiky haircut – his 'punk do', as Martin had it. His clothes hung off him like they were still draped over hangers and pegs, rather than the body of an adult male.

And his fondness for voluminous outfits did not help on this point. He would wear donkey jackets deep into summer, and thick, cable knit sweaters, possibly believing that this bulk would add to the illusion of body mass. It didn't work. Standing at a bar he looked like a child that had been rummaging through the wardrobe of a trades union leader. When the wind blew his trousers and chunky jumper hard against his frame he looked like a stripling that had shed its leaves.

None of this stopped him thinking he looked rough and manly, of course. Or rather, it didn't stop him trying to give *others* the impression he was oblivious to the ridiculous figure he cut.

We, his closest friends and flatmates thought we knew differently, though. Just sometimes you could see the frightened flash in his eye as he let something slip, or scowled when he heard a slight against himself that he was trying to ignore. And the fact he was a self-styled 'communist' was the little red cherry on top of the pale icing. Fifteen years too late for real student rebellion, this son of a modestly prosperous carpet showroom owner took himself just a touch too seriously.

In conversation he was funny and occasionally intelligent, but never self-deprecating. Any comment that seemed to cast him to a disadvantage was quashed immediately and savagely against the wall, as if once a concession had been made – however small – others which had accumulated in the background over many years would break through and explode out the tiny chink that he had allowed.

This was why he became a figure of fun to us, the fool of our little world. And I suppose we were cruel to him behind his back, but in front of him it was enough to catch another person's eye, sharing the moment and the joke. We did not find him so funny because of his failings, but only because he was so desperate to cover them up, to disguise his shortcomings to the world, as if he thought no-one would notice the constant sleight of hand and misdirection that this approach necessitated.

The fact that Martin was so incapable of laughing at himself enthralled us. We would speculate about the strange psychological conditions that had produced the odd relationship of his ego to his material body; the way he at once both denied the obvious to himself, and also knew himself so well as to have control of this denial, foreseeing the danger that it posed to his self-image. It was as if he was always on the run from himself, always keeping one step ahead of the irrefutable in order to avoid the discomfort of refuting it. If he never met himself head on, but instead kept fleeing from the obvious, he could keep moving away from his shadow, even while it followed, attached to him like a tail to a dog. It was a cyclical conceit, and we suspected he knew this too. But if he affected the ruggedness of a binman just home from a hard morning's shift, none of it mattered, he seemed to believe.

Martin had practically lived in that sitting room at university, even typically sleeping down there on the patched sofa. We believed that this was not simply slothfulness, but was something even more abject; fear. We posited the idea between ourselves that he was afraid of being alone in his room, and so would hang around the communal area until the last person went to bed, all the while coaxing people to stay awake, pushing on through the night until morning.

***

Unfortunately, pushing through and moving on seemed precisely what he had failed to do in the years since I knew him. He had returned home to Bristol, no distance from where he attended university, and had gone to work in the family shop, selling flooring – dimly aware of what he was sweeping under the carpet along with the socialist posturing he'd cultivated while earning his degree.

This I knew from other sources, all who had congregated in the area, none of whom, tellingly, were still living with their parents. After leaving university, many had returned to their spawning grounds, but had at least made it out of the family home once they had a job, and some had come back together. They were living now in a few small groups, modifications and evolutions of the original student households. Of course, we all continued to laugh at him behind his back, digitally sharing anecdotes and well-loved routines. Still, those on the scene reported that Martin seemed happy.

That said, his latest email had, in addition to his usual guarded regulation of personal information, a new strain running through it:

How is the land of the rising hemlines treating you? Are you yet enamoured of schoolgirl chic? Have you fallen in love with Hello Kitty branding? (Have you fallen in love with schoolgirls' cheeks?!)

I'm working for the man saving up all my readies for an extended bit of back packing next year. Maybe I'll drop by on you on my travels…

Bristol is sound at the moment. I go to the footie with my mates every Saturday. Everyone goes out at the weekend and gets leathered. Just like old times. Good times.

I've just started seeing this girl. Had to whittle down the interest in the end, make a choice. Anyway, she's top. She's well into the same sort of music as me. We go out to gigs together and things are looking pretty good. What about you? Have you found any sweet honey in the Orient?

I've got to go now as we're out tonight as usual. The fun never stops.

It was hard to know if this was the driest of satires, or if the breezy, aggressively positive tone was overcompensating for the feeble reality. From my other correspondents, I knew that the majority of this was embellished. A steady girlfriend was stretching the truth to breaking point. So I took the main thrust of the email to be the gentle offer for the pleasure of his company in Japan. I decided to do him an even bigger favour.

Let's see, I wondered, if he's capable of shaking himself out of this secure, limited life that he is leading. Can little Martin escape his mother's embrace to make good on his threats? I knew that there would be jobs coming up in the new year, when the charismatic Jay and Jeremy would be set to leave the protection of Takada's education board.

I sent him a reply suggesting that I pass on his information to Mrs Masada, and that he thinks about packing for an extended holiday. I didn't expect him to take me up on it, of course. I honestly didn't think that he could tear himself away from his eerily settled family life.

After all, we'd long joked about Martin's relationship with his parents. He would always talk about what a fantastic guy his dad was, how they'd crack jokes together as they watched the football, talk in unrealistically gritty terms about politics and break wind to the displeasure of Martin's mother – of whom they were united in their common dislike.

Was it possible for a son to have an Electra complex? The adoration that he afforded his totally unremarkable father was completely out of all proportion to the invective he seemed to shower upon his equally average mother. She was on the one hand an impossible nagger and a wily old witch, but also breathtakingly stupid, if he was to be believed. When she had shown herself at the digs she'd appeared to be an ordinary, rather frumpy, but helpful middle-aged woman. There must be something else to the story, we figured. With her reported penchant for cleaning, we concocted some fantastical stories involving her predilection for rubber Marigold gloves and clinical assaults upon her son. It would at least explain his dislike for her and also his own cloaked self-loathing. Oh yeah, it also made us laugh.

We would wind Martin up by calling him a mummy's boy – undermining his sense of solidarity with his father, while infantilising Martin into the mix. Young men can be cruel. But with much of the standard abuse meted out between friends off limits due to Martin's fragile ego, this was one thing we could gleefully get behind, interrupting his attempts to chat up women with 'a message from mummy'.

And like an actual child squawking to unshackle itself from a mother's apron ties, he protested too much in his enfeebled state. This made us laugh even more.

10

In the mountains, my new cadre of neophyte teachers weren't having an entirely wholesome time. True, I was maintaining an admirable attendance record at school and making it to sometimes as many as three classes a day, a smile of wonderment on my face. But I still found time in my busy schedule for the baser pleasures of the exile's life. In fact, all of us settled nicely into a strictly observed rhythm of existence within weeks of arrival.

In this microcosm of society within the wilderness, strong relationships began to develop from the start. The weekends were a riot of unpleasant gaijin fun, where we took our cues from the locals in their impressively escapist diversions; their willful eradication of the working week once Friday evening rolled around (and all over the pavement) once more.

The most commendable in their search for oblivion in the whisky bottle or tall beer glass, were the suited salarymen. Walking down the main street of *Chuo Dori*, the town's middle avenue, sombrely attired yet absolutely smashed out of their nine-to-five supplication, they managed to transpose a regimented, rather sad daily existence, into a night time of romantic debauchery. They were the greying fleurs du mal of the main drag, the dingy petals on the wet, black bough of doorways along the evening strip.

So if these poor souls, flogged out of their skins Monday to Friday, were giving it their all in the over-priced bars of Takada, we creatures of leisure had to match them. With seemingly every other private backstreet dwelling offering up its front room as an impromptu saloon by nightfall, the choice of drinking venues was large, but not being in the know, we tended to be a little conservative in our selections. Anything that looked like you might be sitting down to drink with more than two generations of the same family, we tended to give a miss.

What this left us with, in effect, were a handful of solidly dedicated bars and a smattering of *izakaya*s, relaxed restaurants where you could order many small dishes of food along with a healthy selection of beers. For the most part, the dedicated bars had a depressingly western theme to their names, echoing the English mania for single word titles, such as 'Elvis' (there was a child's guitar hanging behind the counter and the heated toilet seat made one, once perched, eager to linger) or indeed 'Cock' (sic) which thankfully proved an arbitrary naming choice as far as anyone could see. Expanding their language and literary horizons somewhat was 'Paradiso' (it was located up a short flight of stairs).

One night, a few weeks in, when all the teachers across the full range of private language and state schools had finally arrived, and everyone who was leaving had got the hell out, we had a big meal at one of the izakayas. Word had spread, and someone had hired out the large, traditional room at the back of the restaurant with its two long tables. We sat on the floor, either with our legs crossed beneath us, or in the Japanese way, sitting on your heels, or with legs spread to one side; both styles ergonomically designed to cause extreme pain to unaccustomed, tight limbs.

The waiters and waitresses brought the food on a succession of dishes and plates, laying them out on the low, broad tables. Everyone was helping themselves, the threat of a split bill causing the less generous to sluice their fill down throats on a river of beer. Every so often it was incumbent upon a reveller to step over a sea of sprawled limbs and make their way to the truly appalling toilets, putting on the approved plastic 'toilet shoes' before clip-clopping across the slick floor to an evil-smelling latrine area.

There were, of course, two methods for coping with these necessary inconveniences. The first was sensible. It meant keeping to a merely moderate amount of alcohol from the communal jugs and their flat, yet peculiarly frothy blend. The second involved a systematic dulling of any senses likely to produce a gag reflex when brought face to face with lavatories left to self-purge since the reign of the previous emperor. This was the preferred choice of many of us who were experiencing a second flush of youth.

And unlike the majority who had fled a brief courtship of the adult world, Michael, squatting next to me, had never made much of an effort to leave his childhood behind. He had skated by on charm and good nature until now. So it was ironic that, contrary to our little band who prowled the lukewarm backwaters of the state education system, he was now working like never before at his private language school.

"I can't believe you bastards," he said, indicating the backs of Neil and Brian at the table parallel to us, and fondly including myself in their ranks.

"I have to wrack my brains thinking of new and ingenious ways to entertain spoiled little kids, while you lot are pissing around all day teaching teenagers how to say 'good morning'."

"Actually," I said, "We've moved on now as part of a government-backed initiative to extend understanding of the customs of the West. They now say 'good afternoon' between the hours of 12:00pm and 5:00pm."

"Wow, that's a real step forwards for Anglo-Nippon relations," Michael said sarcastically.

"It is. There doesn't appear to be a translation of the phase in my guide book. We are exploring new concepts of time with these children."

"You're still living out of the guide book?" Michael asked. "I'm looking for a taste of the real Japan," he said, leering at the pretty waitress who smiled back coquettishly as she lay down yet another plate of food.

"You'll do well," I said. "Tell me if you ever do get that taste. I'd like to see what a Japanese wedding looks like. You'd look nice in white – flip-flops and dressing gown too."

He did have a point though. There was something intriguing about the decorous grace of Japanese women. That fact that this could also be allied with a strange independence and frankness was as beguiling as it was unexpected.

I looked around the room. As well as myself, Michael, Neil and Brian, there were Jeremy and Jay. However, to counteract this overwhelming sense of boys abroad, there were a couple of American girls who worked at another small language school in the town, plus numerous old hands who had lived around and about for years and had never really moved on. I felt sure that they would appear and reappear out of the woodwork from time to time, bringing an avuncular turn to proceedings. There was no immediate need to ingratiate myself there, I thought.

I reevaluated this slightly as one of the American girls' friends came to sit down at our table opposite me. She was a smart young Japanese lady, modestly yet elegantly dressed in her work uniform, a slightly more flattering version of the office girl's trademark waistcoat and tight skirt. It had just gone ten o'clock, though she had only just arrived.

"Hi there," she said brightly, with the ever-present twang of Americana rattling over the cobblestones of her teeth. "I'm Mayuka. I study English." A big smile.

"Hello," I replied, my voice catching in my eagerness. I looked at the stumpy madness of her tiny canines, breaking out at all compass points from her good natured face.

"Are you on your way to work now," I asked, joking.

"I've finished maybe 30 minutes ago," she said. "I came from there to the meal here."

"I see. Do you only work in the afternoon and evening then?"

"No," she said, flatly. "I work all the day." She gave a small frown, as if this was an unusual question.

"I only work for maybe half a day tomorrow though," she said gratefully.

Tomorrow was Sunday, as far as I could remember, but I left it at that. She was a busy girl, it seemed.

"How come you speak such good English?" I asked her, not in flattery, but in genuine surprise at her facility. I was already in the habit of judging a person based more or less solely on their command of my language. A poor thing to do, but I was powerless to resist.

Her face brightened again.

"I lived in Australia for two years after I graduated college," she explained. "I worked for Mitsubishi cars there. I have forgotten so much since then though. I now go to lessons to remember and to meet people who speak English."

I assumed she meant other Japanese people with a shared interest, but I soon understood what she really meant. She was showing an uncommon interest in a drunken foreigner with a decidedly impaired capacity for conversation. Me. Michael, who had been listening in, nudged me under the table. He may have wanted this shot for himself, but he was generous enough to back me from the sideline.

I sat back and smiled at her, clearly the worse for wear. Her long, slender legs were stretched out to her sides, and her feet wriggled in her dark tights.

"Where do you work?" she asked me.

"Takamori *Chugakko*," (middle school, or junior high school, to use the US lexicon in which it was commonly rendered) I replied, unable to contain my pride at pronouncing the Japanese words with the correct inflections as I had been taught by Izumiyama sensei.

"Wow that is so coincidental," she said breathlessly. "That was my own junior high school.

"It was a very bad school when I went there. But it is better now," she added, seeing surprise at the slight spreading across my flushed face.

"I heard a really good teacher went there and turned English teaching around."

I was struggling to think who this could be…

"Shimoida sensei – that was his name!"

It was my turn to be surprised, but I took the comment on board, again noting Shimoida's fame in the town. I'd still barely met the man. A quick smile in the corridor, or a brisk handshake, had to suffice for a welcome from the head of my own English department until now.

Mayuka shifted her position, stretching out her legs, then hugged them underneath her chin. Clasping her hands together around her calves, she leaned forward over the table, cocking her head to one side so that her soft fringe fell around her face.

I was impressed by the display, though in the moment lacked the wits to see that it was entirely calculated. She held up a large bottle of beer. Blinking her soft eyes, she offered the bottle in my direction.

This is fantastic, I thought, they encourage you to keep on going, even when it's patently a bad idea. How indulgent this Japanese hospitality is. I reached out to take the bottle.

"No," she laughed, shaking her head. "Hold up your glass and I pour the beer for you."

Embarrassed, I offered up my tide-marked glass to her and she poured, honouring the Japanese custom of serving one another drinks.

"Now you pour mine," she said, holding her own glass towards me. I obliged and we both sat there, grinning dumbly.

"Do you know what to say when you drink beer with someone in Japan?" she asked me.

I screwed up my face in thought. It was the only word that Brian had yet mastered, and he had been shouting it all evening as he diffused himself like an oil slick over the buffet of food and the never-ending supply of beer, spreading a membrane on half-discarded glasses. All around his place were the remnants of what looked like an industrial disaster, seeping across the table. Skewered pieces of poultry off-cuts swam in beer spillages, random nuggets of sushi stood precariously on the edges of bowls ready to dive in...

…I was drifting off, and couldn't pretend I knew the word. I was desperate to impress Mayuka.

"What is it?" I asked her eventually. "I promise I do know the word. I've just forgotten it for now."

She smiled again, her dark eyes sparkling above her sharp, gleaming canines which overlapped the slightly recessed lateral front teeth.

"Campai!" she said simply, raising her glass into the air and taking a long draught, holding my gaze all the while.

Not wanting to be outdone, I followed suit, downing the (admittedly rather small) glass in one. She too finished hers, taking a couple of more ladylike swigs. We put our glasses down on the table and looked at each other. Once again she offered the bottle towards me, and I took up my glass, meeting her halfway, then returned the politeness to her. This time we were not so quick to discharge the contents.

"Are you American?" she asked suddenly, with the characteristic upward lilt in her voice, the offspring of Australian Question Intonation and the natural tendency to a Californian upspeak in non-native speakers.

I couldn't believe the question. I leaned forward in disbelief, my eyebrows testing the elastic limit of my face.

"Is that how I sound to you?" I asked her, genuinely taken aback.

In the background Brian was picking at his toes with chopsticks, trying to master this strange new skill. His pasty, hairy legs poked out from his baggy shorts. At some point in the meal he appeared to have seasoned his right ear with soy sauce.

"Well, I don't know. Yes?" she said in a straightforward answer to my question. "Maybe you are Canadian?"

It seemed perfectly obvious to me, looking around the room, where the western people were from, who were English, and who were from the US. Not all the Americans were like Brian, it's fair to say. But even before each of us opened our mouths, our attitudes, bearing – even our clothes – spoke loudly on our behalf. I realised, however, that this glib prejudice might not come as naturally to a young Japanese woman.

"No, I'm English actually," I informed her, trying not to sound too haughty. An inkling that my conceit may be founded on very little beyond my shaky sense of self, flashed across me.

One of the American girls pricked up her ears in the direction of our conversation.

"I come from a city called Brighton and Hove, on the south coast of England."

"Is it near London?" came the inevitable question, for which I was amply armed.

"Yes," I answered quickly. "It's about 100 km directly south of London, by the sea."

She looked surprised.

"Oh, I didn't realise that you were English," she said with what looked suspiciously like a twinge of disappointment spasming at the corner of her mouth.

"I was sure that you were an American man."

"Well, I am very interested in England also," she said, keeping on unperturbed.

"In Japan we know a lot about England. We know about Buckingham Palace and Big Ben and also David Beckham. Do you like David Beckham?"

It was a question that I had fielded many times in class, and I was able to give the official answer.

"Yes, he is a good footballer. He plays well for England."

She changed tack. Now she tucked her legs underneath herself, sitting on her heels in the upright position that suggested both eagerness but also watchfulness.

"You know that teacher is a very good job in Japan. Will you be a teacher when you go home to England?"

"Um, I don't think so," I replied, truthfully. "It's not a bad job there also, but maybe it will be a bit more difficult than what I am doing here. Being able to speak English is sadly not the only qualification for being a teacher in England."

She looked disappointed. Perhaps I was a waste of space after all. But there was time for one last criterion to be measured.

"You look so young," she said, smiling fawningly once more. "Maybe you are too young to be a teacher!"

Then, after laughing at her little joke, her face became serious again.

"Tell me," she enquired, her voice suggesting a question that was less than innocuous, "How old are you?"

She stared directly at me, waiting for my response.

"I'm twenty-four. Why, how old are you then?"

"Oh, I am a little older," she said, visibly stiffening, less from my question, I felt, as she had posed it rather bluntly herself, but from a perceived incompatibility in our ages. The poor girl must be in her thirties, I assumed, to produce that reaction.

"I am almost 25," she said wistfully, turning abruptly to the side to latch onto a conversation behind her coming from the next table. Clearly I'd breached some unwritten rule, though I did not quite have the acuity to pick it out yet.

I crooked my head towards Michael who was busily talking to a burly man who appeared to be the chef, given his headgear. The material flapped as he talked, mesmerising me in my drunken state, until I realised he was wearing a bizarre puff of a sailor hat – and was speaking English with a languid Confederate drawl.

That was that. Mayuka was gone, and it looked as if I had failed some kind of critical test. Neil shouted over, not even raising his eyes; ever the interpreter.

"Youth-obsessed culture, matey. And conservative. Wouldn't do for the man to be younger than the lady. Bad luck."

I raised a hand in his direction, then poured myself another beer. The reciprocal process had dried up now, and unshackled by convention, I downed the thimble-like container once again in a single slurp. I stood up and searched for the toilet shoes once again.

Before I could clamber over the supine bodies littering the tatami mats to the very edge of the room, a beautiful round head appeared around the partition that cordoned off our communal area. I stopped and sat down again, watching the newcomer, alert now.

The sleek black hair and sharp fringe moved forwards and a tall, graceful body followed into the room. Across the other side of the two tables I watched her stop and talk with the American girls. She must work with them at their private school, I thought. I continued to watch.

At that moment the big sailor stood up and waddled off, wearing his hat with an ostentatious pride low on his forehead. He swaggered out of the restaurant, raising insufficiently stifled laughs from the staff on his way. A chorus of hysterical guffaws followed his departure through the main body of the izakaya, lighting up the room with the excitable screams of Japanese middle management's drunken soldiery. At the door, the figure tipped his hat – his face still concealed, now by a podgy pink hand – and walked out into the night, incognito still, giving away only a flash of ruddy jowls and a wisp of blonde hair.

"Who was that exactly?" I asked Michael, who was now sitting alone, twirling the ends of his hoody drawstrings absentmindedly.

"That," said Michael, a quixotic look on his face, "Was a very unusual man. They call him Ahab round these parts. Beyond that, I'll let you find out for yourself when you meet him. Besides, you look like you're more interested in someone else."

"Oh, I'm just taking in the new faces. You have to get a feel for the standards in a new environment, don't you?"

He was right, too. I hadn't torn my eyes away from this latecomer since she joined the party. She moved between a couple of groups at the far end of the room, everyone receiving her with warmth. I caught a touch of modesty and reticence in her lithe frame as she mixed with the others. In spite of the sociable rounds she was making, there was something self-contained, almost self-conscious about her manner which made her appear terribly and sadly winsome.

Nevertheless, I didn't want to acknowledge this on a beery night out in the early days of life in a strange country. The possibilities were surely too interesting and too numerous to pay all my attention to one person.

"So, who brought the nun along?" asked Michael, as he motioned towards the girl.

Uncharitable, maybe, but it was not entirely unfounded. There was something self-abnegating about her, which nearly amounted to a silent piety. Michael's perceptiveness could surprise you at times.

With her thick, dead straight hair, her big eyes with their mysterious, heavy folds, and her pale skin, her appearance seemed the point where east and west met. But her bearing and graceful reserve, not quite Japanese – and far from Anglo Saxon – made her look out of place in the room. I remembered her for later, hoping we would move on to a bar when we had done picking over the corpses of the platters.

When we got outside into the warm night air and people dispersed, several of us Brits who had yet to grow tired of the novelty of pubs remaining open all night, stood around discussing where to go. It was a largely fruitless discussion, as we had barely been there five minutes; scarcely long enough to have a favourite, and besides, probably incapable of finding our way home alone after a heavy night. We sorely needed a local.

As we were about to take the plunge and go for an inaugural session of karaoke, the four boys together of myself, Michael, Neil and Brian were joined by others coming out of the izakaya to make a more balanced party. The pious girl, her American friend and two of their Japanese students joined us.

She took the lead, walking quickly with head slightly bowed, directing us up the main avenue to a side street with a public garden and peach trees running its length, like colonnades lining the road between intersections. We skipped up some steps. It was our first time at 'Paradiso' bar, solely named on account of being slightly physically closer to the hereafter, rather than because of any particular Dantean leanings. In this way it complemented the 'Purgatorio' bar-cum-nightclub which was underneath, slightly below street level.

Sitting down between Neil and Brian, I noticed for the first time the obvious mistake.

"Brian, what's happened to your hair?"

"Ah man, it had to go. Did you see the look on those guys' faces when I turned up that first day?"

"I did," I confessed gravely, as Neil sniggered to my side. "But you've just buckled to Japanese conformity? You're not going to fight the power?"

"Ahh, it's not worth it," he scowled, taking the theme rather personally. It was a most peculiar look he now sported. Long at the sides and back, but with a severe fringe cut into the front.

He continued. "After that first meeting I had Mrs Masada show up at my house."

"Yes, I've had that pleasure. You always feel it's something more than a social call," I said.

"Yeah, exactly. This one certainly was."

He shifted in his seat and ran his hand down the back of his head, soothing the bulk of hair where it was cut longer on top, hanging heavily. The story continued.

"Anyway, she comes in – literally lets herself in – and my apartment is a total clusterfuck, what with all my stuff still in suitcases or spread over the floor. This all happens at about 9 o'clock this morning, by the way, when I'm lying in after my first frazzled weeks in the job. She comes in and sits down next to my bed on the floor and explains that the education board have been 'holding talks' about my hair. She says that she has come to help me with the 'problem'. I couldn't believe it – I mean, how rude are these people? She then says that she will wait downstairs in her car for me and that she'll take me to a barbers to 'make it nice'."

Neil swilled then swigged his rum and coke, which he had been languidly drinking, and burst in with one of his expository talks. He brought down his glass with a self-important jangling of ice, and prepared to hold forth.

"Now when the Japanese have a problem – and they have many little quirks like this, Brian – they have two basic ways of dealing with it. The first way is the one that we traditionally associate with them. They will talk around a subject, the discussion moving in a circular motion, with each revolution bringing a new degree of nuance, a slightly greater stress, subtle as it is, designed to nudge an inference from the person who is causing the problem, hopefully resulting in an end to the matter."

Brian was not necessarily following the thrust of the subject, but this was rather Neil's point. He leaned back in his chair regally, sweeping a lank lock of hair behind his ear.

"They have deemed, rightly or wrongly, Brian, that this soft approach is redundant in your case. They haven't even given it a chance. You may take this as a compliment or an insult, it's up to you."

Brian smirked sideways and broke wind contemplatively.

Neil continued.

"The other way is quite different, as you have discovered. It involves so direct, so apparently tactless a course of action, that the prey is bamboozled by sheer candidness into complying."

Brian understood this part. He slowly nodded, blinking his large, glazed eyes as Neil adopted his more usual, bird-like position, perched at the edge of his seat, smiling contentedly to himself.

"Well, I guess that's what happened," Brian said.

"I came down to her, half asleep, and she takes me around the corner to this hairdressers. It's called *Captain Kangaroo*. I think you can see where this is going. There's a menu outside ranging from a couple of thousand yen for your basic spit-shine, right up to 10,000 for the full treatment. You know what it's called? The Kaptain Kut."

And that was that. Brian's hair would no more be falling in his eyes; but he now resembled a desperately outdated children's TV presenter.

And yet, one whose fame lived on in Japan. At that moment, one of the bartenders hailed a customer, then motioned over in our direction. The customer shrieked with laughter, giving a thumbs-up to Brian.

"Very cool! Captain Kangaroo!"

Brian just shrugged phlegmatically. We had already elevated a state of fatigued, good natured perplexity to an art form.

So we carried on drinking until early the next morning. We changed round seats as people went up in relay to buy drinks or to choose CDs from the selection in the bar. Young Japanese men came and went, dressed in their bizarre clothes, one part rapper, one librarian, a third cosmonaut. Girls tottered around on their high heeled mules, swinging hand bags from the crooks of their arms, drinking little, but ordering bar snacks long into the night.

Eventually the nun and I were sitting together. We talked coyly. All her features were ripe and round close up. Large, circular, dark eyes, a small round nose right in the centre of a round head; vitruvian perfection. When she talked her graceful hands moved, caressing her soft voice into the world.

Her sensitive mouth split into a slightly asymmetrical, perfectly white smile when she shyly laughed. Of course, she was no nun, but a warm, gracious girl, perhaps a year or two younger than me. In the noise of the pub we spoke little. When we did, we looked away, then back at each other.

It was enough for me for the rest of the night. Her coyness was catching. I also caught a little of an accent I couldn't quite place. Deciphering it through the haze was quite impossible.

When we finally all left together, Michael stumbled out into the street, in a playful mood. He nodded his head to a couple of 'Chanelahs' walking opposite. The French label-obsessed local dolly birds clattered down the pavement across the street.

"You, know, I think I could get used to it here," he said. Everyone ignored him. Then in the silence, the air seemed suddenly alive with perfume. Maybe it was showing off in front of my new friends. Perhaps I almost wanted to provoke something. Whatever, I tilted my head back, nose pointed in their direction, sniffing the air sharply like a dog.

"You can almost smell it, can't you?" Michael said, his tongue curling over an exposed canine, and rasping the bristles on his chin. I let out a sudden howl, while Michael panted repulsively. He knew how to get anyone onside, but was almost childishly unaware of how his enthusiasm could upset others at times. Across the street, the girls looked back, frowning without moving their eyes then bent their torsos lower as they jogged across a junction of the deserted main road.

When we stopped laughing and turned back, our new friend was headed after them, leaving us standing in the night. I shouted after her, but she refused to look up.

The first traces of morning were settling on the sky. Myself and Michael were left alone in the empty street. I felt sick, disgusted.

There was nothing left to do, but walk back down to our apartments, wasted after the long night and the heat of the day before that. Already we could feel the humidity building. We sat on the step at the 7-11 across from my block, porch-monkeying with a Pocari Sweat.

"What was that girl's name?" Michael asked after a minute of silence.

It was Nadya, even then. I just didn't know it.

For the time being she had gone back up the mountain to where she lived. We, stuffing our cans into the recycling bins outside the convenience store, went to lie down on our low beds and sleep it off. By the time my head hit the pillow, I'd already forgotten my behaviour in the street, and couldn't place that hollow feeling of remorse which already was growing inside me.

11

The next day I passed my usual lazy time at school, falling asleep during the long hours spent between lessons in the English teachers' room. This was punctuated only by my getting to know Shimoida sensei – the man famed for bringing new standards to the ailing school. Initially he had been keeping his distance, it seemed to me; courteous and quietly interested, but professionally and somehow personally distant.

This world weary department head, a cherubic faced, yet prematurely grey devotee of the school system, wore the same dusty jacket and chalk stained trousers each day from term's beginning to term's end as an analogue to his unadorned dedication.

So far, a peculiarly strangulated relationship had developed between us. Shimoida would ask me occasional keen, intelligent questions. The answers I gave today, above all, felt like they were being carefully stored away, if not for analysing right now, then certainly kept in an annotated recess of his mind should they be needed later.

He was immaculately polite for the most part, though in class Shimoida applied an even more rigidly definition of my role than the female teachers. It made me uneasy. I felt sure that here was an interaction which looked to my untrained eye like deference, but was really hiding a cauldron of discontents. This was probably easily picked up by the oriental sensibility, I thought. With Shimoida sensei, I had more than ever the sense that I was merely there as another of the boxes to be ticked in the endless bureaucratic miasma of school life. I was there to be used, and as such I would be put to work from time to time, but the purpose and the benefits were at best intangible, and in any case, better left untouched.

His authority in the classroom was immediately more palpable than that of the women. Perhaps this was because he was a better teacher with a more finely tuned grasp of how to handle the dynamics of a class, or due to the atavistic Japanese respect for rank which meant the children looked up to him. Or even more simply, maybe his power rested in the fact he was the only male teacher. In any case, it rested beyond my judgement to tell. I could merely observe and discern the realities of the phenomena; not peer behind into reasonings beyond my understanding.

In pool hall conversations, Neil had scientifically shot down the supposed inscrutability of the Japanese by pointing out that, conversely, it runs down a track of perfectly delineated actions and reactions. In response, Bryan had unwittingly recited what I felt sure was part of a US propaganda film when he talked about being "in the heat of battle, looking a Japanese in his dark, pitiless eyes", stating that you simply cannot know what is really going on. The calculation and explanation can come later, he seemed to suggest: but shoot first, whatever you do.

The fact was, my presence put Shimoida in an uncomfortable position. I am sure that I was a perpetual challenge to his manhood and his position. I did not intend to be, and played my role without edge; without arrogance or any confrontation to his worthy practices and methods.

But despite all this, there was something in the way of an understanding between us. Something which lay awkwardly outside of his facility with verbs, prepositions and sentence structure; something stretched behind his impressive vocabulary and beyond his acute mind.

The short walks between the English faculty and the classroom had turned into incalculable distances of strained relations; the couple of straights, perhaps a single flight of stairs and a turn in the shadowy end of a corridor became great journeys of misapprehension and searching after a common rallying point. As we walked, our mouths stalled in the act of masticating platitudes, each pair of eyes searched the hillside of the lower wall, the south eastern face of the Isu valley, taking refuge in the panorama. When we arrived at the appointed room we were suddenly glad of the company of 40 others in an enclosed space.

And when we got there, despite his brisk style, his impressive English and his attention to detail beyond that of the other teachers, Shimoida sensei tended to conduct even more of the lesson in his native Japanese than was usual. As he ran through the points there was again that feeling of detachment, a paradoxical distance from the subject. I watched him carefully in lessons and began to notice his mannerisms – cool, relaxed and light hearted as he coasted along in Japanese, scribbling out in kanji a constant explanation to the few English words which surfaced occasionally like unwanted, bobbing solids.

I noticed how Shimoida's manner changed when he spoke the foreign words, how he turned slightly to one side, almost in a spasm. He almost physically recoiled from pronouncing English. It was there in his body language and his expressions for the onlooker, even as his eloquence cloaked it when engaged in direct conversation. As a detached observer in the classroom I could finally see this, and it embarrassed me.

At the end of the lesson, having called on me somewhat less frequently than the female teachers, Shimoida sensei would turn stiffly to the class, and almost sardonically implore them: "Please thank Willu sensei for teaching us the correct use of English." It left me hanging out to dry, and distinctly uncomfortable. I felt as if he was intentionally depriving me of a platform, but was noting down my inertia, my lack of connection with his classes. I thought back to Jeremy's endorsement on my first day, praising Shimoida sensei. I was dubious back then; and now I simply assumed Jeremy had been winding me up – a joke by the bigger boys at the expense of the new inductee.

Then dismissing me with a curt bow, as he lowered his grey, handsome head, I always caught a grim smile pulling at the corner of his mouth.

12

While Shimoida grinned, Nadya was only scowling. I bumped into her the next weekend. We had a brief, stunted conversation in Paradiso; with a self-contained frown she elegantly turned down my attempts to find out anything more about her background. Later we brushed past each other at the bar and she glided past me without a word, wearing a blank expression, leaving me rubbing a burning ear. An instant warm sickly flush washed over me, and I'd tried to catch the bartender's eye to order a beer and dampen it. I caught my hand scrunching the 1,000 yen note into a sweaty ball.

Spending time with Izumiyama sensei was the perfect antidote to this. Standing at the front of the class, asking every child a different question – but only intermittently receiving even a cursory answer – I was obliged to gut it out through to the last man. Izumiyama sensei chipped in to help me out towards the end, asking the most crushingly boring questions imaginable, a tactic that annoyingly seemed to enthuse the children more than my well meaning attempts at invention. Each time she chirped her ditty, her sing-song twitter, there appeared a gleam of sentience in the child's eye that I had failed to arouse. The pupil gave their formulaic answer. For "What is your favourite food?" the set answer was "I like sushi"; for "What did you do on Saturday and Sunday?" it was "I studied"; and for "Do you like baseball?" it was always "Yes", and when prompted to finish the sentence properly, "I do".

I concluded that I would never understand this strange phenomenon. I'd always found it acutely embarrassing to follow things precisely to the letter, repeating the same litany day after day – as if I would be found out at any moment. However, in time I was coming to understand a new way of thinking, dictating that sedulous application of rule was the key to happiness for all parties. Only a few weeks into the year I was delighting in fulfilling the timetable obligations, arriving at precisely eight in the morning, as the baseball practice was coming to an end, and leaving at five in the afternoon, having observed my scant duties in between. At morning break I was required to return to the general teachers' room and pretend to enjoy the raw, pickled vegetable delicacies that were pushed upon me. Lunch was taken in my own English room, locked away out of sight, as I had refused to eat the school meals and was bringing 'inappropriate' western-style food in. Cleaning took place twice a day. Order is good, then.

Really though, it was difficult to feel too much annoyance at these sleepy kids. It was certainly a lot easier to become swept along with the mood of absurdity that they were feeling. To them, English must have seemed a faintly ridiculous subject. More often than not, I simply allowed myself to float in the irrepressible current of futility that coursed through the classroom, smiling stupidly into the middle distance with the students. Why were these kids, whose country had known nothing but isolation for hundreds of years – and had thrived very happily on this insularity, thank you very much – being forced to learn an alien language? I could see it from their point of view. It had a bitter and ridiculous taste on their tongues, like a pickled radish on my own.

When they were sitting down again, spared the humiliation of standing in front of their classmates to chew around and spit out this gum of opinions, adjectives and verbs, they were different people altogether. At their old fashioned single desks, arranged two by two in long columns, boy, girl, boy, girl, they looked happy enough. In fact they never shut up. Once the spotlight had passed them and their brief moment of silence had come and gone, they were possessed by an animation unthinkable, given their demeanour under fire.

Children were up and down in their seats, suddenly remembering they had important business with a colleague on the other side of the class; cutesy mirrors were produced by girls who felt the need for some retouching of make up after their tribulations, and impromptu games of 'scissors paper stone' (known as 'Janken') were breaking out all over. Such industry generally went unheeded by the teacher.

Of their own accord, things settled down, and the ever-patient lady at the front of the class, still beaming, set about explaining to the class the object of the lesson. Now, it's important to understand that Izumiyama sensei, while a delightful woman, was nevertheless a poor teacher in the accepted sense. However, what she lacked in professional imagination, she made up for in enthusiasm. In this way the lesson she had prepared, in between the vast quantities of paperwork she was obliged to carry out on behalf of the school, was nothing more than reading a couple of pages of the set English textbook.

My job would simply be to read from the book, sentence by sentence, allowing the entire class to copy me, trying to pronounce the words as I did. Sadly, for any career I might have envisaged in teaching, this arrangement suited me perfectly. After my first few lessons at school I'd realised that I had little interest in pushing the students beyond their comfort zone. This was because I myself had little or no intention of stepping outside of this safe little world either, and so a nice symbiosis developed between teacher and language assistant, a pact where neither of us would begrudge the other our lack of adventure or flair.

This was just the first act. After this feeble warm up, the little teacher then got down to the business of introducing the new topics for the lesson. It was something about togetherness, or understanding the languages of the world, ending war or curing cancer. It was usually something worthy and rather ill-judged to engage the imaginations of 14 year olds.

Little Izumiyama sensei introduced the topic to the children in a mixture of English and Japanese, trying her hardest to make the class understand the one language, but having to revert all too often to the other. Battling her own vocabulary, her head darted up and down, and she blinked furiously, searching the floor for inspiration, always smiling, as if acknowledging the absurdity of the dilemma. Then, as the apposite word alighted on her tongue, she bounced it towards the class, overcoming the giddy haste of her normal speech; marshalling the girlish recoil of her conversation.

"Do you understand?" she asked. "Do you understand?"

"Yeeeeees" came the drowsy reply from the unspecified point somewhere in the body of the class.

She turned to me, giggling. "I think they understand now," she said. "Would you introduce the new topic using the pictures, please, Willu sensei?"

The picture cards were a rather meagre assortment of second-rate stock photographs and cartoon doodles, all presented in a medium guaranteed unconducive to handling, being manufactured from a 'card' barely thicker than toilet paper, and trimmed to a size more appropriate for furnishing a small yacht's mast.

Taking them up gingerly, I breathed a deep sigh, feeling the familiar beads of sweat start to condense on my forehead, a product not just of the clammy weather, but moreover due to the usual anticipation of the problems ahead. Trying to explain the concepts of a society which strives for consideration towards the disabled, as indeed this lesson would attempt to do, while confining oneself to a predominant use of single syllable words and mindful of the exclusive rights that the present tense had secured over the publication of the textbook, would be a linguistic challenge.

"Well," I said, inspecting with reservation the clownish cartoon of a grinning child in a wheelchair being pushed up a ramp into a building.

"Well," I continued.

"This person is… disabled" I said, indicating with as expansive a gesture as I could the joyous character in the picture.

"I'm sorry, Willu sensei," Izumiyama interjected, "But the students do not understand that word."

"Oh right. Of course. I'm sorry. Maybe you should explain to them what 'disabled' means."

"No. I mean they don't understand 'person'" she clarified.

"Ah yes. No, it's my mistake. Sorry. I'll try again," I apologised.

"This girl here is disabled."

"I'm sorry, Willu sensei," Izumiyama interjected, "But the students do not understand that word."

"Which one?" I asked. The clock ticked loudly, five airless beats.

"Disabled," she said brightly, flashing her little teeth.

"I will explain to the pupils in Japanese," she offered when she saw my dismayed face, turning to the class in a little skip.

She did as she promised, complete with many shades of serious expressions and gently imprecatory inclinations of the head. Particularly so when miming wheeling herself repeatedly into an unyielding staircase. Looking up, still pumping her little arms enthusiastically as she sat on a stool, she handed the baton back to me.

"OK, so this girl is disabled," I said cautiously, looking at Izumiyama out of the corner of my eye; seeing the little crown of errant hair bob in encouragement. There were many students staring open-mouthed at the picture, and an even greater number in a certain state of hilarity. We ought to be familiar with this concept now, I thought.

"Anyway, she is being pushed up a ramp by her friend," I said, pointing to the boy pushing her up the ramp. He was black. Arbitrarily so, but such is the random nature of educational textbooks. I realised what was perturbing the children.

"Excuse me, Willu sensei, but the students do not understand the picture. They want to know if you have many black men in England", Izumiyama sensei asked optimistically. "Do you see them every day?"

"Well, I suppose that most people are white in England, but there are still many African or Caribbean people, probably mostly in major cities," I admitted. "I don't know that many people who are black, I suppose. I guess it depends on where you live."

One boy shouted out from the back of the room in a voice crazed with glee. Everyone fell around him laughing. Izumiyama sensei made no attempt to keep a straight face, no attempt to fight against her natural inclination to laugh with the class.

"He said that he went to Tokyo and he saw a black man last year," she told me.

"He said that the black man was very big and had lots of necklaces like a woman."

I looked at the picture again. The man was wearing a red jumper and sported an ingenuously bouffant afro. Over his arresting pullover he boasted a nice pair of dungarees. I could see where one element of confusion was arising, at least. He was alarmingly tall and skinny. So much so, that the viewer seriously questioned the character's suitability for propelling the wheelchair on the flat, let alone up the incline of the ramp.

"Anyway," I continued, once Izumiyama sensei had exchanged some more gestures of incomprehension with the class. "Look – they are both happy. She is happy because her friend is *helping* her. He is happy because he is *helping* his friend." ('Helping' was indeed one of the new words being introduced.) I looked at my colleague. She was blinking her dark, shining eyes happily, echoing the emotions of the picture. She seemed happy to continue the scenario.

"Look at these stairs," I offered. "These are a *barrier*." (Yes, you've got it now.)

"If we find a *barrier*," I held up the next card depicting the girl struggling to surmount a staircase in her wheelchair, "We must find a way to help."

I adopted an excited face as I presented the first card again.

"The stairs were a *barrier*," I said, ignoring Izumiyama sensei's momentarily downcast face at the introduction of the past tense, "But now we can work together and help each other. When we are *helping* each other, there are no barriers."

As I finished my little speech, I dropped the enormous card, a *barrier* in itself with which no-one was *helping*. Izumiyama sensei's praise for my star turn was as effusive as it was embarrassing.

To make sure they had understood, she ran over the idea again in a mixture of English and Japanese, the ratio of which was creditably in favour of the former. To underline her point she once again assumed a seated position, this time employing the teacher's chair which was mounted on little rollers. Now she beckoned to me, and we acted out the events of the picture cards, with myself wheeling her around the classroom to the amusement of those children who were not asleep in the heavy afternoon air.

After this charming vignette, Izumiyama sensei turned to me, the little tuft of hair at the back of her head wafting in the breeze from the open window. With an appalling gratitude she asked me to keep up my end of the bargain.

"Please, Willu sensei", she emplored. "Will you now read the new section to the students so that they can copy your nice English".

I winced at the sincerity with which she asked me to perform this meagre task.

"Yes. Of course I will. But you really must stop exhausting my powers like this," I joked. She smiled back and apologised.

"Ok then, everyone stand up" I said, addressing the class, trying to stifle any note of guilt growing in my breast.

"Everybody hold up your books and read loudly, please, in a BIG voice." Izumiyama sensei translated my words and feeble half mimes into Japanese for their benefit, raising up on her toes and flinging out her limited wingspan in as broad a gesture as she could summon. There was a gentle grumbling and all stood up once more. I was king in the little classroom, and they all had to follow my lead.

I read the list of new words slowly and exaggeratedly at first, allowing the students to copy me. Then with each repetition I read a little faster, a little more naturally. The students followed, bending their hollow mouths around this strange language, tasting its alien flavours.

Whenever we would go through this exercise of simple pronunciation – which was every lesson, of course – an unusual thing occurred. Instead of becoming more resistant to the drill the longer it went on; instead of feeling patronised by the vaguely pantomime nature of the repetition, they would in fact become more engrossed with each iteration.

This was an unforeseen phenomenon to me. You might expect English schoolchildren to become surly and uncooperative if asked to perform the same task repeatedly, as if it was a challenge to their dignity. But these kids loved it. It was as if the very nature of the drilling bonded them together, keeping the ship and its class of sailors on the straight and true course of the lesson. They repeated with more, not less, energy the longer the exercise was drawn out, repeating feverishly. For the most part they were not understanding these words, mind, nor seeking to remember them. But they shouted them out with the desired level of dedication.

And that, simply speaking, was largely that. This game persisted in ebbs and flows, with more or less attention afforded by the gravity of the class, with greater or lesser amusement; with rising or falling numbers of sleepers among the body of students. Then once more the chime rang through the speakers of the school in parallel, Big Ben's call to the daydreamers to awake. Little Izumiyama sensei turned to pester me one last time before the lesson could close.

"Please, Willu sensei," she asked me with, with her sad, sparkling eyes. "Will you say goodbye to the students please."

It was the least I could do.

13

If there was one positive way to stave off the feeling of letting other people down, it was to be found in the bars of Takada. Here, you were letting just yourself down. We were escaping a mean-spirited England where it felt like everyone was living, self-obsessed, for the weekend. But here too, it quickly seemed like we were doing the same. September was not even at an end, the nights were still warm, but already I felt a certain nostalgia for the summer, and was chasing something in the Takada night.

So we lurched from bar, to izakaya and back again, threading our way along the main drag of the peach town, calling in at Musique Macaque, the biggest karaoke joint. We slumped into it for an hour, here and there, stooping beneath the bright sign above the entrance, where the eponymous primate tilted back his head and held his end-less note.

The owner was Sergo. A trim 35 year-old, and originally from Geor-gia, Sergo had lived for a time in Russia in the late 1990s, before settling into the protection of provincial yakuza as a businessman in small-town Japan. Exactly how he made this transition, we were never sure. But talking over a late night game of pool one time, Ser-go explained a situation that sounded rather like him being run out of the country after he refused to sell his Caucasus taxi company to a local 'businessman'. "That's what they do there," he said. "If they like what you have, they take it. Here, the mafia are more respectful – provided you pay and stay quiet."

He would cruise by the booth we were sitting in, bringing a multi-coloured tray of complimentary drinks, then perch on the backrest of a sofa, shiny black slip-ons up on the seat. Sergo explained how the taxi company became a front for a car-jacking gang who would ultimately prove to have links to local warlords – all of whom held power straight from Moscow. Here was much more civilised, he said with a smile.

He was a nice guy. And having built up a second business from scratch in an alien country, Sergo was clearly a survivor. With his fluent Japanese and integration into the local economy and power structures, he was more at home than we would ever be.

This evening, after a late pitstop at the singing monkey, I headed out into the night with Michael. We were already a few pints deep, and were due to meet Ahab and some of the others at Paradiso. But as the cool air hit me, I wasn't feeling great. I sent Michael on ahead, and sat on a bench in the communal park running behind the Chuo Dori main street. My head was spinning and I was already regretting the pink cocktail Sergo had brought us, grinning seductively, just an hour before. I looked around at the little stone groupings of figures and assorted amorphous pebbles, clustered in thickets and in little corners of the narrow, strip-like park.

I shifted my feet in the gravel, and felt the cold of the bench beneath me seep upwards. Wondering where in the little citadel Nadya was tonight, I heard the shouts and cackles of the people over on Chuo Dori, where the inconsistent selection of buildings ran arrow-straight into the distance, as if into the foothill of great Shuetsu-san itself, in an explosion of kinetic life.

The wind blew gently across the small patches of grass, to roost in the evergreen tree above my head. In the corner of my eye, the bunches of stones with their pictographic markings, little versions of shrines perhaps, shuffled, steeling themselves against some change which they could feel, but was perched beyond the frayed edge of my senses.

For a desperate moment, nothing made any sense. I stood up, walked over to the nearest group and kicked out at them, catching one of the smaller stones flush, and sending shooting pains running up my leg. They all stood, monolithic, each to themselves, watchmen without a gaze; Sphinx-mute.

Even the spiritual world was leaning in to my life and causing physical pain. I walked off, heading up the hill towards Paradiso. Weaving parallel to the main street, I explored the tiny, pavement-less roads which radiated in all directions. I zigzagged up and across, running close to the buzz of Chuo Dori, then away at right angles, picking a route on nothing more than the cadence of my walk. Behind me, shadows lengthened under the bright moon pulsing down upon me; in front, the tangle of electricity poles spun out, binding the micro-neighbourhoods together in a tangle which I could not unpick. As roads gave out into dead ends of houses with their little car ports, their off-camber ramps stacked with empty crates, I wasn't quite sure I was headed in the right direction any more. Squeezing through an impossible footpath between sheer sides of homes, I hungered for the pleasantly heavy feeling of sitting among people I knew, on a comfortable seat, the music and alcohol drowning obligation, raising expectation.

Suddenly, I emerged from a side street onto the main street, crossing it to the transverse-running road which contained the earthly Paradiso. Then, by one of the endless gravelly parking lots, set back just from the road, I noticed something strange. An old, low black saloon car was parked sideways across the entrance, a young man at the wheel, and another two standing outside, leaning against its long flanks. In front of them, a woman. Even at a distance, I could tell from the immaculate bob that it was Nadya.

I quickly grasped the situation. Their ginger died hair, paired with amusing Hawaian shirts and a raucous bearing meant one thing: 'chimpira', apprentice yakuza keen to make a name for themselves. So were these edgy new friends? Should I just walk by?

No. They were barring Nadya, who'd taken a shortcut through the lot, from leaving through the gap at this end of the chainlink fence. Now one of the youths moved behind her. Desperately casting about, Nadya caught my eye. I stopped dead, and immediately there were several more sets of eyes fixed on me; then an ineluctable tightening at the back of my neck.

So, I knew the yakuza existed even in this backwater. It's not like I'd thought them just an anecdote from Sergo. You could see them hanging around the lurid gambling machines in pachinko parlours and pulling up illegally in their black Mercedes outside convenience stores, running in for a coffee, a deep fried octopus ball, or Japanese whisky. But I never expected to have one eyeballing me in a side-street, with a woman's honour – and my own – at stake.

The one standing behind Nadya barked something at me. I didn't follow, but I certainly got the message. *Move on.* I took a step sideways, then one forward. Nadya stretched out an arm in my direction. I couldn't tell whether the gesture meant 'save me', 'be careful', or even 'don't bother'. I didn't have time to think it through; I'd already skipped over, then squeezed through the gap between the fence and the car. In a far corner, one of those identical white micro-MPVs juddered off and out onto the road, as fast as its feeble engine would allow.

Positioning myself carefully to the side of the three figures, I adopted what I hoped translated into a supplicatory smile. I took a step closer to Nadya, simply repeating "Tomodachi, gomen nasai" – Friend. Sorry.

My smile was echoed, twisted into an unpleasant grin by the guy standing next to the car – all focus seemed to shift to him, and I knew he was the leader of this little bunch. He now pulled himself upright, a wiry youth crowned with a tropical flower arrangement of hair, spitting unexpectedly at me, as the barker shoved me from behind. I fell into the car, lying crumpled over it for a moment, dazed. Then, wiping spit from my cheek, I realised how angry I was. Without thinking, I balled my hand and pivoted my hip against the car, spinning my torso round and catching the leader off guard, smashing him across his cheekbone with a hard punch. Nadya shrieked as he fell to one knee, leaving me and the barker looking in each other's eyes, both equally surprised.

For a agonising moment, no-one moved. A gasp of wind cut through the car park while a savage, hot sensation pulsed through my core. Just as quickly, it went, leaving me sapped me of energy, leaving me enough time to pause and reflect on how anything could now happen. Back in the moment, I reached for Nadya, making a grab for her waist and pulling her feebly towards me, as the two chimpira quietly climbed into the back seat of car, quite ignoring us. I stood to one side, like I was a chauffeur holding the door for them. The driver slipped neatly into his seat.

Just as I thought it was over, finished in a peculiarly decorous fashion, a wafer of silver flashed from the window as the engine roared. I crouched down, more from the tension, than pain, and then Nadya was pressing something to the back of my neck, where the blade of a knife had slitted me, cutting a narrow, curiously neat incision.

95

"William, it's Ok, it's OK," she repeated, her accent more pronounced than I remembered.

"What happened?" I asked, then gathering myself; "What would have happened if I hadn't come past?"

Her cool fingers on my neck soothed me, and a couple of quiet tears rolled down her round cheeks. I knew something had passed between us. I stood up, full of purpose once more, leaned in and kissed her, in control of the night once again.

14

In mid-October the weather changed. It happened one day as I was walking home from school. The evening was beautiful, but full of the understanding that summer had long since been stretched beyond breaking point. True, it had never snapped, but simply lost its elasticity and had been withering, the warmth draining day by day a little further over the lip of the horizon, the sun catching its belly a little heavier each time on the peak of Shuetsu-san.

Today was different though. As I walked out into the freshness of the early evening, it was clear that a dramatic change had taken place during the working day. A remarkable smell filled the air. It suffused everything, as if the afternoon had suddenly brought forth unseen blossoms on the trees, which the wind immediately winnowed and diffused. You could open your mouth and taste the ecstatic floating perfume.

The change was so complete that it suggested the date had been long earmarked in calendars as the official start of autumn. And now it had arrived, the Ministry of the Emperor's Seasons had made sure that his subjects respected the event. Along with this cool fragrance came a wonderful freshness. Summer's enervating intensity had gone, leaving behind an airy giddiness, soporific still, but now invigorating.

And I was settling down, self-satisfied, into it. I had my suspicions about Martin. He'd been writing with new stories about his life, alluding to loving and leaving women all over the south west. Nonsense, of course. On the other hand, I felt like I was actually having a fair time with women. It was a novel feeling.

After the chimpira fracas, Nadya and I were quietly, steadily, growing together over the weeks. I didn't share things easily, but in her quiet self-control, I saw a goodness worth opening myself to. I'd learnt from my earlier buffoonery. With Nadya I was now the perfect gentleman, for once making my intentions clear. And while I was no real man of action either, she'd been impressed enough by my car park gallantry.

I'd hardly made headline news in the past, never understanding how to conduct a relationship at quite the right pace. Either too fast and unrealistic in what was possible, or playing it cool with a nonchalance quite the opposite to how I really felt. I'd made a fool of myself a couple of times; recently mangling a short-lived engagement through a mixture of naivety and stupidity. In truth, I was probably fleeing this episode as much as anything in my coming to Japan. So in my own way, I felt as alone and lost as Martin. Of course, he relied on bravado to see himself through; in myself, I diagnosed it as a certain type of stoicism.

Nadya was a breath of fresh air, though – some mercurial breeze I fancied, which had been waiting for me here in the mountains forever, and I couldn't do anything wrong. We simply enjoyed being together, without recriminations, subterfuge, or foolishness of any kind. A look deep into each other's eyes was all it took to diffuse any argument before it really started.

And so we had spent long weekends holed up in each others' apartments, barricaded in to watch endless videos. Just occasionally we would surface to trek across town. It was a generally unhealthy way of life, but that didn't stop it being fun.

One Sunday afternoon, having recovered from the excesses of the weekend with a long lie in, we were hunting around for something to eat. Nadya padded around her tiny room, with its kitchen corner and cubicle bathroom, wearing her checked pyjama bottoms, standing delicately on tip toe to reach the higher cupboards.

"Have you found anything?" I asked her, rather hopefully.

"No. Nothing to be had here. We're going to have to go out for food," she replied, turning her round head and sighing as she hooked a thumb inside her waistband.

As neither of us had a car, and our attempts to unravel the mysteries of the local transport system had been thus far fruitless, we geared ourselves up for the hike. Our search for the correct route had involved sitting at the main bus station in town for an hour every Saturday afternoon, watching 'Yodas' – diminutive, wizened, stiff-hipped Japanese grandmothers – confidently and stolidly board buses, sometimes shouldering a huge sack for good measure. Any enquiry to which bus went to the Peach Road shop area on the edge of town met with surprise from the driver. After all, we were gaijin – what possible reason could we have for engaging in an outlandish activity like a weekend trip to the shops? Besides, we would be consigned by law to take up seats on the back of the bus if we ever located the correct one – Brian was sure he'd read this somewhere. So now we had given up on this, and simply took the direct approach each time. Shanks' Pony.

Nadya got dressed, and we set off, from the citadel where she lived, near the main station, across the plain of the Matsugawa river, and up the other side of the hill to the shopping strip. We walked past the array of Japanese restaurants on the upper side of town, turning down their fishy delicacies. Their awnings fluttered in the afternoon sunshine, beckoning customers in with their slogans we weren't even close to understanding. We peered through the sliding doors at the alien scenes. Some were tiny family businesses, which operated out of the front room of a house. More up to date restaurants took this personal theme and extended it to modern needs, where the warm simplicity of the old world was fused with a brisk efficiency, the shuffling familial aspect replaced by ranks of identically clad young men and women, called quickly to the table by electronic bells and a witheringly keen sense of duty.

Here too the incredible smell of autumn was dying on the air, but you could still taste it. The flavour made us more hungry, as if invisible flowers were settling on our tongues and cleansing our palates in preparation for a feast. We passed the government buildings and headed down the terrace of the slope to the broad plain of the river.

"I love walking out like this, when there's no pressure, and we can just spend the day as we want," I said, giving her my arm.

"You know, we would never be able to do this at home," Nadya said. "Too much empty space, no pavements. Too much... dirt," she said.

By now I understood that slight accent I'd heard on our first meeting. Nadya was not English, or American. In fact, English was not her first language – or even her second. She was from the east of Ukraine. She spoke Russian first, and Ukrainian – while fluently – a distant second. Where she was from, people remembered Soviet times as an age of plenty, the citizens of a socialist state bound together by a single language which stood proudly ahead of any national tongue.

While she spoke English virtually fluently, it was certainly not native. Nadya came from the enormous mining centre of Donetsk, a city built in the mid-19th Century by a Welsh industrialist named John Hughes. He had brought out with him workers from the Welsh valleys to mine the virgin anthracite seams of the Donbass basin. Gradually they stayed, were integrated into the Russian Empire, and the area eventually became one of the major production centres of Soviet industry.

And Nadya, whose surname was Williams, was descended from these Welsh miners, heir to a history largely forgotten in the Soviet years, when anything smelling of the outside world was immediately suspicious.

It wasn't until Ukraine's post-Soviet independence in 1991, when Nadya was ten, that her parents learned much about their roots. Several letters from across the decades were suddenly released to them by the authorities; letters written from South Wales, by a distant relation doing genealogical research and trying to establish contact with any branch of the family still left. As she explained to me, these letters had almost been destroyed, but in the 1970s found their way into a KGB file on Nadya's father, Leonid, by then the only Williams left in Donetsk. Years later, he collected the letters, bemused – and quite incapable of reading them – when the state apparatus was in the process of dismantling itself. The day before, a quixotic intern hovered his hand over the bonfire where most secret police records were headed, then cast the bundle into the vast bag of mail awaiting collection from the central office. "Your history almost went up in smoke!" the official laughed cheerily, as Leonid dropped the bundle into his pocket and turned away.

A miner himself, Leonid was unsure what to do at first. Then, with the help of Tatiana Nicolayevna, a family friend and English teacher at secondary school, he replied. Over the months a gradual correspondence built up, changing Leonid and his family's impression of the West. Finally, in the mid-90s, Gerald, the great-great-nephew of expat miner Thomas Williams, came to stay in Donetsk with Leonid, his wife Lyuba, and the teenage Nadya.

These relationships, once discovered and now strengthened, led to an enduring bond between the families. When the Russian world's economy fell apart in 1998, Leonid was paid in coal, Lyuba in sugar from her job at the sweet factory. Nadya was due to go to university, but the family had no money. So Gerald stepped in, offered to sponsor her to study in the UK. The visa situation was not easy, but eventually the right palms were greased, and she spent three years studying international relations at University College London, working with a tenacity she'd never quite witnessed in British students.

Although Nadya returned home to Ukraine, she took back with her a cherished possession: dual nationality, granted based on her family. And the one thing the Russian people know how to do is to work connections, she told me. Able to travel more freely than many of her compatriots – and trading on her name – Nadya got a job teaching in Japan through her old university friend.

Now, after six months in Tokyo, she had moved within her language school franchise to isolated central Japan. She explained that, after spending her life in great industrial, financial, and technological centres, she yearned for clean air and the mountains. She'd found Shuetsu-san, and the Peach Road.

15

"We all begin things we can't hope to finish," said Neil, turning to look at me.

I instantly felt accused, though knew secretly he was only seeking some form of encouragement to continue. I raised my eyebrows expectantly. I actually enjoyed his perorations; it was good to benefit from autodidact Neil's investment in the Japanese mindset.

"We set off at tangents trying to find that escape from the present, or worst, the past, but we always come back to ourselves.

"There is no escape, which is why we must stop fighting.

"The Japanese understand. Eastern philosophy and religion is characterised in the West as an escape from the world, an abstraction into a spiritual state so pure, everything else is transcended. But this is only partly true."

He leaned in further, enjoying the moment.

We were in Paradiso. It was Friday night. Actually it was Saturday morning, but the night was still comparatively young.

Neil looked like an old preacher, looming over a lectern, building the horror of his flock. *I'm invested in this, right up to the elbows in the muck*, he was saying, and delighting in it with an almost scatological fascination. *I am the way...*

"The real story is living in the world, in the moment, in such an immediate and diligent way, that you are consumed by the whole. That is, in itself, an abstraction.

"But it is also an integration, and this is what sits at the heart of modern Japanese society; this desire to be part of life to the extent that you are consumed by it."

Neil smiled and swept his slick hair back, exposing the deep lines on his forehead, befitting a much older man. He took his thick glasses off, rubbed them perfunctorily on the lapel of his flannel jacket, then slid them into an inside pocket.

Myself, Michael and Brian took draughts on our small, very Japanese glasses of beer.

Comparison of cultural notes after a long week teaching often crossed over from amused wonder to philosophical exposition when Neil was around. He still hadn't come close to a woman since arriving in Japan several months previously. Brian, his particular – and somewhat unexpected – confidante, had intimated this to us after a long night recently.

I looked at Michael, who was running his sweat band across his forehead. The bar staff had cranked up the heating at the first hint of the oncoming cold weather.

"What about you?" Neil continued. "You'd better be careful that you don't finish what you've started with Hanako. You might get more than you've bargained for."

I had already suspected Neil was aiming a fragment of his monologue at Michael, who had just started seeing the gamine Hanako, one of the groupies from his private English school. Neil knew Michael's intentions, and he didn't care for them. He himself was fond of the girl and was setting himself up as the avuncular friend who was in Japan for the long haul, should anything else develop over time. He suspected that Michael was after nothing more than a bit of fun to get himself through the long winter months.

At least Michael, charming rake that he was, had no problem with candour.

"Don't worry. We've driven past that wedding hotel Marrywell a couple of times and I saw her eyes light up. But it's OK. I shot her down pretty quickly, and so far I've avoided meeting her parents, so there's no worries there.

"But I tell you, Japanese girls have some special talents."

"What kind?" I asked quickly, putting into words the expression which was clouding Brian's glazed eyes.

"Oh, I'm not sure we have the vocabulary to explain," he said with a mischievous smile. "Well, definitely not in Japanese, anyway. And I wouldn't want to lower the intellectual tone of this table by sounding off in English."

Neil walked away. He had developed a taste for White Russians at Purgatorio, and with his general levels of frustration slowly escalating, so was his once feeble capacity for alcohol. He came back with a cocktail which he sat peevishly cradling.

Arranging his extravagantly proportioned legs under the table, Neil took the most chaste of nips then began again.

"There is always a discrepancy between what a Japanese expresses and what they truly believe – especially when dealing with a foreigner. Tatamae and honne it's called; what they express face to face, and what the true feelings are which they keep hidden away."

I felt it would be worth another go to rile Michael. I could sense the tension on Neil's part and felt sure that beneath Michael's laidback demeanour, Neil really grated on him.

I took on the role of the mediator and explicator of the holy mysteries of Neil.

"I think Hanako's just playing you for a sucker. I reckon she just wants a western boyfriend to butter up so she can improve her English on the cheap, then do a runner and find a real man to take care of her abroad."

This almost certainly wasn't the case – at least not long term, for it was plain that tiny Hanako was a traditional girl at heart, even if her rumoured predilection for throwing herself at foreigners suggested otherwise.

Michael was unperturbed.

"Man, as long as she makes her gratitude very clear to me each time I smuggle her out of the family home, then I don't care.

"The girl can play me any way she wants."

Brian choked on his beer.

"Well said," he grunted. "That's what I've got to find me, a willing, eager Japanese girl, not like these witches who make you pay for every pleasantry you manage to cajole out of them."

Brian had recently been taken for a ride while trying to do the decent thing as an American abroad; flashing his wallet. He had paid almost £100 for a gentle rub down with a masseuse round the corner from his apartment block, after walking out late in a stupor, looking for some action, and finding Hot Hot Massage open for business.

The thought of him lying flat out with just his sandals on, negotiating his table stake through a phrase book, was a scenario we had enjoyed, both behind his back and to his face.

Anyway, the language barrier had brought him up short of whatever he thought he was getting that night, and for the time being Brian was down on women. Everyone laughed at the image still flashing itself round the hive-mind of the table.

All except for Neil who was twitching as he always did when he was desperate to say something; shuffling in his seat and bouncing his crossed legs so that he was literally beside himself with impatience. He couldn't hold off making his point clear to Michael.

"Ah, so Mrs Masada's talks about having a reputation to live up to haven't quite sunk in yet? I thought you would have been trying to impress her, what with that cosy relationship she has with the private 'educators'.

"Surely this isn't the face you present at school?" Neil goaded, a broad grin stretching toad like across his face.

"Tatemae and honne, isn't it?" Michael shot back.

He had got to grips with the way the system worked pretty quickly. Michael may have played the eternal student bum, but he was no-one's fool.

He would have picked up the gravy train whiff in his job early on. Terakida, a private language school, ran more on the exotic and pretty faces of its western staff than on the rigour of its teaching methods.

Even though Neil was several years his senior, which can seem a lot in those early twenties when boys are still developing into men, Michael was not letting him go before the pay off.

"Perhaps other people have more sympathy with the natives than you would think. I've certainly got a lot of sympathy for Hanako when she comes sniffing round in need of some attention.

"And if she gets the wrong end of the stick and thinks I care for her a little more than I actually do; well, I guess that's just something lost in translation.

"If she *really* wants to believe that I love her when she's staying the night with me – well, it's tatemae and honne."

He gave a defiant glance at Neil before accepting an ill-aimed high five from Brian.

Neil just ran his fingers through his thin hair, downed the last of his white Russian, and stalked out into the cooling night. He was here for the long haul.

16

It was just as well Neil had made an early exit, because he could never hold his own in the dog eat dog world of the karaoke suite. We headed once again to the neon collection of sights and sound which was Musique Macaque, its name possibly inspired from the sounds reverberating around Takada in the early hours.

Along the road from the rusted gates of Takada Zoo, from which arose the hooting of monkeys, along with the lethargic cat calls of the birds of paradise and the wheezing bark of the baboons, we floundered our way in, nodding at the watchful Sergo, and collapsed into a private booth.

Here indeed we met up with Michael's bright little Hanako, four foot ten with a tail wind, always overdressed for any occasion in a ludicrous confection of ball gown sleeves and skyscraper heels. Tresses rolling like a fishing net tumbling from a trawler completed the impression, the bouffant, teased curls and light brown highlights bouncing straight from an outdated soap opera.

She played the role of the accommodating Japanese woman to perfection, welcoming everyone before sitting down to attend to her man, at once part of both the public and the private.

Accompanying Hanako was her older friend, 29 year-old Yui; straighter, more reticent. She was the eldest sibling of two brothers, a traditional girl bred into the traditional expectations of their parents. And she was disappointing and even worrying them by not being married already.

Yui had learned to keep her mouth fixed into a gentle smile, showing a white expanse, offset by a dappling of brown freckles across her nose and cheeks. She'd bitten her tongue for the sake of her younger friend, covered for her with her parents and was only lately catching up to her in terms of the freedom she enjoyed.

Her rebellion was the mute reaction of Japan's secret life. Hanako openly sought after western men in a loyal yet somehow changing caravan of boyfriends. But Yui, not suited to this by both natural inclination and upbringing, allowed herself nothing more than the clandestine ministrations of the mercurial Ahab, himself several years married and many more her senior.

Ahab was one of the old guard. Originally from Salt Lake City, he had lived in Takada for a rumoured ten years plus; a period lost in history for us newcomers. He breezed in and out of scenes, disappearing for months at a time. Expats routinely joked he'd gone to find the white whale.

Ahab believed the decade service he'd put in was sufficient to do away with his real name for day to day purposes, and more than enough to reinvent his Mormon upbringing. Depending on who you spoke to, he'd transposed it in the retelling to a Louisiana seaport, an Oregon fishing town, or Naval Station Norfolk in Virginia.

Anyone who knew the real story whispered about how this land-locked Ahab had only put on the sailor's hat during a weekend break in Tokyo. Returning to the mountain town from the big city, he reappeared fully formed as the salty sea captain, and had weaved his shifting stories, numerous and changing as the ocean waves, age-old and hard bitten as shanty ditties, ever since.

Ahab had enjoyed taking his time finding the right woman in Takada. Eventually settling in early middle age on a demure and pretty homemaker who would keep the base running smoothly, he'd prepared for a respectable life of boring marriage and children. Ahab knew enough to understand the church and state of Japanese married

110

life; the fawning attention of the wife which atrophies into devotion to home and first born once the time comes. So he started secretly thumbing through his old Brigham Young texts as he expanded his teaching business and awaited the birth of a child.

Only then his wife went off on a tangent. Tapping away on her mobile phone one day, chatting with her oldest friend, Mrs Ahab experienced a tiny, prurient revelation. She started describing some lurid fantasy scenarios through an extended sequence of texts, titillating herself, and initially alarming her friend. Just like that, she had found her creative outlet and her perfect medium. When keitai shousetsu – cell phone novels written in instalments barely a hundred words each – started to take off in Japan, she was in the vanguard, describing a world of excitement and forbidden love which chimed with thousands of young Japanese women. A novel followed from this, and suddenly the housewife from Takada became the home's main earner – and a minor local celebrity.

In the space of a few months, Ahab's wife was keeping him in the style he craved; with a smart dinghy he awkwardly rowed out from a diminutive boathouse, across a lake at an exclusive leisure retreat in the mountains. But as he sat in the prow each weekend, reading his wife's work alone in the middle of the lake, the nuances of the Japanese language settled on him, perching heavily on his hat as he bobbed on the water. Each carefully measured word within the narrow cloister of the novellas became a silent scream which weighed on his ego like a dropped anchor.

So Ahab's cultural assertion of the strutting deckhand on shore leave, initially born merely of a striking yearning for his homeland, became more absurd, more desperate. It manifested itself in an aggressively mannered dress – the trademark hat was suddenly amplified by bell-

111

bottoms and shiny black leather boots for casual wear, a handkerchief knotted about his shoulders. When he sat out on the porch of his home, built with his wife's money, the accordion he inexpertly caressed with his bludgeoning hands drowned out a present where he was the denatured husband; muted a past recollected in other old timers' photograph albums. Ahab, then just plain James, his hair cut in a mullet, caressing a low-slung keyboard bass in a tight vest, plastered in a shit eating grin.

But Ahab was no Melvillian invention. If all of his history was a fiction, then he was acutely aware he could do what he wanted with it, and with impunity. He didn't pin its capricious spirit to the sails of a Nantucket whaler, a 19th Century hulk of seafaring romanticism. No – Ahab's fantastical sense of self was rooted in the atomic age; the attack on Pearl Harbour and all that followed.

So when he walked among the Japanese, his sailor's swagger was infused with the condescension of the conqueror; the just dealer of retribution, who spoke quietly and carried a big bomb. And the further he took his persona in clothing, in jokes, in pontificating, the stronger his animus grew against his adopted country, its people; his wife.

His stories underlined and formed a counterpoint of fantasy against those of his wife. The more she tapped her world of make believe into her mobile, the more Ahab inveighed against the 'treacherous Japs'. It was difficult to imagine how this casual unpleasantness could be warranted; how they complemented his last memory of the States – cruising suburban Salt Lake City in the late 1980s. This insouciant racism of the foreigner long abroad in an alien climate could almost be taken for a tedious mannerism, were it not for the fact he routinely referred to Yui, as his 'paddy chimp'.

Like many others who had been too long in Japan, he had stagnated into a caricature of a westerner, a simple visual indicator that held meaning in a few broad strokes, like a kanji character, but whose origins were argued over and never quite what they seemed. And so Ahab, lost to his fabricated naval history, would tonight be the singing seaman, taking on Petula Clarke's Sailor as he stood, legs braced apart and one hand tucked into his white trousers, imagining himself being called back to shore by a siren song from across the waves.

Though I pitied her, for all I knew Yui was happy with this state of affairs. She enjoyed her man at the weekend, relinquishing him to a wife who had her seafarer by the mainsail from Monday to Friday.

***

We would pour over the telephone directory-sized catalogues with their immense lists of songs, many in Japanese, with a generous yet uneven selection in English from the early years of rock onwards.

Bands which had sprung up and enjoyed their fifteen minutes of fame two or three decades before, here lay preserved deep in the un-fathomable workings of the metal box beneath the TV screen. Third rate teddy boys pranced alongside rave MCs and the one-hit singer songwriters, whose only lovelorn ballad played on, occasionally, in the karaoke houses of the orient, years after the composers had found that elusive love, raised families, or simply died.

Songs which had barely caused a ripple on the surface of the British charts at the time here were preserved for posterity, along with a clutch of other obscure songs, exhumed from murky vaults of indif-ference. The aphorism 'Big In Japan' was not without justification.

We keyed in the numbers of the songs we wanted to sing, taking lib-erties here and there by lining up a medley of own choices if others were slow to rifle through the books. We searched out the perfect, almost forgotten tune that would seemingly be beamed straight from our intimate record collection on another continent into the TV here, the words overlaying dull cityscapes through which clean cut oriental lovers frolicked. In those days, before digital music put a lifetime of music in your pocket, such discoveries seemed significant.

It was always a race to lay claim to a particular favourite, setting it aside for an individual performance. Otherwise it was a given that you would be singing an unintended duet with buzzkill Brian, who would keep hold of one of the microphones all evening, unintentionally policing it in a well-meaning drunken haze.

And we would always sing the same things each week from our own personal tracklist; Michael with a baritone take on Cream's White Room, or the occasional ill-fated venture into the few rap tracks the machines contained. Brian picked from a bizarre collection of appalling high school rawk, and myself going with Neil Young (I brought my harmonica along), REM, or the Rolling Stones.

And on this last selection we were all in agreement.

There was nothing better than crowding everyone around the microphones for a rousing stab at Paint it Black, thrashing away demonically on the courtesy tambourines and jumping on the upholstery.

Other favourites included a sweaty-browed growling, arms round each other's shoulders, through Springsteen's Thunder Road, or Van Morrison's Madame George. Did I alone contemplate the irony of singing these hymns to thwarted dreams and lost youth in our oriental sandpit?

Conversation was difficult in the private rooms, each barely 15 feet square, dimly lit and pleasantly disorientating, with jagged swathes of mirrors and eccentric mixes of décor, dotted with occasional pot plants, and always clustered around the table which held the innumerable empty glasses.

Tonight in my solitary, thrillingly abstracted world, broken by the splinters of glass refracting countless visions of the spectacle, I looked to Brian. In his hunched form you could still see the bullied teenager, the bedraggled child. I felt a sudden warmth for his hopelessness, his own sorry warmth of spirit. I thought of Martin, of the prank we pulled on him once during the boisterous evening in before a night out. I'd taken my bike lock and, while four others – all much bigger men than Martin – held him still, chained him to the banisters in the hall. We popped a can of beer on the flat top of the newel post at the bottom of the stairs, just beyond his comfortable reach. When we came back an hour later, ready to leave the house, his forcedly amused aggression couldn't hide the redness at the corners of his eyes. The incident cast a strange atmosphere over the rest of the evening, and without talking about it, we understood never to bring it up in front of Martin again, not even as a joke.

I came to my senses mid-way through Brian and Michael's wonderfully doleful rendition of the Springsteen's melancholy River, Brian bowing his head down low, locks of hair obscuring his face as he held onto Michael, unsteady due to drink and the precarious footing on the sofa.

During the harmonica break I held mine up to the mic and blew like a man possessed, drowning the synthetic version on the backing track. Neil simply sat in the corner, abstrusely fingering chords on an phantasmal guitar.

Nadya looked on, not quite fitting in with the other girls who shyly sat to one side, occasionally springing into life to order drinks through the intercom for their men. And she looked still more bemused as Hanako and Yui started singing together, their tiny voices struggling to rise to the occasion as they took on the chiming backing of Eternal Flame, singing in that bizarrely unselfconscious way we could never emulate, even after all the cocktails the Macaque had to offer us.

It was affecting seeing them line up, cheek to check and perfectly composed, motionless and serene, their accurate but reedy voices in tune and in unison, at once so deeply incongruous with the alien words and yet also so perfect in this setting.

When they were finished each went to her man. Having done her turn, there were now more important matters to minister. Nadya edged closer to me.

Walking out into the crisp morning, we split into two groups in the last traces of night. Ahab, playing captain as taxi driver, took the girls home in his erratic pick up, while Brian, Michael and myself set off back down the hill to our apartments.

Everything was still.

Even the coordinated groups of Texs – the counterpart to the mountain Yoda, dubbed thus because of their saddle-sore, bandy-legged gait – would not be out on the streets for their civic gardening for another hour.

The only other sign of human life were the bartenders through the window at the Macaque, settling down to lie across lines of bar stools rather than make the journey home at this early hour – having drunk as they worked the graveyard shift – while the occasional salaryman passed out on a step in a cheap suit, snoring soundly.

Even the animals at the zoo were relatively quiet, the muted whoop of gibbons and the sotto voce chatter of the monkeys dampened on the air.

We too walked for a couple of minutes in silence, past the small theatre and the rows of identical hostess bars with their awnings like little hotels, and hopeful English names promising the finest in hospitality.

"So are we still enthusiastic about it all then?" I asked, the question rearing up in my mind, apropos of nothing. It felt like an apposite moment to take stock; it was the end of November, the weather was changing – the honeymoon period was over and we all knew where we stood now.

"Sure," shot back Michael. "Everything's good, isn't it? I've got a nice little set up with Hanako, which is winding up that old bird Neil, so everyone's a winner.

"I mean the jobs are a piece of piss, aren't they? Especially for you two – paid to sleep half the day and play the talking clock to a room of kids when you wake up."

Brian felt his professionalism called into question.

He answered Michael without taking his eyes from the pavement in front of him.

"We have to do some work occasionally, you know, man. We might be paid to sleep, but you aren't so much better, getting a pay cheque to look up teenagers' skirts."

The attack had coaxed from Brian the perpetual defence of his Dick Whittington adventures in the East; escaping from the horrors of post 9/11 America and the tidal wave of conservatism which he believed was keeping everything on a knife edge. Those in power – from the lowly yet secure jobsworth upwards – arranged warily against a generation of college leavers unsure of their future.

He again drunkenly recited his inability to find anything worthwhile; the dead-end computer repair jobs he drifted into. Brian was only a couple of years older than us, but he had acquired a man's bitterness in that time.

It was as if he had accidentally got Mary pregnant and been given a wedding coat with his union card sticking out of the top pocket – and the flight to the world's edge was his response to this impasse; his own personal River.

He concluded his tirade with a curt nod of his matted curls and wheeled off to his room, in a block perched on the edge of a drop, on the outcrop of land high above one of the main routes back down to the valley floor.

Michael laughed. He was happy if he was getting paid to be a pretty face. He would use Hanako as he saw fit, but in reality no lies would be told. There might be a card sharp's quick-fingered modulation, a sliding scale of truth, but never a distinct separation of fiction and fact.

I'm sure Hanako knew what she was getting.

We came to 7-11 and sat down on the big step outside, porch monkeys escaped from the zoo, a final beer in each of our right hands, me just fifty yards from my bed. I thought of Nadya, now tucked up at home in her one room apartment, in her own bed just inches off the floor.

There was not much to say. We were the ones getting ahead in this alien world. There was no worry for either of us; we were safe, mated up and immune to a future of possible disappointments.

"What do you think – will Neil and Brian sill be here in five years?" I asked.

"I don't know what to say, William," Michael replied. "I mean, they kind of seem like losers who don't have a whole lot of options available. So they'll probably just take the line of least resistance. If that means hunkering down in the mountains, then so be it. They're running away from something. Now they've found somewhere to settle."

"Are we doing any different?" I asked honestly.

He didn't even look away for one moment from the Kirin, giraffe brand beer, in his hand.

"No. We're young and foolish, but we don't care," he said, heroically throwing the can into the recycling bin next to us on the step. "We can do what we want. Take it or leave it. And if we get bored, we go home.

"*We* are not the exiles."

He got up and set off down the hill for his current, temporary home. I loitered for a couple of extra minutes, sucking the last froth from my beer, then pitched my can in the same way, from a slightly closer distance.

I still wasn't sure quite how young or foolish I was.

17

While we went throughout the week immured in our own schools, spread out over the dribs and drabs of Takada, our Wednesday team teaching in shogakko – elementary school – shook things up nicely.

I had drawn Neil, while hapless Brian paired up alternately with either Jeremy or Jay, whichever one had sunk the most in Mrs Masada's affections that particular week.

This was an adventure in itself, and gave us a pioneering zest to buck up the flagging week as we moved around a variety of schools, some of them quite remote. I was thoroughly glad Neil was my wingman for this. Not just because Jeremy and Jay were such faceless souls, or Brian so inept, but because being paired up with Neil meant necessarily seeking out the parts unreached by less intrepid teachers.

Neil, by dint of his eccentricity and reasonable facility with Japanese, both the language and the people and their customs, was assigned digs some miles outside Takada in a little settlement plum on the broad, shallow Tenkyo river, exactly where it is squeezed into the bottleneck of a series of dramatic gorges, the high rocky cliffs funnelling the water down towards the sea.

Here it emerges almost at the midpoint along the 53 staging posts on the Tokaido – the route of the eastern sea – connecting the ancient capital of Kyoto and Tokyo. When these waypoints along the great journey were immortalised by the artist Hiroshige in a Japan still closed to the outside world, he became an instant celebrity, for surely he had caught the spirit of something ancient in the grooves of his wooden printing blocks.

But beyond this, Hiroshige presaged a Japan which the world would come to know in the 20th Century; a vertiginous, crepuscular landscape where man seems superimposed on a backdrop alive with fleeting light and the incessant possibility of night.

Tenkyobashi village stood at just this liminal juncture, where the brightness of the valley took on the dark tones of the wood and was swept away down to the plains and the sea. Its two sections stood on either side of an iron bridge, orange with rust, colossal supports inlaid with a filigree of spider webs and green bodied arachnids picking their way on delicate long legs.

Next to the bridge was an incongruous hotel, huge and out of place in this backwater village, overlooking the mouth of the gorge. Beneath were schools of bare fisherman's boats moored at pontoons, and a couple of the long, narrow motor skiffs which were used for taking day trippers down river to see the system of gorges.

This way, just around the first headland, through the chasm of water and rock, was the pride of Tenkyobashi, a suspension footbridge, high above the river, by an ancient stone fountain and a wooden beaker for cleansing hands before stepping out into the dank air.

The struts and the delicate webbing of cables was a parody of the spider structures woven into the road bridge, though in itself this structure went nowhere, simply linking one side with the other, where the path terminated abruptly at the edge of the wood. Beneath was a meagre wash of shingle, twenty metres wide, used by gangs of twos or threes during summer to spread their towels while they leapt from the rocks to splash in the water. At these times the gorge resounded with the cries and laughter of teenage boys, shattering its usual peace.

Walkers could stand in the middle of the footbridge, craning their necks to see back around the village, or turn their gaze to the waters beneath them, suddenly aware of the trembling cables and flooring which sounded out a hollow echo, reverberating up static legs to explode inside the balloons of chests.

And in the stillness of the ancient forest, high above the eternal wash of the river, when a companion was just out of sight behind a tree or a rock by the path, it would take an insensitive ear not to hear the incessant, eternal voice, echoing from the water and up between the cliff face of the gorge, calling out to join it.

At these times a walker would feel the indifferent hostility of nature at its most persuasive, its most gently reasoning, and grasp the handrail with a renewed urgency. In these forests, darker and more Jesuitical than anything I had ever known, there were presences alien and intimate, oozing from water, sap and mulch as surely as from each pilgrim's own heartbeat.

***

Due to Neil's geographical isolation I would make the thirty minute train journey out to meet him at Tenkyobashi station. I would loop round the back of the citadel of Takada, going considerably downhill in the process – how the train remained in control, I know not – to cross the Matsugawa river, down through the length of the city to the midpoint of the valley's depth where the Tenkyo ran.

The train would then follow this line, past the limits of Takada, through the industrial area and out across the plains of grasses, dropping off schoolchildren by the carriage load at stops until it hit the middle of nowhere, just before Tenkyobashi village.

Neil was always there waiting in his little white Suzuki minivan – the imaginatively named 'Carry' – hunched over the steering wheel, or outside, incongruously leaning against the roof like a movie cop.

When he saw me he feigned a coolness, staying in character, only meeting my eyes at the last moment with a brisk salute as he ducked his head into the amusing vehicle with the impossibly dismal grey interior.

It was always a similar drill, but one time involved a singularly amusing farce as we met at the station.

Neil was struggling with a tangle of cables spewing forth from the tape player, connecting his minidisk to the feeble frame of the car.

"What have you got in it?" I asked, knowing the answer could be petrifying, and certainly unconducive to the next stage; finding the elementary school hidden somewhere in these hills.

"It's a bit of Zappa today, William, I'm afraid. "I know how you love it."

"It's true, Neil, you know I love it every bit as much as Phillip Glass or any of the other esoterica you play."

Neil smiled to himself.

"Well you've got a special treat today then, because it's not just Zappa, but a live Zappa double album with spoken word sections.

"You'll be in heaven."

He was still mashing the gears while trying to set up his minidisk. We hadn't moved an inch, and the driver of the single taxi parked on the diminutive rank outside the station doors was looking ever more perturbed, with his pristine white gloved hands resting on the steering wheel and head tipped back, bracing against the lace covered headrest.

The minidisk kicked in eventually to Frank's sonorous voice interjected with spats of laughter, like Lawrence Ferlinghetti's anachronistic hipsterisms overlaying The Band's Last Waltz.

Neil finally found the elusive first gear and the car swung round, barely in control, coming within a doily's width of hitting the taxi, and we set off over the iron bridge, past the hotel and up the hill. As usual, we had little idea where we were supposed to be going.

Neil had typically received some half-arsed instructions faxed to him at chugakko from Mrs Masada. Included were the usual scribbled imprecations to be polite and try to chug back as much of the lunch as was humanly possible, which for Neil, being vegetarian, was usually very little.

"What's up then?" I asked Neil.

"Do we have any idea where we are headed?"

"I haven't got a sodding clue" he admitted, honestly, yet not reassuringly. "As ever we are going to have to use a little inspired guesswork and our latent white man's compass we are always presumed to possess."

"Well, we were running half the earth while this lot were distilling the limits of their worldview into a teapot," I said provocatively.

Neil grinned his broad, sickly amphibian smile.

"And my nose tells me to keep going until we crash into a wooden hut," I offered.

The winding, potholed roads combined with Neil's appalling driving to make the whole experience a challenging way to start the day. Every road we turned down looked the same as the last; the dense ranks of pines stood ever more vertically on top of each other.

Neil handed me the instructions which were patently not detailed enough to allow us to win near to our goal.

We spotted a doughty Tex cleaning the windows of a decrepit family run convenience store halfway up a deserted mountain road. The excellently maintained tarmac was presumably the product of some pointless recent initiative to connect nowhere with nowhere else.

Neil came to an undignified halt to ask him directions.

To his credit the Tex unblinkingly took us in and gave his reasoned response in a heartbeat, leaning into the car and pointing vigorously with a sharp hand back up the hill.

We knew we had surely exhausted the opportunities in that direction, but we thanked him and continued in the direction he suggested. The long morning was wearing on. It was already 9am and we were supposed to be taking our first class in ten minutes.

Neil, under the reproach of Mrs Masada's written encouragements to make a good impression, was feeling the heat.

"It's every frigging time!" he burst out, uncharacteristically. "They just seem to think you know all the back roads as well as they do. Peasants who have never been further than the next frigging village!

"Pushing their bloody little wheelbarrows up and down the same bleeding cart track and then giving us these shorthand instructions."

He had blown himself out.

Sure enough a Yoda came pottering along the way, large rocks piled in a wheelbarrow, coming from the hinterland of god knows what, and headed for the arse end of nowhere. Her floral pinny rode the stoop of her back and hung down to her knees, her eyes fixed on the floor in a glaze of steely purpose.

She was a woman who knew where she was going.

As was often the case, on the third or fourth time we retraced our steps, certain elements started to fall into place – stone-monument-by-side-of-road-brought-back-dim-memory-of side-turning-not-yet-taken; particularly-forlorn-house, door-opening-straight-into-traffic, signalling track-glimpsed-through-trees which offered a different route up the mountain.

Through a combination of Neil's buttonholing of peasants and sign reading, and my own vague nose for direction, we would find our way.

This morning, however, we had clearly missed our first lesson as we pulled into the pitted gravel car park outside the long, low familiar hulk of the school, beautifully nestled in a copse of fir trees.

The cold sun broke through in the mountain air. It was almost winter proper here. The incredible smell of autumn had long since faded, but the weather had not yet fully changed to the striking cold we were bracing ourselves for. We had all been promised we would be very sure of winter's arrival when it finally settled over the Japanese Alps, anointing peaks up and down the valley as far as eyesight held and bringing a recurring slush of snow to city streets.

For now though, we stepped out into the crisp morning air to be greeted by a delegate from the school, waiting in the foyer to ensure we removed our shoes and squeezed into the homogenous unwearable green slippers with their unintelligible gold embossed logo.

Neil stepped in to smooth the way, assuring her we were indeed the same Neil and William as mentioned on the portable blackboard inside the entrance, the ones who were so 'happy welcomed' by the school, as the message joyously declared.

Always sensitive to the precise level of English understood in any given moment, Neil and I snatched a few seconds to appraise the situation.

"These bloody slippers!" Every single time I meant to bring my own, but never quite remembered. "I can't spend another day sliding around these polished floors on the verge of losing control."

Neil agreed with me, though in one of his uniquely unexpected flourishes he demonstrated the danger by skating and sliding ten feet on the rich, shiny wood, riding close up behind the homely shimmying bottom of the delegate. She was dressed in the slovenly fashion of the rural shogakko; a mix of sandals and tracksuit bottoms, topped by layers of cardigans.

"Yes, they are awful, but rather fun. If you take them in the spirit they are intended," he said, looming like a pond skater over the darkly reflective floor, the surface polished to glassiness.

"I wouldn't worry about the fashion aspects – I'm sure we'll be straight into the action. They will want to maximise their assets, after all."

He couldn't have been more wrong.

18

We were ushered in to meet the headmaster, the kochi sensei, in the cavernous, twilight world of his study, the honour we were being extended evident in the reverence our guide approached the door and announced our presence, hands folded in her lap and eyes not daring to hold his.

He offered us a seat on one of his squeakily fake leather sofas, where we sat facing him, taking in the bizarrely preserved 70s pallor of the room. The panelled walls were in a ribbed teak, along which huge cabinets with glass sliding doors held countless files, and an ostentatious clock which sounded out throughout the room with an oppressive, hollow tick.

As noted, Neil and I could spot the ones that weren't going to latch onto our remarks and winks, and this guy, with his grey suit and dour aspect, moving slowly about a living mausoleum, was ripe for the taking.

"Jesus," I whispered. "We're getting the full treatment today."

"I think they dug him up specially for our visit," Neil shot back.

Fujimoto san (by this stage, even I was capable of reading the more common kanji name badges) creaked his way around his austere desk carrying two files slowly before him. He moved to the mantelpiece and examined the clock in a laboured manner, turning his back to us. Neil rolled his eyes, angled his watch in my direction and twice sharply tapped the face.

Mr Fujimoto turned around slowly and took up his place once again behind his desk, moving on gentle footsteps and sinking with arid certainty into the unpleasant black plastic of his large office chair. He opened the first of the files and groaned deep within his composed body, setting hands down on the table.

"Sooo…" he breathed to himself with a weary satisfaction and slowly turned the pages of the file.

Still he did not look up.

Neil was beside himself.

If Mr Fujimoto was not going to break the silence, then Neil was. His head was ticking from side to side and the sofa squeaked under the continual shifting of his weight.

Neil coughed twice in rapid succession then burst forth in Japanese.

"We are sorry we are late. It is very difficult to find the schools sometimes. It is confusing…" he offered to the headmaster.

Mr Fujimoto waved his hand in a dismissive gesture.

"Ehhh…" he said, easily breathing the economical Japanese version of 'don't trouble yourself'.

"Neil-san", he said immediately, "English?" (This in English.)

Neil-san was caught off guard by this deceptively ingenuous question. All things were perhaps contained in this file. Was he merely starting with the most obvious?

"Yes," Neil said (in English), "We are both from England."

A look of dismay crashed onto Fujimoto-san's face. Neil responded quickly, offering up the information again, this time in Japanese. He craned his head to try to sneak a glimpse at the file.

Mr Fujimoto seemed satisfied with the answer. Still he poured over the file, opening and closing pages at random and nodding quietly to himself. His breathing was even and metronomic, mirroring the ticking of the angular Seiko clock on the mantelpiece, his placid features flavoured with the hint of a raised eyebrow from time to time.

Neil was slowly turning a livid scarlet, his feet dancing uncontrollably on the parquet flooring. He turned to me in desperation, panic in his eyes.

I felt like I wanted to pat his head, to reassure him as one would a schoolboy who has misconceived the scale of his crimes under the unforgiving scrutiny of his headmaster.

Suddenly, and for once with a vigorous and wholly unexpected flourish, Mr Fujimoto shut the file on Neil. He slid it silently to one side.

Neil's relief expressed itself immediately in a physical fashion, as he breathed out, his legs stopped their antic dance and he slumped backwards into the sofa.

Fujimoto-san looked up for the first time and caught my eye. I felt sure I saw the traces of a smile tugging at the fine lines around his mouth. He opened the second file, this one surely devoted to the history of my life, with both fantastic conjectures and disorienting insight into the more recherché aspects of my psyche. Nodding his head, he now picked up the file, and walked towards us, sitting on a chair directly opposite our sofa.

"William-san," he began, exactly measured, his arms parallel with each other once again on either side of the file, his tie bisecting its spine.

I felt a frisson of the pressure Neil had been under, but was determined not to give anything away. I smiled back, saying in practiced Japanese my standard spiel – where I was from, where I was working, where I lived.

130

He let me have my say this time, half raising his hand, then thinking better of it.

(In Japanese) "How old are you, William-san?"

Unusual question. But I answered. I was ready and prepared for anything he had. I was running through my National Insurance number in my head, trying to recall the date I passed my driving test, and composing a potted educational history using the rudiments of the language which I possessed.

Again he nodded, expelling air evenly and loudly through his nose, a sigh which travelled down his body, gaining momentum and force, until it reached a critical level as it reverberated in his torso. It finally forced its way outward in another monumental 'Sooo…' wrenched from his very bowels.

"*Sooo…*"

Then, in a gesture previously unimagined to lie within his range, Mr Fujimoto deftly looked up, his head remaining bent over the file in his lap, but his eyes dancing to catch my own gaze with a sure intensity.

Perhaps he caught horror in my expression as our eyes locked. Suddenly his hands came to life, springing upwards from the table, where they had been laying so passively until now.

They were whirling and twisting with a manic intensity, the slender fingers performing arabesques, compelling our line of sight, while Fujimoto-san stared still straight up at me, loving the power his sudden digital ballet was having over his appalled audience, his dark eyes shining in the airless, dusty study.

"Meat," he suddenly shouted in English, causing Neil and I to jump in our seats.

"Meat, William-san, meat?"

I realised it was a question, and the demonic twirling movements of his hands were a mime of the cyclonic shovelings which took place at lunchtime in schools, where everyone from the teachers downwards contended with each other in a silent, voracious race.

I was transfixed. It dawned upon me slowly that I still had not replied.

"Meat? Meat, William-san?" Mr Fujimoto was still asking.

"Yes, yes!" I shouted, "Meat OK!"

I had been sucked into the street theatre and was now hammering phantom chunks of glorious flesh into my gaping mouth, spinning my hands like I was struggling to land Santiago's marlin adversary out on the unforgiving sea.

I tempered this with my usual caveat – "*Demo, sakana wa tabemasen.*" (Something hopefully recognisable as: Yeah, but I don't eat fish) which usually met with open mouthed amazement, but in this setting was forgiven, as I had qualified myself as being at least partly human. I was simply surprised at how easily Neil had proved his own humanity.

Now I was determined not to slow my hashi spinning movements before Mr Fujimoto. We were both still going at it, smiling grimly, locked in a standoff, with Neil, I could see in my peripheral vision, looking on in horror.

He knew what this was leading up to.

Eventually Mr Fujimoto slowed his energetic movements, the colour and the diabolical smile drained from his face, and he stopped, wheezing slightly. I made sure he was flagging before easing my own cartwheeling hands, staring at the crown of his head in triumph as he once again returned his vision to the file.

He coughed and took up a red pen, drawing a circle in the William file with the typical Japanese marking flourish, where a large round spin of the biro cutting across the majority of the page stands in for the sober tick in the bottom corner which does nicely in British schools.

I had passed the first test and my papers were laid to one side in this strange museum of a room.

"Here we go…" Neil hissed through his teeth while smiling at Fujimoto-san, showing a remarkable gift for ventriloquism. "I knew the ordeal wasn't over."

Neil's vegetarianism had been a stumbling block behind the scenes, he knew, furrowing brows the length and breadth of the valley. As long as it amounted to no more than looks of amazement over his refusal to eat pickled bees in the staffroom, Neil could handle it, but this new turn preyed on his sensitivity towards Japanese conspiracy theories.

Mr Fujimoto retuned to his desk. He adjusted his dark tie and once again opened Neil's file. This time he quickly homed in on the page he was after, avoiding the preamble. But still he couldn't help himself, leaving a chasm of a dramatic pause, daring Neil to interrupt.

Neil needed little encouragement for this. He was already back on with his spectral dance shoes, tip tapping on the spot like an armchair Riverdancer.

"Yes, yes, I'm a bleeding vegetarian," he whistled through his teeth. "What are you going to do – string me up?"

Mr Fujimoto was all business now.

"Neil-san," he barked sharply, "Meat – no?"

Neil smiled broadly, again the toad.

"Meat no!" he affirmed, beaming angrily, determined to face up to this test.

"Sooo…" said Fujimoto-san; "Meat, no…"

He began to take out his pen once more. Neil leapt into action with a writhing twist of his head. He spat out a defence against an imagined crime in Japanese.

"I am a vegetarian. I do not eat meat or fish. I am allergic to them."

(A probable lie).

"If I eat them I will die."

(Definitely a lie; possibly an ill-judged one.)

Fujimoto-san instantly bridled, and rose to his feet, shutting the file on Neil – but not before he had scratched a couple of final marks in his red pen.

19

Out into the hallway, and toward our first class; Neil still spitting feathers as we walked in on a scene straight out of Takada zoo.

Were we prepared? Despite a rather steep learning curve, after a few months Neil and I were beginning to hit our stride with how to deal with the nippers at shogakko.

Initially we had comically misjudged what was expected of us, leaving a string of confused faces on pupils and teachers. Now we had taken down our own expectations several notches and cynically performed the same ridiculous routine each week, minstrelling our expected roles to rapturous responses lesson after lesson.

Crucial to the establishment of this new confidence was a magical briefcase of tricks, tat bought on the cheap from the 100yen shop, or made out of scraps of card pilfered from chugakko. And yet the wonder which the children greeted this feeble bag of assorted nonsense was touching. Eager faces crowded round, intrigued by the contents of the old converted laptop bag, jostling each other to peer inside.

Neil and I marshalled them and blundered through our usual routine, involving cunningly executed sleight of hand card games, and Simon Says tomfoolery with Neil making a prat of himself. Then there was our favourite – alphabet noodle relay.

In this ingenious game, which I claimed as my own invention, two teams of children passed small foam letters along a line using chopsticks, thus providing a clever mixture of multi-faceted learning; sight recognition, manual dexterity and an all-important competitive spirit.

In addition it afforded Neil and I a damn good laugh as we watched the friskier members of the class attempt to consume the foam letters and the less coordinated children come dangerously close to poking themselves in the eye. Granted, sometimes the teachers looked a little perturbed, but the trick was ignoring this, and soldiering on through.

At break time Neil and I were corralled into the guest relaxation area, a *washitsu* traditionally decorated room, incongruous – to my eyes at least – within this institutional building.

The delegate had collected us cordially from our lesson where we had taught no more than twelve children and shimmied ahead of us down the silent corridor to the relaxation room. She slid aside the paper paned and wood framed door with a gentle bow, staying low to ensure she policed us removing our slippers before entering.

Then we were alone in the placid stillness of the chamber. We seated ourselves cross legged on cushions at the low table, facing each other, yet both gazing out through the window onto the garden. A pond with koi carp ran alongside the windows, with judiciously placed stones connecting islands of vegetation. Beyond that, the familiar military compound scene, rendered more serene in this isolated setting.

Neil broke the silence.

"Did you see them spearing themselves with the old hashi? It's unbelievable – like personal injury lawsuits never existed. To think of being able to get away with that in England, or God forbid, America! Imagine Brian conducting a class of chopstick wielding chimps in Murka – a terrifying thought!"

"They seem to have a higher pain threshold than us. A fact exploited by gameshow franchises before now," I countered archly. "The teachers just stand back, scowl and let them, and us, get on with it."

"Still it's great to be able to cut loose and do something fun for once," Neil said, clearly one of his enthusiastic moods bubbling over.

"Well, we do serve up that same steaming nonsense every week, don't we," I said, still trying to come to terms with Neil's mood swings. "And anyway, I thought you were hating the shogakko experience again this morning after the interrogation."

"Oh, that's just standard bullshit, isn't it? I mean you can't let it annoy you."

I sensed a philosophical interlude barrelling my way, like a small child running the length of a classroom with its mouth full of foam alphabet shapes.

"When you've been used to your boss – who by the way is supposed to be showing you a little encouragement after your two hour commute to sit like a dog at his feet – screaming two inches away from your face, getting a bit of heat on your eating habits from a placid old buffer who doesn't even dare meet your eye is not so bad."

Even when I sense melodrama and sniff the odour of affected world weariness, I nevertheless cannot help but be impressed by the tales of a former existence from which the storyteller has drawn experience and profited. Still so young, so inexperienced, I was in thrall to the grafting Neil claimed to have done in his time.

"It was sheer misery, William," he continued, enjoying his customary position of minister to the captive audience. "Running pointless, demeaning errands, compiling lists of targets for your own assessment – so fashioning the noose for your own neck – and being told in no uncertain terms when you are an inch out of step with the grand plan of your bastard overlord. No, I tell you what, give me Japanese nuance and infinitely subtle grades of disappointment rather than a gobby, uptight manager any day of the week. In fact give it me just from Monday to Friday. They can all piss off at the weekends."

He had whipped himself up into a self-righteous frenzy and needed reining in back to the professional matters at hand.

"The thing I don't get, Neil, is the strange attitude to living things. I mean, our own children are little buggers. Indeed we have a keen culture of general neglect for a supposed nation of animal lovers, but I was led to believe things were different here."

"Are you referring to the turtle engaged in his endless misery in the fish tank?" Neil asked.

I ran my hand slowly along the edge of the low table.

"You saw it too then."

In the previous classroom I couldn't take my eyes from the most basic of open top fish tanks, less than two feet square and pickled with foetid water. Around the inside perimeter of this boundary a sorry turtle maintained a ceaseless patrol, raising up out of the water to claw ineffectually with front flippers at a world perpetually in sight yet beyond reach.

The tips of these appendages were rubbed raw by continually grubbing at the plastic as the turtle opened its slow, stolidly uncomprehending beak at the dark shapes flitting around the room. Children came with a metronomic insistence to tap at the plastic walls and laugh indulgently at its plangent anthropomorphic gestures, as the turtle hopelessly tried to broaden its horizons.

The teacher had smiled at me when he saw us taking a horrified interest in the spectacle, as we searched for an explanation for the unchanging tableau which ceaselessly played itself out.

"Children really love tortoise," he said simply, grinning broadly and turning away. "They like to say hello."

Back at the low table, and I was pumping Neil for information.

"I'd read of this intimate relationship with nature, far beyond our western conception of mere love for cute animals."

"It is something I'm afraid neither you nor I will ever come close to understanding, save an about turn in religious ideals," he replied. "You will hear many accounts of the reverence flowers are treated with – how cherry blossoms at festival time are left alone to hang naturally on the trees, even with the multitudes of crowds viewing them and the vastly greater multitudes hanging higher on the branches. Who would miss a handful picked as a fleeting memento? It's all part of the uniquely Japanese notions of *mono no aware*; an exquisitely tuned sensitivity for the transience of the world, and a greater respect for everything you find in it because of this.

"And I think despite everything, you *will* find a greater respect for living things here. But it is something quite different to our notions of a sentimental love for our pets.

"This is stoical and therefore standoffish; animals and plants are not separate kingdoms from each other as they are from our own. They may romanticise nature in a childish fashion, with cutesy animals, but beneath that silliness is a deeper acceptance of things.

"We are all in it together, I think, is the Japanese view, and man makes do with his lot with the same still religious core as does a cherry blossom. Or a turtle."

"Still, from our point of view it's a poor bloody turtle, isn't it?" I asked, keen to press home my point in the face of Neil's explanation.

"Yes," he conceded; "It's a pretty poor bloody turtle."

Around the walls of the room were artefacts, quite possibly replicas, beyond the telling of my inexpert eye, of Japanese culture. Beautifully sparse paintings bearing the familiar, yet always striking vertical and backwards, right to left, alignment of characters, providing an oblique illumination to the meaning and state of mind of the artist.

They were to the painting what my conception of Neil was to the cultural secrets of Japan; a refractory commentary – the mood along a journey to enlightenment, rather than befuddlement at an instruction manual; a paradigm as opposed to a narrative. Perhaps this is just how it should be. I stood in relation to Neil as he did to the cultural island of the Orient, further stepping stones to an unrealisable higher feeling.

An opening in the wall, called a *tokonoma*, lay aside from the table at which we were seated, populated by traditional stringed instruments with their long necks, and the tempting displays of items approximating to spears, with lacquered black handles and elaborate steel heads, finely turned and engraved with more characters.

The tokonoma could reliably be found in the corner of a traditional room considered the most worthy, fairest site, away from the relative clutter of whatever else the chamber contained, resplendent in its own simplicity.

This one was embellished by a weeping peony in a chastely decorative bowl, standing on a low table. The flower bent and gently swayed to a rhythm unheard by anyone in the still room, yet as surely present as the cold steel of the spears hanging in their brackets, or

140

the paintings with their delicate colours and broad stokes of calligraphy.

I took it all in with the same wonder as Neil, not knowing the words or the rhetoric but feeling the underlying forms to the same degree, but intuitively; not intellectually. The room was an entity which could be contemplated, if that was what one wished to do, but more than this it could be *partaken in*, absorbed as if through the pores of the bodies inhabiting it, until all matter in the room floated together, occupying the same space within a void.

As we sat there and the sharp winter sunlight pierced the room, each individual strand, each friable beam was visible as it penetrated the glass of the windows, and the dust danced in space as we became drowsy, transfixed by the strokes of the *kakemono*, the writing on the wall in the characters of scholars and poets.

The atmosphere of the room, abstracted and yet immediately present, lent itself to lazy, indulgent discussion.

"If we can't understand the cruelties of our own culture, we'll never get a handle on the finer, or rather the more savage aspects of another one," I said.

"Those are wise words," Neil replied. "And it's something I'm coming to realise after years of reading about the country. Nothing, absolutely nothing, can prepare you for the blow to the head of living here," he continued.

"Why is that though?" I burst in. "I mean we have a clear enough caricature of Japanese insanity which has asserted itself as a sort of cultural token or symbol in the West."

Neil nodded and patted down my interjection in an avuncular fanning motion.

"One of the reasons is that the Japanese feel no need to interpret their reality – as we are attempting to do here – in an intellectual way," he said. "We start with the personal and try to fit it into a general schema, but for them the process is totally in reverse.

"They understand the universal instinctively, and out of this all-encompassing form grows a measure of individuality, even if it seems limited to us. The universal is implicitly understood from childhood, it is not necessarily even taught or inculcated, so there is no need for explanation."

Neil thought further on the subject as he glanced towards the tokonoma. I followed his gaze in the silence of the room.

"There's a real contradiction and tension between our view of the Japanese and the reality, as you might expect. The world sees them as inscrutable, half-crazed with a kind of indecipherable, wilful madness.

"In fact the opposite is rather the case – what I now see is that they operate to a code which is strictly delineated.

"Rather than acting in a scattershot, random manner, they conform to rigidly defined rules so proscriptive, that their behaviour, once you have any sympathy for their modes of thought, is utterly predictable."

"Perhaps the best thing to do, then, is not to worry too much about the theory and just enjoy the ride," I said, feeling as ever as if I had learned something from our cosy chat.

"That," said Neil, "is probably the wisest conclusion one can draw. And if you have realised this already, you are doing OK."

The bell, once again an electronic rendering of Big Ben's chimes, shattered the silence, incongruously cutting through the room.

"Shit – I was just getting comfortable," I said, stretching my legs to shake some life into them, numbed with pins and needles at the low table. It didn't matter whether we were abstracted or enmeshed; we all had to crack on just the same.

We needed some brisk relief before we were sought out once more for our travelling salesman's bag of tricks.

As I looked out of the French windows, which made increasing sense in the context of the room, echoing the sliding traditional doors found for centuries in Japanese rooms, an incredible sight met my eyes, ever the mixing of the serious with the absurd. Children had just broken up for playtime and we could hear them tearing through the corridors outside our sanctuary. Now they appeared, criss-crossing each other, cutting one another up and T-boning their friends on unicycles.

"Bloody unicycles!" I shouted, in a sudden ecstasy of joy.

It didn't get any better or more typically tangential than this.

We both leapt up and pressed our faces to the window, beaming at the children. Neither of us had seen this before, despite being warned about it by Jeremy and Jay, which we had taken to be a dry joke, aimed at mocking the greenhorns.

Some of the older children were proudly mounted high on the saddles, shooting around the cloisters of the entrance hallway with its sheltered colonnade, doing laps of the little quad, then turning round the end support and coming back again, heads held imperiously high.

Younger ones, only a couple of years into their training for the putative big top, were less steady on their steeds, teetering precariously as they held onto the wall while mounting up, then rocking backwards and forwards as they see-sawed slowly down the concrete path, stopping here and there to make a desperate grab for a ledge or a post as they overbalanced.

The smallest, six year olds barely weeks into their elementary school career, were nevertheless not shy about giving it a go.

And bless their little rubber bodies as they came crashing to the floor – and picked themselves up time after time with a remarkable dedication in pursuit of mastering so seemingly trivial an ability.

Neil and I felt sure we would see a serious injury before long, and yet ghoulishly committed ourselves to this sentry watch at the window for some minutes, never once taking our eyes from the action.

That there were no adults on hand to rigorously survey the antics and censor the approaching danger would once have shocked us on our immediate arrival from England. There was a refreshing laissez faire attitude to health and safety, located at the midpoint between our modern preoccupation with eliminating any possibility of danger to children, and the perils of a Industrial Revolution factory.

The children were simply playing, and if they fell a thousand times, then they would eventually learn how not to fall. It was a refreshing attitude.

"Look at that little bugger!" I cried, as a particularly precocious child, no more than seven or eight, undertook his pal, weaving frantically through less able classmates.

He was forced to leave the walkway to avoid a head on collision, something clearly laid down in statute as being both undesirable and forbidden, and an older girl, quite possibly some species of pre-teen prefect, forced him to jump down from on high, pointing out the repercussions of his zeal, now the tread of the tyre was soiled with the ubiquitous clay of the military drill ground.

"It's remarkable – quite remarkable," Neil was repeating to himself. "How do you reconcile the fact they have no central heating in schools with the notion there is a unicycle for every child at shogakko?"

"They breed them tough out here, I guess," was my only suggestion.

"I mean, can you think of anything more pointless than learning to balance on a one wheeled vehicle?" Neil asked.

"Well, perhaps it's some form of state-sponsored drive in anticipation of the moment when Japan becomes too crowded to afford four, or even two wheels per person," I said, "And they are breaking in a new generation with this way of thinking.

"The Yodas may be beyond saving – I can't see them saddling up on one, though the mind does boggle – but they're getting started on the younger generation before it reaches crisis point. In any case, Tex is probably up for it after spending a lifetime in the saddle."

Neil smiled, considering the hypothesis as a serious idea.

"You know, from what I'm learning as time goes on, that might be the most rational explanation to a typically Japanese conundrum."

"Which conundrum do you mean?" I asked, "The pressure on Japan's resources and land, or the educational merits of circus act teaching for pupils?"

"Both," said Neil as he stood in his military stance, hands folded behind his back, pigeon chest thrust upwards and outwards.

"As ever in this country, probably both."

20

There was little time to further digest the scene before us; digestion of a different sort was to be put to the test with the trying experience of elementary school lunch. This presented itself as a farce in three acts – mirrored in the tripartite nature of my club sandwich – and performed solely, I imagined, for my own viewing pleasure.

Whereas I had let it be known from early on that due to my distaste for fish I would be supplying my own food, vegetarian Neil put himself – by way of attempting cultural integration – in the firing line for all manner of unpleasantness.

While I would tuck into my lunch, with its pork and chicken and delicious garnishing, my little tub of crisp fingers, my string cheeses and fruit in jelly, all washed down with some chemically begotten pop, Neil would tip toe through the platter before him, picking his way uneasily between untold species of recently deceased critters, presented with all the bounties of the sea.

However, before lunch was served, we went through the usual rigmarole, endlessly entertaining to me, but endured with less grace by Neil. Anyone who has witnessed the show will feel quietly confident that the phrase 'too many cooks spoil the broth' has no Japanese equivalent.

As soon as Big Ben signalled lunch was due in the mountains, there was a flurry of activity as dozens of small feet kicked into action on hardwood floors, the echoes reverberating through the hull of the school.

Neil and I were dragged off to the tiniest children's class, just in time to be honoured guests at the ceremony of the preparation. The commotion had died down by the time we arrived and took our seats – designed for six year olds – offered with decorum unusual in a child.

Now eight kids were being solemnly suited up by their peers in what looked like surgical attire; long white robes, white head pieces to cover their hair and again what can only be described as masks designed for infection control.

When this was done and eight pairs of unblinkingly serious eyes looked back at the teacher, he dismissed them and they scurried off to the bowels of the school. When they returned, they looked for all the world like they had been on an alien autopsy jaunt, but got sidetracked into bringing back the steaming pan and vats of lunch instead, by way of a performing a favour to the caretaker.

Children came in, cloaked to the nines in the garb which was deemed appropriate for the potentially lethal exercise of serving up hot food, but with little toes dancing all the while precariously in their flip flops. The piping contents of the great metallic vats sloshed backwards and forwards and minute hands struggled, two to a handle, to control the combined weight of food and serving apparatus.

Other attendants followed the magnificent caravan of delights, bearing ladles and racks of bowls, dishes and victual trays, the sincerity implicit in the concentration of their faces beautiful to behold. They arranged themselves in an assembly line along a row of tables set up for the purpose and apportioned the various prizes in precise amounts to every member of the class, tidying the slop if ever it was placed imprecisely into a section of the compartmentalised trays.

These held the main meat, tempura fried vegetables, fish – tails poking boorishly out of their sleeping bags of batter – the cold sliced cucumber and sour radish with its nut accompaniment and the slimy, tasteless buckwheat noodles.

In a separate bowl huddled the clammy rice, this the only part of the meal where children could have an input into their appetite. The delicate girls took their moderate quota, while the fat kid (and there was always one rather obese boy per class) and the sprightlier children had their daily ritual of classmates' laughing encouragement to pile up their rice above the brim of the bowl.

When all was finished, when all had taken their seats once more and the mask wearers, their ritual performed, once again exposed their faces, the intercom sprang into life, as if divinely ordained, with a blast of Beethoven's Sixth Symphony underscoring the frolicsome mood.

Gradually the rite of spring faded out to be replaced by young voices reading lists of names and other data without humour – or more strangely given their age, any hint of self-consciousness. What they were saying, despite the ritual being repeated day in day out at chugakko as well as shogakko, was indeterminate.

What was clear from the tones was the gravity of this enormously important task, given the formal flourishes characterising each new cadence. Each measured phrase both began and ended:

"Please excuse me/I beg you to pay attention/Thankyou for listening to my humble words."

Possibly not a strict translation, but I would like to think the tenor was something like this.

Then, so quickly I missed it every time, there was a swift handclap and expostulation of their version of the *'For what we are about to receive'*, and they slipped their oppressive shackles of decorum.

Maintaining an immaculate stillness throughout their torso, the initial scrum of child versus lunch, each a uniquely personal affair in this country of psychological unity, nevertheless embraced a ferocity of movement unseen in the rest of society.

148

Chopsticks dove into rice, spraying it in all directions while shovelling mountains of the sticky substance down throats, rent small pieces of sesame seed coated chicken asunder while held in an accusatory dagger manner; gripped with a feral dexterity the slimy pieces of cold pickled vegetable.

Occasionally faces would rise from the tray of food like pigs raising their downcast eyes from a trough of swill. Clinging tenaciously from noses, cheekbones and even eyebrows, could be seen doughty rice sherpas, blazing a trail to the dark summit of the crown.

Contrasting with this scene of unfettered gorging were Neil and I. For my own part I ate with moderation, not wanting to offend any further having already got away with my western lunchbox.

Neil, however, fussily picked his way through a school meal like a haggard old bird prowling the seashore for morsels, sifting and discarding, alighting on a titbit, testing it gingerly, rejecting one, then bolting another. Our eyes met several times over lunch and I always found myself wondering quite why he put himself through this charade as I caught his weak smile from across the classroom.

Then, with quite the same suddenness as it began, the meal ended, again with a curt handclap, slight head nod and word of formal acceptance.

Robes were donned and platters sent back with chaperones to the school bowels from where they had come, and the moveable feast disappeared out from under us, Neil and I left once more stranded on tiny chairs, as if the sea had departed too quickly and left us beached, our dignity ruptured with our ungainly bodies broken on the sand.

One final act was left to accomplish; that of the post lunch teeth cleaning, something I would have understood, but for the twin facts that firstly Japanese toothpaste is as ineffective as mud, and secondly, they didn't use toothpaste anyway, but simply brushed using water and the perfunctory zeal normally associated with these hollow rituals.

The rest of the day passed without great significance, until home time, when we were called with much ceremony over the school loudspeaker to the gym – in the direction of which we had heard the better part of a hundred juvenile feet rushing.

"What do they have in store for us now?" I asked Neil, who had adopted his traditional springing gait.

"A coordinated unicycle display team?" he suggested through the corner of his mouth.

We walked in on an upscale game of musical chairs, involving the entirety of the student body with associated teachers, several of whom encouraged us to join in. This was not quite my cup of tea; less so in fact than the allegedly refreshing green blend of macaque pee which passed for a hot drink at shogakko break time.

But once I gave in; to the absurdity of the situation, to the warmth of the people and to the reassuring small voice which told me no-one would ever see me again alive on this particular mountain side, it was actually quite fun. Neil started to exhibit the excruciatingly premature avuncularity which would define his interaction with children through the rest of the year, and I skipped and played with the little chaps as we jostled for seats.

When we finished our games we learned what all this had been leading up to, and any cynicism left was dissolved when we received a lovely gift of a collage of pictures, taken that day as we danced and shouted to keep their attention focused.

Dominating the centre of each photograph, the two of us stood over six feet tall apiece, Neil, skinny and avian, and myself appearing all the chunkier beside him, we towered over the cherubic faces in their brightly coloured shorts and T-shirts, mildly bemused expressions on our faces, pulling ironic victory 'V's to echo the energetic finger poses of our comrades.

Finally, we expressed our gratitude in languages both familiar and foreign and then we left. As we walked out into the beautiful dusky sunlight, children wheeled about us on unicycles pressing little paper cranes, folded by their own hands, into ours.

We took them with a smile and a bow and climbed into the little van, slightly more confident of the return journey than of the outward leg. Neil, concentrating on avoiding a koi pond as he reversed, did not see the last of our day's teachers, head bowed in conversation with Kocho sensei, both for the moment abstracted into the same twilight wood block picture the mountains had become.

21

Meanwhile at big school everything was proceeding apace and in the Japanese way – that is to say slowly and comfortably, with much circumspection and even more circumlocution.

The English teacher's room – a desolate bunker fortified against the rest of the school, seemingly constructed from an alloy of exposed steel, formica and David Beckham posters – became ever more my haven.

But even this microcosm of school life, through which the students passed with their baskets of books and pained expressions, had a rich bass of characters.

Shimoida was still all pained reserve, acquaintance shorn of affability. He would pass unseen in the corridor, harried and hurrying along, coming out of nowhere to breathe a brisk, sinister hello from behind, then disappear before you could turn around. It would always leave me disconcerted, slightly disorientated.

At the other end of the scale was Iwabata, the much put upon junior member of the faculty. But she was certainly not the runt of the litter. Weighing in at something approaching 20 stone, and standing the better part of six feet, Iwabata sensei embodied the full fat flavour of the Japanese schoolchild, the one in ten marked out by their genes for a miserable time in the harsh world of school life.

And just like an overgrown schoolchild she sought to conquer this deficit through the counter-intuitive method of drawing attention with bright colours and luminously branded clothing. Completing the look was an overkill of Beatrix Potter animal motifs, starting with feet rammed into bunny shoes, and Tom Kitten ankle socks choking the life out of colossal calves.

No jewellery or adult accoutrements offset Iwabata's childish effect, just a prodigiously broad and perfect smile, all the more remarkable given the inconsistencies of Japanese dental standards; teeth shining inside the folds of her waxy, lumpen face, perpetually on display beneath her bizarrely permed hair.

She was the archetype of the young woman, marginalised by her own lack of appeal to the grown-up world. And so she did as many others, making a virtue of a necessity and running with the infantilised theme, intentionally rooting herself in an adult Neverland she could never hope to transcend.

Iwabata, fighting a workplace war on two fronts, battling firstly the limitations of her sex and secondly the obvious shortcomings of her lack of sex appeal, was the whipping boy of the office, getting the fag end classes, the extra baskets of book marking and, I was assured by others in oddly compromised confessions, an unfair 50% teacher's salary into the bargain.

The gentle condescension with which she was treated by the other members, though codified in structures of speech and inflections, was still visible even to my alien eye.

But Iwabata was happy in the cloying world she had created. Even the constant spectre of her diabetes did not get her down. Dashing off for a pee in between lessons, she seemed to live an engagingly full life, whatever social barriers she had to drag her bulk over.

Even though she lived at home with her Christian parents, occupying quite possibly the same Potter-themed bed she had slept on since she was prised out of a cot, Iwabata would delight in making the most of our time together by filling me in at great length about the latest intrigue of her internet and speed dating.

"William sensei – could you just mark these books for me?" she would ask, breaking into a gargantuan instant messaging session I would inevitably be holding with Neil.

This was merely an ice breaker for the main topic of conversation she was twitching around in her oversize Jemima Puddle-Duck (I would imagine) briefs to discuss.

"I have got a very big problem right now, William Sensei – did you know this?"

"I'm sorry to hear that," I replied, knowing as surely as the hourly timing of her regulation toilet breaks, what was to follow.

This would never, for all manner of reasons of decorum and personal shame, be discussed in front of the other teachers, and though I longed to make her squirm by alluding to her intrigues with them around, I would never have gone this far for fear of some diabetic inundation, leaving her to deliquesce into a pool on the wooden floor.

In truth I knew it was something of an honour, being confided to in this way. After all, I was a triple stranger of workmate, man and foreigner. Besides, the bizarre rituals of Japanese dating was a mystery I felt I owed it to myself to penetrate at least some way into.

"I want to know what to do – I have met a man… he is nice guy, I think. I spoke to him when we went on a trip to Disneyworld in Tokyo."

"I see," I said. "Well that's all rather charming. What is the problem then?"

"No problem, I don't think. He is maybe a little shy, but very sweet, I think, *ne*?"

Did the way she inflected the rhetorical suffix suggest she was reassuring herself?

"He said he liked me and we could maybe meet up for dinner. I think he works hard and has good job. And he shook my hand very nicely when he said goodbye. Because I am Christian, ne?"

"Well I am sure he is a fine man if he shook your Christian hand at the end of the date…" I began.

"Not date – not yet," she assured me. "Maybe I want it to be date – we will see."

"Well go for it then. I mean it sounds like he has the total package; good job, firm – yet respectful – handshake, likes his amusement parks. All clean fun. When did you meet him?"

"In June," she said, beaming more radiantly than ever.

"Um, but it's almost Christmas."

"I know – the time when Jesus died on cross for human sins."

It sounded much like her ineffectual prince charming had long ago taken his last ride down the log flumes before bailing.

"I gave him my number, you know, for my mobile," at this she got out her phone, presumably an essential prop to my understanding, and waved it triumphantly, the pendant Mrs Tiggy-Winkle dangling from the stubby aerial, fixed in a pose of spiky rotundity.

Fat little Hiromi Iwabata, unchanged in nature – if not stature – since the first grade at shogakko, looked at me expectantly as she replaced the phone in her oversized handbag.

"Do you think he is going to call me?" she asked, with no edge whatsoever in her voice.

It was a pretty silly question.

155

"When else have you seen him," I asked, trying to find a shred of evidence that could keep her hopes going.

"Just once," she beamed.

"Oh – what happened, where did you go?"

"I already told you, to Disneyworld."

"Oh, so you have only *ever* met him once, then. Is this correct?"

"Yes!" she shouted, this time in a sickly state of happiness whose pathology was beyond my understanding.

"Why don't you phone him?" I ventured, cunningly placing the onus upon her to make her own destiny.

"I cannot do that," she said.

"Ah, because you are the lady and it would be insulting to you both for the woman to chase the man?" I guessed, getting into the game.

She shook her head and laughed.

"Because you are Christian, and as such this would be unbecoming behaviour for a young woman, privately bred?" (If she wanted a personal conversation on the finer points of dating, then an Austenian flavour was in order, I felt.)

"I am Christian, ne(?) but I cannot phone him because he did not give me his number. I asked for it. But he forgot to give me."

No, he does not love you, my dear. Let us count the ways… ah, they would be more numerous than the seeds in Squirrel Nutkin's stash.

"I don't know. Maybe he should have called already. I mean, it's six months ago now. In England we would think the time has kind of passed. We talk about 'windows of opportunity'. Well, metaphorically, that window became a catflap, then a letterbox, and now I rather fear it has disappeared entirely."

Still Hiromi beamed her smile, unperturbed.

"I think he will ring maybe one day soon – next week, ne? What do you think?"

"Perhaps," I had to concede, powerless in the face of such ill-founded yet vigorous optimism.

"And I have another man who I met the other day. I think maybe he will call me soon…"

The long day wore on, my appraisal and input of dating mores totally superfluous to the remorseless tread of day trips, outings and intrigues stone dead before they had begun.

Hiromi was 33, she said. When did I think she would get married? Soon, Iwabata sensei, very soon. Though let us not forget Jesus himself died at 33…

I wandered out into the long, dark corridor, chuckling about Iwabata. I was still smiling to myself as I swung around the corner to the toilet, to see Shimoida sensei leaving a quiet office, deep in conversation with Mr Oni – the emissary from the ELT education department at city hall.

What were they doing together? They could only be discussing me. Plotting, even. That's just how Oni would operate, I was sure. And Shimoida too. I couldn't trust him.

I watched as they smiled and bowed to each other. Oni turned on his heel and scurried away in the other direction. I weighed up whether I could make it into the toilet before Shimoida saw me, and I bounded towards the door. Not so. The head of English raised his gaze and we locked eyes for a desperate moment, each searching the other's intentions for a split second. We'd caught each other in the act; him going behind my back to confer with the ultimate powers, and me snooping on them. I leaned into the toilet with my shoulder as Shimoida's forced smile turned to a scowl; the closest he would get to admitting I'd seen him, and acknowledging the moment of understanding which had passed between us.

22

Christmas came and went. Everyone else appeared to have somewhere better to be. Neil and Brian, evidently feeling flush, went on a break to Tokyo while Michael barricaded himself in his room with little Hanako.

Nadya, after carefully weighing up the expense – and the danger – went home. She stayed through the last week of December, for New Year and her Orthodox Christmas on 6 January. The Ukraine she returned to was in turmoil.

Just weeks previously the country held its general election. When the widely expected win for the lenient, westward-leaning candidate didn't materialise, people took to the streets of the capital. They felt cheated. And as Nadya went home to the east of the country, people had already been occupying the central square in the capital, hundreds of kilometres to the west, for nearly a month.

But in her own city she found folk protesting against the protestors, reminding everyone there is always another side to a simple story of cause and effect; the angle of incidence and its reflection are not necessarily predictable. Her own family were fractious. They lived close to the border of Russia, and like the majority in the region, instinctively felt more Russian than Ukrainian.

***

She called me from her parents' apartment in a lull before their traditional New Year celebrations began. I was hours ahead; for me it was four in the morning, the end of December.

In fact, it was already the start of the New Year for me, and just a few others in the world. I was bored, and colder even than these wintry protestors on the fringes of Russia. Snow had settled in the empty

Japanese streets to a whimsical timetable, hanging around for just a day after a heavy fall, disappearing for an afternoon or two, then settling in for the New Year after a seemingly innocuous flurry.

My apartment was, almost literally, freezing. The oil-powered fan heater was my only way of staying warm. There were no radiators in houses, at least not in the accommodation I knew. The digital display on the device regularly registered 3 Celsius in the mornings before I had fired it up, following a mercy dash to the petrol station up the street to buy a huge orange tank of gasoline.

The oil heater was a strange beast, at once both high tech and utterly backward; with the bulk and weight of a large TV, it featured an incomprehensible digital readout with an army of functions. But then it also ran on a decidedly old fashioned, and highly combustible liquid – petrol essentially – eating up power in its struggle to stave of the Japanese winter.

It always made me feel slightly nervous, especially as my traditional rooms were entirely wooden, and I gave the plastic gasoline container the respect it deserved by pitching it outside onto the concrete balcony after I had filled up the reservoir each time.

School had finished for pupils on Christmas Eve – generous given the circumstances, because teachers came in on Christmas Day itself for a rigorous cycle of meetings. I was not invited to these, but instead had to sit on my own in the silence of the staff room. I passed a Buddhist Christmas, then.

Feeling a bit sorry for myself, I looked out of the window at the snow covered sports field on its terrace above the Iizu valley and the distant mountains to the south, themselves not yet snow capped. Even hardy teachers, bred in the mountains of Nagano, had taken to wearing coats throughout the unimaginably cold school day. Happy there would be no stigma to following suit, I did the same, my previously respectable wardrobe (thanks, Mrs Masada) becoming more practical with the onset of the uncompromising weather.

Also without central heating, the school eschewed the relative safety of my oil heater for a far more primitive option.

So once the education authority had ascertained that indeed this winter was no different to the historical hundreds which had gone before – and it indeed was going to get damn cold – a primeval structure was assembled in each of the classrooms.

Put together with much ceremony and with a quasi religious fervour on Christmas Eve, the final job of the children before disappearing for their week-long holiday was to assembles an infernal machine in the corners of their various classrooms.

The *stove-oo* as it was cutely named, was square as a washing machine and invariably positioned, with scant regard for practicality or safety, directly inside the main entrance to each room. Not used to their sudden appearance? Not on your toes as you entered a new room? Then you may easily have collided with its demonically hissing surfaces.

Looking like a relic from early 20th Century industrialisation – and therefore not entirely out of place in the almost Art Deco hull of the school – the stovu was not the most efficient of beasts. It relied on raw power, rather than subtle and economical diffusion to heat the rooms, and was essentially a portable boiler, exuding heat both through its lethally hot carcass and through the wide gauge pipe which erupted from its bulk straight up to the ceiling and then ran the length of the classroom, suspended every few feet by what looked like wire coat hangers, the individual segments of tubing fitted together and hung by no lesser engineers than the children themselves.

On top of the stovu a pan of water constantly evaporated with an insinuating plume of steam and a window on the side of the machine gave out onto a view of the flames raging within.

Naturally there was no barrier to keep idle limbs from brushing the sides of the stovu. More than this, though, it actually became an impromptu piece of climbing apparatus. In fact, teachers at elementary and middle school alike would smile on absent-mindedly as their charges jumped from a desk on to the top of the heater, sending boiling water splashing onto the floor.

But today, without children careering around, Iwabata showed more chutzpah and a more conniving mind than I had given her credit for. With minutes to go until five o'clock home time, when I had packed up the debris from a day alone, having observed my silent and pointless vigil, she came in to catch me standing forlornly at the window.

"Willu sensei – what are you doing here?" she asked with mock incredulity. She was more than familiar with the rules.

"I'm enjoying Christmas Day," I answered. "Can't you see the festive smile on my face?"

"Why do you come in today – last year the ELT did not come in at all during Christmas?"

"Well he was either a more religious man than myself, or the rules are getting stricter," I said. "Either way, here I am, doing my job. It doesn't matter, I'm off home now to sit in my cold little apartment."

Iwabata's dark eyes lit up.

"Where is your girlfriend? Are you not spending Christmas with her?"

"I'm afraid she is back in Ukraine and most other people seem to be off somewhere else; I'm the only Englishman in town at the moment

162

and the only one who had to work over Christmas," I said. I was milking it. In truth, I knew I was probably better off here than twiddling my thumbs in my room.

I'd taken it as a directive from on high, quite possibly a personal test from Oni to see if I would crack and bring shame on the system by invoking the gaijin card and refusing to come in on Christmas Day. In any case, I indeed was the only foreigner who was deemed essential to the slick running of schools. It looked like I was getting Boxing Day off – purely by chance as it fell on a Saturday – but would be expected to be seated at my desk at 8am in the run up to New Year.

It was a simple, mute battle of wills, of the kind I was sure happened between millions of Japanese every day; arbitrary dictums were laid down and underlings swallowed the bitter pill while fulfilling their duties to the letter. I took a perverse pleasure in joining in the game, refusing to exhibit any of the unbecoming petulance others could show when faced with a similarly raw deal. Brian wouldn't have stood for it, by god.

Stories abounded among the longer serving expats, of teachers who fought the holiday system and won, securing an extra day off here and there, but were forever tarnished with the unseemly reputation of being an uppity foreigner. I was determined this would not be my fate. In a Japanese culture of slavish dedication to duty, where assiduity and grinding out the long days was rewarded, I was not going to blink.

For a start, it was impossible to tell from which direction the inflexibility came. Was it the old farts at the board, fussing with implementing the finer points of contracts; the Kocho sensei, principals of each school, engaged in a tacit battle with each other to see who could

163

extract a greater share of their pound of flesh? Or was it even Mrs Masada herself, sacrificing us as a face-saving measure rather than fight an embarrassing war on our behalf against a world order she implicitly believed in?

The order, wherever it had come from, came from above. That is all ye know on Earth, and all ye need to know.

"Maybe you can come to my house for some food tonight" Iwabata suggested, breaking into my reverie. Her bright, oily face shone even more under the fluorescent lights.

"It is OK, you know, because my parents are Christians, ne? They love Christmas. I think they would like you too," she added.

I should have turned down the invitation, but a combination of loneliness, gratitude for the honour of being invited home – and downright curiosity at what I would find chez Iwabata – assaulted my normal judgement.

"Well, that would be very nice, Iwabata sensei," I said, genuinely touched. "I shall go and put on my Sunday best."

"But it is only Friday, Willu sensei," she pointed out.

She was right. I was always out of step.

I shook my head and swivelled to the screen of my laptop, looking at the message I'd just received from Martin McQueen back in England.

Another hopeless case, turning a brave face to the world, Martin didn't even have the salve of Iwabata's attention, I sneered. His acute awareness of his shortcomings and his aggression in hiding them kept him permanently on his toes, fighting to keep one step ahead of assumptions. Perpetually on edge, ready to sidestep any jibe he anticipated.

But buried in the self-consciously breezy tone of Christmas greetings, there was something else. Martin alluded to hard times in the Bristol carpet trade. And he complained that, in those early days of the new millennium, the consumerist timbre of the country was also at odds with his politics. This *soi disant* socialist was feeling out of touch with the Labour government, and the direction of the country. He'd always enjoyed talking himself out onto the margins, of course.

This time I felt Martin was building up to something. I read on. Then, just as quickly he signed off. Things to do; people to see.

Same with me.

23

Later that night Iwabata picked me up in her generic spinstermobile; a tiny glorified shopping trolley with an outlandishly proportioned gear lever seemingly imported from a London bus, and the sit-up-and-beg position favoured by young Japanese women behind the wheel.

An army of soft toys clung tenaciously to the dashboard, peering out over the bonnet to inspect me as she drove up and stopped outside the stairs to my apartment. She beckoned me in as ten pairs of eyes followed me suspiciously.

"Willu sensei, my parents are very excited to meet you!" she said. "They are looking forward to meeting a real English Christian."

"Well, I wouldn't quite say that – what have you been telling them?" I asked, willing to go along with the joke, but slightly concerned at the billing I had received from Hiromi, and the possibility I may be gatecrashing a quiet family gathering under false pretences.

"I told them you are an English gentleman – we know in Japan how all English gentlemen are Christians."

I looked at her, genuinely confused at how she had received this impression, whether from some throwaway remark I had made to her, or an outdated notion she had gathered from fighting her way through an ancient novel.

Iwabata doing Jane Austen in the mountains I found a particularly surreal notion, imagining her crashing out of the rigmarole of Japanese social convention headlong into the deeper rigmarole of 19th Century provincial British niceties.

"You showed the pupils your lovely school with the church where you had to go each morning and sing songs and pray."

Well, sort of. In an attempt to capture their attention and ride on the coattails of the Harry Potter Hogwarts zeitgeist which was proving a mild sensation in Japan at the time, I had shown them pictures of my old school, with its dour mid-Victorian austerity, all grey flint, gables and flagstone floors the colour of the grave.

The fact it had its own chapel was something which provoked much consternation in the resolutely unreligious school system in Japan, confusing the pupils and evidently sending a frisson of misunderstanding jolting through Iwabata's ample frame.

She turned to me, flashing her prodigious smile which I returned rather weakly.

No further protestation needed; just fervent Protestantism, then.

"It was something like that, I suppose," I agreed, weakly.

I held on to a bar on the dashboard while Iwabata piloted the car blind across the backstreet junctions which filled the residential areas of Takada, enmeshing the irregular islands of houses in an elaborate and unpredictable net of non sequiters. As she drove she took one hand off the steering wheel every now and then to vigorously pet the soft toys lined up behind the windscreen, smoothing down fur and tweaking velvety ears with a plump hand.

Soon we pulled up in a little carport with a corrugated plastic roof, attached to a modest, neat house on the corner of two quiet streets, standing no further than six feet from the road surface at any point. Iwabata led me gleefully up the two steps of the delicate garden path, lunging between carefully cropped hedges; an immense amount of greenery packed into the shallow front garden.

Before we could reach the front door, it was tugged open from the inside and the house's two occupants stood side by side, slender enough to both be framed by the modest doorway.

Iwabata père et mère were not what I had expected. Facially I could see the resemblance; the big, innocent eyes and incongruously immaculate teeth had clearly been inherited from the mother, likewise from the father the luxuriant curls.

But beyond this, Hiromi's defining characteristic was a feature unique to herself.

The parents stood there at the threshold of the house, their beaming faces sitting atop scrawny necks and puny shoulders. Each crossed their thin arms in front of themselves, bowing slightly from their slender waists as Hiromi bustled towards them, greeting them in Japanese, turning sideways to navigate the porch columns.

She gathered them in a loving bear hug and then beckoned me up close and personal in the Japanese style, sausage fingers drawing the viewer in like a cat paw; palms turned to the ground.

I approached, ready to return my carefully practiced bow, mindful of the correct degree of bend so as not to be too formal in this social setting, while also being careful to show respect for the honour of an invitation into someone's home. I came within arm's reach of the father. Hiromi began the introduction and I began the slow bend from the waist.

But before I could execute the judicious bend, a wiry arm shot out and snaked around my shoulder, drawing me with unexpected strength into the old man's bosom, as the other limb patted me in a disturbingly paternal manner on the back. I was held in the embrace for several seconds, until, unsure of what to do with the redundant arms dangling at my sides, I returned the hug, patting the strangely warm old chap gently on the back. Still held in the clinch, I turned my eyes to the side and saw Hiromi's mother, her eyes moist, grasp her daughter's hands. As I was let loose, the mother then repeated the father's embrace on me, with only slightly more restraint.

Hiromi was shouting something over the outpouring of emotion on this doorstep in the backstreets of Takada.

"Toshiyuki and Chihiro are their names. You can call them by their first names, their *Christian* names, ne?"

For all their conservative dress, Toshiyuki's immaculately parted hair and the prim restraint of Chihiro's doily fringed shirt, nondescript skirt and brown granny tights, Hiromi's parents were clearly a progressive couple.

In the hall two strands of tinsel pointed the way to Christmas dinner. Once a new round of introductions were out of the way, I understood quite how merry proceedings would be. The rectangular table overflowed with pizza, pasta and salad, crusty focaccia and ciabatta bread with a selection of cold antipasto meats.

Crowning the effort they had made, the dining room table sported, as its centerpiece, a plastic Jesus sitting astride a shiny green cracker, in a pose redolent of the climax of Dr Strangelove. The Lamb of God looked happy; it seemed he had come to love a modern Christmas of superabundance after all. Or at least he had reconciled himself to this unique festival; a confused Tuscan feast beyond the borders of Christendom.

The dining table was simple but resolutely western, as was the rest of the decoration of the house. Though there was a tatami matting area at the far end of the kitchen dining room, it contained no trace of a tokonoma, no family shrine or traditional flourishes. Instead there hung a crucifix on each of the three walls. I looked closer at the

169

fourth wall in the kitchen – all pantries and appliances. Then I spotted it, squeezed in between a shining white cupboard and the microwave, a final Jesus in metal presiding over the harmony of the modern kitchen.

"Wow, is this what you normally eat?" I asked the family through Hiromi.

"I remembered you told me Italian food is your favourite and you really hate fish. We normally eat fish at home – Jesus was a fisherman, ne? – but I don't think you would enjoy this."

"Well thank you very much," I said, turning to Mrs Iwabata, able to express absolutes of opinion now in Japanese.

"I like this food very much." Screwing up my eyes with the effort of recall: "As for me, Italian food is number one."

I held aloft an index finger to demonstrate my enthusiasm, then lowered it, realising the odd pose I was striking, pointing to some particularly pious looking angels, thronged about the light fitting. Mrs Iwabata smiled her appreciation.

"You are welcome. But really it was nothing – please enjoy the food," she said, indicating her husband with an expansive gesture.

"My father was the cook tonight," Hiromi said, beaming. "We know how men do cooking in England. This is not so usual in Japan, but my father wanted to make you feel comfortable."

I acknowledged Toshiyuki's effort on my behalf.

"I am not such a good cook. But this is a beautiful meal. Let's eat," I offered.

Mother and father discussed something lengthways across the table and Mr Iwabata entreated me in his most formal classical Japanese.

I had no idea what he was saying, but could understand from the use of certain tenses and voices that he was making a solemn imprecation of the highest politeness. I looked across the intimate table to Hiromi, whose knees were pressed up against mine beneath its width.

"They are asking you to kindly say the prayer as you are the guest. So please go ahead."

"Good god," I said to myself in an expostulation which was supposed to be under my breath.

"Yes, that is a good start. That is what we always say," Hiromi smiled.

I turned helplessly to either side of the table. Expectant, gently encouraging eyes smiled back at me.

"Please, to begin," Hiromi said again.

There was clearly no way out of this, so at risk of causing both social and religious offence, I spoke the words of the school dinner prayer.

I could tell the occasion was going to be more of an ordeal than I had reckoned on and I cast my gaze about idly, imagining an escape route. Perhaps Jesus had slipped something into the salad. I resolved to steer clear.

Throughout the meal I was the victim of overly generous attention to my every desire: what dishes I desired to try; in what order and magnitude I would try them, and quite how much I enjoyed each facet.

It was charming, and as ever the attention to detail and the solicitous care for the comfort of the guest was quite breathtaking. However, I was beginning to feel there was an agenda here and I was being piloted inexorably towards some unfathomed harbour of intent.

Once we had established that I had burned out my linguistic powers on expressing gratitude for the meal, and that Toshiyuki and Chihiro were patently unfamiliar with English – save the supposed piety of its native speakers – Hiromi assumed the central role, acting as conduit for the conversation.

"My parents want to know all about you – your age and...I don't know how to say it... your background and experience. Please tell us."

"Am I facing an interview panel, then?" I asked, amusement concealing the certainty I now felt that I was being sized up.

Hiromi laughed.

"Please explain to the pupils," she said, mixing her words out of habit.

Faces wracked with attention followed my potted history, interrupting at regular intervals to further explore ambiguities, seeking clarifications of the manifestly obvious and itemisations of the already enumerated.

"Excuse me, Willu sensei," Hiromi said, "but they want to know what you are going to do when you go home to England."

This brought me to a halt. It was something I banished from my mind whenever it popped in there.

Officially I was there for the year and only the year, I told myself, not wanting to indulge my otiose inclinations too far into the future. I would return to my native land at 25, a man of the world which would lay spread open before my experience and imagination.

"Well really, I haven't thought much about.." I began.

"Perhaps you would want to stay in Japan longer?" Hiromi offered, cutting me off.

"My parents are saying maybe that would be good for you. My father said he would like to cook for you again soon."

"Ah, well that's quite charming, but I couldn't trouble him too often," I laughed.

Hiromi was translating as I spoke and mother spoke urgently back to daughter in a desperate staccato, the veil slipping.

"No trouble! No trouble at all, she is saying. Anytime you want to come round here and have a tasty cooked meal, you must."

Still more asides burst out between mother and daughter, as if colluding. Hiromi listened intently, nodding and then exploding in agreement.

"My mother is asking about my friend who goes to a dating club with me, you know where we go on trips together to Disney and things like that?"

"Yes, yes…"

"Well my friend is really fat, you know."

I tried not to raise an eyebrow, though I was aware of it being a simple physical fact that this happened.

"I am a little *chubby*, ne? But my friend is really, really fat!" she laughed, staring me down.

Toshiyuki and Chihiro burst into laughter, recognising a word.

"Fat, fat, fat!" they cried.

"Poor girl!" I said. "She must really want a boyfriend as well, I suppose."

"Not really. She is huge, but she keeps getting men and it is really annoying. She doesn't even want to keep them very long. She just has one boyfriend and then the next week she has another."

"Good lord. How big did you say she was?"

"Massive!" Iwabata moved her hands in an exaggerated gesture of smoothing the contours of a colossal frame, then realising it was simply a mirror image of her own body, frowned and repeated the motion, this time with more hyperbole.

"She is REALLY fat, ne?"

"She certainly is," I agreed.

"I mean, I am a little porky. But this girl is really, really big. I don't think I like her very much, you know? How come she has so many boyfriends?"

This was not a traditional topic for Christmas dinner.

"I really don't know, Hiromi. Perhaps she is a very demanding woman and she only wants the best. Perhaps the men just aren't measuring up to her needs."

"Yes, I think that is it," Hiromi said, latching on to my unintended innuendo: "They are too small and do not 'measure up' to her – she is really, really fat!"

Under the table her knee again rubbed against mine as she smiled at her joke with – was I imagining – a new coquettishness?

I stopped and took stock of the situation. We had made our way through the majority of the feast. I had eaten heartily, but this was nothing compared to the absolute carnage wrought by Mr and Mrs Iwabata who had become quiet as their daughter held forth.

Their skinny bodies packed away the alien food with an unimaginable voracity, while Hiromi herself nibbled coyly around the edges, perhaps to avoid the fate of her detested friend from the Mickey Mouse club. A few errant curls of hair which had unfurled from Toshiyuki's temples were the only sign of the devastation he had wreaked upon the meal, while Chihiro had subtly unbuttoned the sleeves of her blouse at some point, rolling them up to the elbow.

They sat there smiling, sated and happy.

Suddenly Chihiro leapt to her feet, forgetting her role as hostess, and a bottle of warm sake was brought for me to try.

"My parents want to know if you can drink Japanese wine. Do you like it?" Hiromi asked, genuinely interested, as the Japanese always are, as to whether western digestive tracts are capable of processing their native peculiarities. The word *Nihonjinron* – the idea that no-one but a Japanese is fully fit for their unique culture, explained at length by Neil – flashed into my mind.

"Well, I've tried it a few times and I think it's quite tasty actually."

Shock and slightly condescending encouragement lit their faces. Chihiro poured the glass for me, reverently, then all eyes fixed me as I took a ginger sip. It was quite nice, once you got over the fact sake is usually served warm, compounding its initially disturbing sourness.

"Ummm – it's delicious," I said in Japanese, stunning Mr and Mrs with firstly my capacity to drink their wine, and then pass a favourable judgement on it in their native tongue.

Each time I finished the little earthenware tumbler I was rewarded with gasps of appreciation followed by a hasty refilling.

"Yes! Yes!" encouraged Toshiyuki, joining in every third beaker of mine with a chaste nip of his own, clearly getting a little pissed on this inconsequential amount.

I began to experience that all too familiar feeling of uneasy drunkenness, catching my mind floating to the corners of the room, detachedly looking down on the scene, yet not following quite what was unfolding.

It was something which was taking place all too often over the past few months, as I slipped into the easy round of excessive drinking every Friday and Saturday night. But this wasn't due to the hideously British characteristic of living for the weekend, enduring the torment of the week only to reach this endlessly cyclical promised land of leisure. Instead, it was for the simple reason that for the first time in many of our lives, we all could properly afford to indulge our indolence; purging the slothfulness of our weekdays at the weekend.

I drank tumbler after tumbler as a second, then a third container of sake was brought to me. Then Mr and Mrs retired to get themselves ready for bed, assuring me I was welcome to come back again "any time – sooner is better."

Hiromi and I were suddenly left alone at the table. I was smashed, and unpleasantly so.

"Won't you drink some sake?" I asked her.

She laughed, flashing her lupine dentistry, her grin huge and imbued with a peculiar gravity in her shapeless face.

"Don't be silly! I cannot drink alcohol because of my insulin, ne?"

Of course. No respite there, then.

"Are you very drunk right now?" Hiromi asked, no hint of concern in her voice; the same upbeat intonation which marked every question, the same mildly astonished expression puncturing the folds of her face.

"I am, as we say in English – but be careful, as this word is a little rude – absolutely wankered," I replied.

"I can say wankered?" she asked. "I have never heard this word."

Indignantly she took out her electronic dictionary which she always turned to when doubtful of a word I used with her.

"How do you spell this wankered?"

"I don't think you will find it in your dictionary," I said, laughing. "It is a colloquial word."

"I know colloquial," Hiromi said. "It means I must be careful when I use it with the principal of the school."

"Well, quite," I said.

In a language which has few equivalents in terms of our lexicon of profanity, the concept of a swear word was not always grasped.

My mind flashed to the discovery, when marking pupils' work, in which one boy was writing a simple dialogue between himself and a friend, practicing the use of time and places to set up a meeting. Inadvertently, he had turned a straightforward Saturday morning shopping trip into an extract of a Tarantino script. It served as a remarkable lesson in the way base profanity does not translate across the language divide.

It read as follows:

Me: Are you free on Saturday?

Ryu: Yes. What shall we do?

Me: Let's go to Jusco supermarket.

Ryu: OK.

Me: What time shall we meet?

Ryu: How about 10.30am?

Me: Nooo! Fuck! Fuck you, motherfucker!

Ryu: How about 11am?

Me: OK. See you then.

This piece of homework was handed in by a relatively assiduous 14-year-old boy.

Not wanting to get the little mite in undue trouble, but feeling I needed to at least make the teacher, Izumiyama sensei, aware of what was being said in the skit, I tried to explain.

"Yes! I see!" lovely Izumiyama said, laughing.

"It really is very rude," I said, babbling when confronted with her lack of concern. "You would get in a lot of trouble if you wrote this in an English school."

"I think maybe he doesn't understand what the words mean," she said, herself perhaps not understanding what the words mean.

"Just give him a big circle for his effort," she said, giggling her good nature.

I laughed too; there was nothing else to do and no translation would suffice. I circled with an even thicker red pen than usual.

But now Iwabata was tapping away in her little dictionary, the results of which would always need further explanation from me.

"How do you spell 'wankered'?"

She typed it in.

"Willu sensei, there is no wankered, just a noun – I will look it up."

No fucking way! Motherfucker! In my weakened state a complicated discussion about the etymology of the state of being wankered seemed a touch too far.

"Willu sensei, I don't know if this is the right translation, but it says wanker is really something inappropriate."

"Oh, Jesus, I don't know Hiromi," I said, feeling suddenly precarious upon my dining room chair.

"Maybe you are asking for some help? From me?" Hiromi was now not even feigning coyness, but simply turned her lurid smile to full wattage, an appallingly fascinating sight.

Moving in one leap from knee to knee fondling, Hiromi ran her foot, prised from its usual Potter shodding, up my calf. Transfixed with horror, I watched dumbfounded as she swung her great arms beneath her leg to hoist the slab of meat higher, winching her plate of a foot to continue its journey up my thigh.

I came to myself just in time and jerked backwards.

"Iwabata sensei!" I said, suddenly formal again. "What are you doing?"

She stood up and lurched round the table. There was now no solid construction between us, and I was scared. Still, I had a few trump cards in reserve.

"It's Christmas, don't forget – the time of the birth of our lord, Jesus Christ."

"I know," Hiromi said, an exclamation mark of saliva punctuating the far side of her mouth; "And we are both Christians, ne? It is good for us to be together."

Somewhere outside, an unidentified creature kicked up an enormous fuss, whining and squealing as if it could pick up on the raw animal distress flooding the room from the pit of my stomach.

"What the hell is that?" I asked.

"It is my pet," Iwabata replied.

Before she could elaborate, I guessed. A pig.

"It is Pigling Bland!"

A slender trotter flickered through the back of the doorway, where I made out the edge of a trough.

I composed myself.

"We should not be doing this in your parents' house" I pleaded, rocking back on my chair, fighting for ground.

"They will be very happy I have a boyfriend now. They have told me they are tired of waiting for me to find a man."

Still she approached, running a plump hand seductively along the table top and leaning her corpulent bottom, swathed in an unflattering ankle length denim skirt, against the edge.

"But I already have a girlfriend – we love each other." I lied a little.

"I know you have a girlfriend, but many people have girlfriends and boyfriends and then they go away. It doesn't mean so much, I think. We will be married and nothing can stop us from being happy forever. And anyway, where is your girlfriend now you need her?"

Excellent question. A more precise one was 'where was any other member of the human race' – literally anyone would have done at that moment.

The only creature sensing my pain was Pigling Bland, perhaps feeling a kinship with another poor object of his mistress's desire. He knew what was to come, and he didn't like it one bit.

I shot a gaze at Jesus, riding the cracker to oblivion.

"You're on your own here", he seemed to be saying. "Expect no divine intervention – I'm on holiday."

"What about the children?" I asked in desperation. "The pupils should not have teachers who are boyfriend and girlfriend. And the other teachers will know as well. It will be very unprofessional."

"No one will know – we will not show our love to anyone else at school. We will only show love to each other in private. Like now," she said, ripping her Mrs Tittlemouse blouse open at the front, buttons popping and whizzing across the room.

As she did this there was a change in the pressure of the room, as if something major had happened just out of sight, beneath the surface; a shift of an almost tectonic magnitude. Hiromi dumbly looked down to the floor between her legs and I followed her gaze. Jesus astride the cracker looked down as well, making it a silent trinity of the grimly enthralled.

The denim which clung to her legs was now framing her thighs and calves with a hideous tenacity. The material was changing texture and colour, dark patches forming, the crisp, taut denim becoming oily and clingy as it soaked up the tidal burst which flowed freely down Hiromi's monstrous legs.

Her bladder had given out under the strain of the situation. And once she popped, she certainly didn't look like stopping anytime soon.

Neither of us could wrench our attention from the steaming pool which was collecting at her feet, running into the dark valleys and cascading over the dark cataracts of the flooring.

As the tide reached the back legs of my chair, upon which I was pivoting, I swung to one side and leapt upright. Swiftly coming to myself, shocked out of my drunkenness, I started for the door.

"Thank your parents for the meal, Iwabata sensei," I shouted over my shoulder, formal again, not a trace of a smile. "I think I had better go home now – see you next term."

And I left her there, open mouthed, 33, and standing in a puddle of pee.

24

The next day Nadya called me from her parents' tiny flat in Donetsk.

"People are really angry here," she explained. "They think that some power is trying to change our president."

As I bombarded Nadya with half-questions, I heard her mother rolling away the bed, folding it back into the living room sofa, as they had done for decades in the old days when they all lived together.

"Russian news is talking about 'provocations'. People say America is getting involved in our elections, trying to put the candidate they like in charge. My parents are talking about moving to Russia."

The line went quiet.

"What does that mean? I just want to know when you are back."

She sighed down the phone. "It could mean I won't stay in Japan for long. I'd have to help them."

"Nadya, I'm sure your parents will be able to make the right decisions. You just concentrate on getting back here. We can go skiing, enjoy the best bits of winter here…" I didn't know what else to say.

Silence once more.

"When are you back?" I asked again. I'd almost looked forward to these few days alone, relaxing. Things should've been simple with everyone away or holed up. Now I felt like something out of my control was pulling part of me in another direction.

25

We didn't speak for another couple of days. I emerged from under my floor-level blanket, where I was wrapped up playing computer games, as the phone rang. Sweeping a selection of rented videos and ramen pots out of my way, I slid across the four tatami mats of my living/dining/bed room to grab the handset.

Nadya from another continent; that vast, dark landmass we'd flown over just a few months before. She described a situation balanced on a slender pivot, rocking between two realities. The western, Eurocentric part convinced some dark power had snatched an election from their grasp. And an eastern one which viewed ongoing protests and American pronouncements on the corruption of their beloved country as the thin end of a wedge which would soon be driven between them and their Russian heritage.

Nadya sounded weary as she tried to explain it.

"What is that shouting in the background?" I asked her.

"Oh, the TV? He's just a politician. Very popular. He is famous for saying all the things the Russian president can't say about Ukraine without getting in trouble with the west. Anyway…"

I tried to concentrate on Nadya's soft voice, but it could not hope to compete with the row coming from the TV set. Nor what I took to be her father's disembodied commentary on what he was hearing from the politician.

"Is your father offended by this man?" I asked Nadya.

"No, no – he loves Zhirilyashky. Thinks he's very clever and funny."

The explosions coming from Nadya's papa crescendoed, sounding for all the world like he was violently remonstrating with the heedless screen.

"What the hell's going on?" I laughed, wincing, as he climaxed in a shout which reverberated around the room, before bouncing down the wires into my tender ear.

"Ah, he's just happy," Nadya said, flatly. "We are a passionate people, you see."

I went away and searched him out online. Zhirilyashky, or ol' fat thighs. Populist demagogue. Known for venomously abusing liberals, professional women, or indeed anyone who did not share his point of view – a point of view which usually ran to honest-to-goodness Russian chauvinism spiced up with conspiracy theories. Specialist topics seemed to be lionising the build up of military might, and running down the legions of variegated 'fascists' forever poised to bring Russia to its knees.

With his tie hoiked down into a tight knot, unruly collar and suit jacket sleeves turned back, he looked like an ill-tempered schoolyard bully. Ok, so I didn't know much about politics. But if this beetroot-visaged dumpling was riding high in a region's affections, I knew it could only be a bad thing.

26

Nadya came back from her Christmas at home. In one sense, we picked up right where we left off.

Seeing her again was a sight for sore eyes, frozen and weeping from the cold. We settled into the guts of the winter, tucked up at one or other of our apartments, making a virtue of their pokiness by telling ourselves we were cosy in our little world.

In another, naggingly real sense, we were back together but with a new feeling between us of distance, as if part of her had stayed behind on the outskirts of Europe. Before she had left, I could tell Nadya was tiring of the experience. Now I was worried by what had gone on back home; how she would feel about returning here, so far from her family.

"It's really confusing where my parents live right now," she told me. "There's a lot of tension. Not just in Kiev, but in my neighbourhood. My parents hope that the country will split. And they can return to Russia."

"What do you mean 'return'?" I asked. "They aren't Russian, are they?"

"They feel Russian," Nadya said. "This is what matters. They remember when things used to be good in the Soviet Union. They had long holidays – they had *money* to go on holiday. People respected their jobs, and they knew most people were working together."

"For what?" I asked. "A communist future?"

"They are not interested in politics," Nadya whispered. "They just want to work hard and live quiet lives."

We went quiet ourselves. At length, she jerked her head up, the huge fringe sliding across her brow.

"But I had a reason to return and I couldn't get back to Japan quick enough in the end."

"What reason was that," I asked.

She skipped over to the low bed, little more than a mattress on the floor, where I lay. Nadya leaned low over me, hair hanging down in my face.

"You, my darrrrrling," she said with a comically exaggerated accent. She dipped her round head with her soft, round brown eyes, and kissed me.

She was the first to say it, deep in the heart of January, at the end of my hundredth season of life. "I love you," she told me, and I knew she meant it, finding refuge here, despite the discomfiting news about her family, and worry about her place in the world; our tenuous foothold on this edge of land, rimmed before the Pacific expanse like the finest edge of a wine glass.

I knew she meant it because it was the first time I had ever heard these words with any truth, any resonance. They struck me hard, and I knew I felt the same way.

"I love you too," I told her, the first time I had ever spoken that simple, indulgent sentence, with its impossible glassy profundity, like a shimmering surface of water tremblingly concealing activity below.

27

As January turned to February, the warmth and tenderness I found in her flat each time made the walk up through the winter snows not just something to be endured, but even something to be enjoyed.

Rain, hail, sleet and snow, I would climb the hill from my apartment, either heading up Chuo Dori, the central street up through the the citadel to the station, or run parallel to this, past a park perched on top of an underground car park, a long, forlorn open air swimming pool on the next block, followed by an arcade of high end shops – always empty – which ran up to the corner of her little road, tucked at the top end of the Chuo Dori.

Whichever way I went I would have to cross Peach Avenue, as even the Japanese called it – with no translation needed. This wide road, running breadthways across the citadel, ranged from a dual car-riageway at one end to an almost pedestrianised section where it terminated opposite the city zoo.

On this second section, Paradiso lay tucked away, bordering the cen-tral cultivated section where Peach trees grew, among a dotting of benches, small fountains and wooden structures around which the rose vines twined themselves.

A centrepiece for the city of peaches, this bit of town planning was pleasant, if not inspirational. The people had laid it out in the wake of a major fire which destroyed the ancient wooden heart of Takada immediately after the Second World War. Once an important castle town, Takada saw its historical, residential and business sectors re-duced to ashes.

Like the graceful, upbeat civic layout of Hiroshima, albeit on a dif-ferent scale, Peach Avenue proclaimed the Japanese ability to move on, mindless of an empty heart ravaged by catastrophe. Now the peach trees were left in the hands of the city's junior high school students, who turned out in spring and summer, heads swathed in do-rags, to tend the branches full of fruit.

At the other end of Peach Avenue lay another important symbol of the modern city, the kite-makers clock tower. Takada's kite festival had become famous throughout Japan, and as it grew, a gleaming new landmark sprung up from the rich soil on Peach Avenue.

Twelve feet in the air, doors opened with the clock chimes and puppet characters – their significance lost on mere gaijin – frolicked in the mountain air. On the pyramidal peak of the tower sat a jaunty everyman kite maker, towing a metal kite through the sky, rakish hat on his head and cheeky ribbon in his hand; the mascot of the city.

I always came in from the cold into Nadya's apartment with parched lips, cheekbones feeling as if they were protruding through, and the strange mountain smells frozen onto my skin, my hands reeking of pine smoke and giddily fresh air.

I would collapse onto her bed after a long day doing nothing at work while Nadya pottered about her micro kitchen, still full of energy. She would go to bed early, after her hard day teaching, but first – while I flopped out – Nadya would busy herself about the tiny room.

While she moved from stove top to electric worktop oven I listened to music. With no TV reception there were lots of long, lyrical silences unless I popped on a CD and stared up at the ceiling. Nadya had brought me her favourite music, the Russian singer Bulat Okudzhava. I put it in her cheap disc player and settled into its warm intimacy in the tiny room, listening for the first time.

He sang 'Old Jacket', and Nadya explained the words to me.

"It's about a man who takes his threadbare old jacket to a master who fixes clothes."

– "A tailor," I interrupted –

"Yes, a tailor. And he asks the tailor to make it all new again, almost as a joke. But the tailor takes him very seriously. He works hard, like he believes when his customer finally puts the old jacket on once more, old love can come alive again. It's a very ironic, sad song – of course, this is impossible. The singer knows it, and calls the tailor a strange, funny man."

In the sombre, matter-of-fact, voice, you could hear this tension. It was tempting to think of this in terms of the black humour of a long-suffering people.

Nadya walked elegantly across the kitchen, as that strong, clear voice reverberated around the room, bouncing off the stark materials of the identikit apartment block, then slowly permeating the concrete and steel; stopping up the broken window which wouldn't quite close.

It was a voice of deciduous, poetic beauty, set against the backdrop of Shuetsu-san; this land of the evergreens and recurring life. Nadya sat down at the kotatsu and folded her hands on the table top.

"Do you like this music?" she asked. She explained some of the lines a little more. It was intensely personal, the everyday conversation elevated to a universal sense of loss.

"It's really quite beautiful," I said.

"I think if you enjoy this, you can understand the Russian soul," Nadya said. "It's that sense of longing, the deep knowledge that everything passes. Maybe I should say it's the Soviet soul."

Nadya told me about how her parents went to Moscow shortly after she was born. "You see, they abandoned me with my grandparents," she said, joking.

Her mother Lyubov dreamed of the products available for sale in the Soviet capital. Of course, she was used to the towering billboards showing the life to come, posted around Donetsk. In Lyubov's childhood they had maintained an element of believability. People could almost imagine touching the soft fabrics in these lifestyle images, turning the warm, desirable material over in their hands.

Then, as the Krushchev years gave way to the sombre Brezhnev era, to a classic grey 1970s of professional espionage and quiet graft, the life played out above the population's heads in advertising became slightly more muted; though just as unattainable. Wool replaced fur; and boots, high heels.

The centrally planned economy, lacking the signals of supply and demand – the vigorous survival of the fittest of businesses struggling – simply produced more of the same garments, perfumes, tools, kitchen products and all the invisible ingredients from which a resourceful people could cobble together their lives. Its more complicated consumer durables like white goods, which finally arrived to raise the quality of domestic life to a standard enjoyed by Americans two decades previously, were imported from the relative technological powerhouse of East Germany.

Anyway, Lyubov did not care about washing machines. Her strong forearms scrubbed the family clothes in the bathtub like a ritual, each night after her work in the factory. What she wanted was a little luxury – a mere drop – which would wash all this everyday work away. She had heard the stories of Polina Molotova, the headstrong wife of hardy Bolshevik Molotov; how she kickstarted the Soviet perfume industry in the 1930s. Polina Zhemchuzhina – her revolutionary nom de guerre meaning 'pearl' – may have had a better idea than most Soviet women about glamour, but she was no Parisian lady, and her own Molotov cocktails were rough, combustible approximations of French scent.

When Lyubov and Leonid went to Moscow for that one and only time on a short weekend break in late summer 1982, Brezhnev lay dying, and the famous Tretyakov gallery was closed for opaque reasons. Thousands were lined up outside Lenin's mausoleum all through the morning, until dusk fell on the domes of St Basil's. But if Lyubov was going to queue, she wanted something to show for it. Something more than a few shuffling seconds' glimpse of a man who looked more mannequin now than political colossus. And definitely something more than the usual loaf of bread or nylon cardigan in an unflattering cut. So together, they spent an afternoon in the GUM department store, waiting patiently at the perfume counter.

She tried and rejected the stalwart Red Moscow fragrance for being too conservative, and saw through White Lilac as a craven French copycat. The assistant, glum from the start, was on the verge of hostility when Lyubov finally settled on Nina Ricci.

"This was their one holiday abroad, you understand?" Nadya said.

"And it was all one country then anyway, yeah?" I pointed out.

"Well yes. And I'll tell you more. They wish it was all one country again," she added.

I couldn't grasp what Nadya meant.

"So, they miss communism?"

"It was never really communism in the Soviet Union. People gave up believing in all that before we were born. All the aspirational stuff

was just for the political classes' pride. But nevertheless, good people – people who today work hard and hold onto some concept of
society – still associate Soviet times with safety and a sort of comfort.

"Does that sound funny?" she asked. She smoothed the blanket of
the kotatsu over her slender thighs.

It did rather.

"So how did your mother reconcile that with searching out the
choicest French perfume?" I asked.

"There doesn't need to be a conflict," she said, looking at me with
huge unblinking eyes. "People had to hold onto certain parts of their
identity. She was a hardworking mother – but also a woman. I guess
that's what the perfume reminded her. A little reminder every day
throughout my childhood, actually," she added.

Nadya explained how her mother would take a single drop – half a
drop – of that perfume, each morning. She would delicately touch
that tiny, rich bead to her wrists, carefully scooping up any excess
and returning it to the bottle, itself a vessel shaped like a woman.

"You know what?" she said. "Even after the liquid was gone, the
perfume lingered in the bottle. Such good quality – *takaya kachest-
va!* She still has the bottle on her dresser at home. Whenever I go
back home, I quietly open it, and take a little sniff. The smell is still
there, like a memory of my childhood – a different time."

My own mind drifted back. Before arriving in Japan I had come off a
bad year, lost, finishing off my masters' degree, but really scrabbling
around for things to occupy my mind, which was already roaming
ahead – though to what, it could not know.

A short, unhappy affair, just left me more confused. Until I met Nadya I had been forever doubting in the power of another person to make me happy.

Now I was filled with the great faith in the possibilities of life that only love can provide, experiencing this epiphany for the first time.

I had been wrong, through my wilfully miserable, darkly poetic years. Life was not a filtered memory, cloaked in sadness; not the echo of a blue melody, infecting the mind's ear with a sickly nostalgia. It wasn't even the lingering smell of perfume, the ghost of scent in the sweet empty bottle.

I had been wrong all along and I was glad that I knew this now. I drifted off to sleep in the little room.

Hours later I stirred, raising my head slightly to look out the window at the gathering darkness round the base of Shuetsu-san, the great peak which capped Takada and marshalled around it the other hills to face down the mountains on the far side of the Iizu valley; the vast infantry of the vaster landscape, landlocked in the heart of Japan.

Nadya was lying beside me, sleeping soundly. I kissed her and she entwined her slender arms around my neck. She was my angel in the mountains, a redemption for me. How we had come to be in this place, the square room with the toilet screened off in the corner, and the broken window at the edge of the world, was unfathomable to us.

So I lay in the twilight and thought about that icy river, spilling down from the mountains of the Central Japanese Alps, themselves now capped with an enduring snow to the west, up above the town. It would be tamed, then return again to nature, never truly directed at all by man – the lie of the land giving rise to man's self-deception.

Time faded slowly in each other's arms. Nadya remained in my heart.

28

Night tripped over the brink of Shuetsu-san, descending on embers of red and it was time to go out once more into the cold mountain air for an evening in the bars and karaoke booths of Takada.

I ran over to Lawson, the convenience store round the corner from Nadya's apartment and picked up my favourite beer, a litre and a half keg of Kirin Ichiban which came with a tiny gas cartridge, so you could connect it up to a reusable pump handle to give a perfectly pressurized pint each time. For Nadya I bought a small Chu Hi alcoholic plum can. I knew from experience this is all she would need to be well on her way before we even left the flat.

Back outside her building I stopped at the bottom of the staircase, looking at the steps which descended a twist in the corridor with a sickly, claustrophobic lighting. Like many, this modern apartment building housed a handful of businesses, a row of elegant clothing shops and a delicatessan. On the top floor was something which seemed to resemble an occasional office and jun room.

But here, at the edge of the building's stairwell, there was a sign pointing down towards for a subterranean establishment called, strangely – yet grammatically accurately – Nick's.

I'd asked the old timers before about this place, but no-one had ever been there or claimed to have heard of a Nick, and so it was taken to be a random western name, perhaps seen in an old film. No-one ever seemed to come and go on these stairs, and yet the signpost stayed illuminated every evening until the early hours. Nadya herself never heard footsteps on the staircase, or much movement throughout the rest of the building, for that matter.

This layering of living and business, the desolation of establishments which seem to operate silently and without discernible patrons, was something difficult to understand. The coldness and impersonality of Nadya's apartment struck me all the more as I ran back up those cold stairs again, and sat down to the meal of rice and beef curry she had cooked up during the few minutes I was out. I thought of the ghost businesses carrying on in all directions around me, forging ahead in diminished circumstances, without customers or seemingly much hope to sustain them.

Sergo had explained the peculiarly Japanese notion that kept them afloat – that idea of the banks refusing to call in the loans on hundreds of thousands of money pits across the country. No one really knew the extent to which the economy was built on sand, Sergo said, and in truth no one cared to look too closely in case the whole shooting match fell to pieces. Tatemae and honne, you see. While Japanese society had happily existed for hundreds of years on a series of vague injunctions and elegant lies, in the world of economics, where all things eventually become spectacularly manifest, this approach was like a concrete block teetering on the edge of a jetty. And if it toppled, how far the ripples would spread into the realms of the great Japanese corporations was anybody's guess, he added.

But even if it affected just the family run izakayas, the ramen bars and pointless boutiques of the provinces, there was something absurd about the numberless workers going every day to switch on the sign outside their shops, turn on an air conditioner and fill in meaningless paperwork for a business whose existence was an abstraction, an aberration made real in a country where people smile and look the other way.

***

In our own abstraction of our little scene, it was already 9pm, but at least an hour before anyone would think about taking the hand of

197

Beatrice and climbing up to the paradisiacal bar in the sky. It was time for some serious drinking on my part and preparation of a more feminine kind for Nadya, as she made an ample corner of the room her own, spilling her make up across the floor in a surge of powder, then painstakingly clearing it up again before using anything.

So I put on the music we could agree upon. Jumping Jack Flash creaked from the tiny speakers of the bargain basement CD player. I jacked it up to full volume as I carefully popped the Kirin's gas cartridge in its holder and tightened the lid to break the seal, priming the tubes with expectation. I pumped the handle a couple of times, then with a gurgle the rich golden beer began to seep into my glass, at first trickling, then building up to a steady stream, kinetic in the bottom of the glass.

This was my ritual, repeated five or six times until the small keg gave out and the returning gurgle of the gas canister meant there was nothing left to pump but an airy froth. I drank each glass with an earnest enjoyment, savouring this precious preparation time before going out from our little nest to face the world of after-dark Takada.

Nadya meanwhile performed her own brisk ritual, washing her hair, then piling it up on top of her head in a towel as she knelt in just her underwear before a long mirror. She touched the blusher to her cheeks, pulled a little mascara across her eyelashes, and she was done. Nadya's delicately fecund beauty shone out without need of embellishment; just a gentle highlighting of her bonny features; her rounded *goodness*.

Blink, and you miss it. Outside it was raining as we played Gimme Shelter, but indoors I could pause briefly and enjoy the spectacle. She was my beauty, guiding me insistently by the elbow halfway up Shuetsu-san. Whether I carried on or went back down was up to me.

The Kirin was going down well, in any case, and my throat weighed up the heft of the rich drink. Nadya took sips from her can, and by the time she had finished blow drying her hair, had not quite finished the small can, though her cheeks glowed and her brow was flushed.

"Are you struggling a little, ukropka?" I asked her, using the harmlessly unflattering Russian name for Ukrainians – 'dill people', after their love of the herb. She was gracefully slipping in and out of a third outfit option, and frowned at the name which jokingly pegged her as a western Ukrainian; with its suggestion of aggressive nationalism.

"A little – one drink is all it takes."

"Well I hope you are not going to embarrass me later," I winked.

"I am a real Russian, don't forget. I may not drink much, but there's always a little vodka in my blood. There's only one of us who needs to watch out after a few drinks," she said, shooting a gently chiding glance.

"How long are you going to be?" I asked, unfairly, knowing it annoyed her when she was just trying to look her best for me.

"All I've got is an evening listening to you, Neil and Brian go on about this song or that song, or this teacher or that teacher. So maybe it doesn't really matter what I wear…"

"You look beautiful, whether you were in a kimono or a judo suit, that's what I should've said. And you're right – we don't deserve you hanging out with us."

I think I saved the situation, because the next thing I knew we were out the door and she was skipping along beside me, pressing her slight, cold hand inside mine.

29

Nadya was right. Paradiso was a maudlin affair that night. She probably did deserve better than this. Unbeknown to us it was Ahab's birthday – the latest of God knows how many he had spent in the bar at the top of two flights of impersonal, car park-style stairs bordering the anodyne Peach Avenue.

Him and Michael were playing double dates with Hanako and Yui, Mrs Moby perhaps at home, working on the latest chapter of a cell phone blockbuster. Neil was picking his way carefully through a sophomore White Russian while Brian, clearly smashed at 10:30pm, was shuffling from the toilet to the bar as we passed him on the way in. He nodded to us beneath his mop of curls and gave his lopsided grin, shirt open to reveal another strangle of chest hair which was eyed suspiciously by a solitary girl on a stool.

I half turned and thought about joining Brian at the bar, but went to sit down with Nadya at our customary large table on the slightly raised section behind a strange curtain of jewelled plastic beads.

"Brian is looking pretty happy already," I said. "I mean I know it's the weekend and Lord knows I'm several pints deep already, but he looks like he's really going for it."

"He's had a bad week," Neil explained. "It seems the gloves are coming off."

"What happened?" Nadya asked.

"Well, he's been told his work is not up to scratch and he's got to perform a demonstration lesson in front of all the rest of the teachers next week instead of going to shogakko."

"Christ – how did that come out?"

"Mrs Masada paid him a special visit at his school today and explained it – in the bluntest possible terms for a Japanese. She actually took me along to mediate the message. Or maybe she's just circling above my body as well, and it was a warning. Anyway, Brian has to impress the top brass from the city education board or he's on the next plane home. And I have to help him in his demonstration lesson. Cheers."

I realised Neil was actually a little drunk. His control was slipping a little; it could have even been his third white Russian.

"By the way, Ahab, happy birthday," I said, acknowledging him by raising a hand to an imaginary naval tricorne.

He smiled back, playing the strong, silent type as he had done for a decade. The pose was now indistinguishable from the real Ahab, the man and the mask; the façade shown to the world and the feelings within. He had become more Japanese than he would allow for, despite the normal weekend fancy dress of the pseudo sailors' uniform of bellbottoms, scarf and hat perched in his fat head.

Hanako and Yui, resplendent in flimsy, flouncy dresses and looking like they had been clothed in the fevered imagination of a teenage comic book geek, beamed their smiles and shuffled round the table to talk with Nadya about girls' things which never went beyond the three of them.

"Check this shit out," said Michael wiping his forehead with a wristband, brandishing two dark statues. "I bought them from the hundred yen shop, and it's a pretty good piece of business, I think you'll agree."

The hundred yen shop was the answer to all manner of domestic necessities, and was always worth a quick trawl around to pick up an electric fly swatter or pack of face masks to protect others from your shameful cold germs. Until now, however, I was largely insensible to its potential as a source of art. For what Michael had presented Ahab with on his birthday was a rather fetching twin set of statues depicting native Japanese Ainu people, their traditional dress setting off the perplexed look on their faces; half European, half oriental.

It was straight out of the school textbook – I felt sure there must be a chapter examining with wonder the 'primitive peoples' of the northern Hokkaido island – and the perfect gift for Ahab.

I apologised for not bearing anything to match up to this rare find and went to get Ahab a drink to make up for it. Music played at a mercifully low volume through the pub's speakers; some alarming Japanese pseudo dance reggae, very much the style of the times among hip Japanese twenty somethings.

Sitting down again, I took up a position between the opposing parties, Neil and Brian to my right and Michael and the sailor to my left, myself not quite at the head of the table, but rather at its bottom. The surfer and the sailor were performing an Ainu hunting skit with the figures while the girls giggled and Neil looked on with his customarily uneasy disdain.

Hanako and Yui clicked their fingers with a charming lack of self-consciousness. Brian swayed, though not quite to the music. He had his head in his hands, fringe sweeping the table and twisting around the leather bracelet on his wrist.

"I just don't know why I ever bothered coming to this shitty country," he said. "They're all inbred mutants in the mountains anyway – how are we supposed to teach them English?"

He banged his glass down and threw back his head for desperate emphasis. But the routine was syncopated; he wasn't even in time with himself. Neil shot me a glance and then leaned in close to Brian, ever-sensitive to the impact we made as a group and trying to reel in this very un-Japanese display of public emotion.

"You and me both, matey. It's a load of crap – we all know this – but for the time being you will just have to jump through the hoops. It's the Japanese way, you know."

"Well fuck it – if what I'm doing isn't good enough then they are only getting what they deserve. Half the kids are asleep in their chairs, the other half are talking. There's maybe one in each class who stands out because they actually want to learn."

It was hard to credit Brian with frustration coming from a professional sense of performing an educational service. Or even just a general sense of completing a job. He'd shown little to make me think he cared up to this point.

"Look Brian," I said, "What's it to you, hey? None of us are here for the wellbeing of the youth. We are just pissing around filling in the space between the weekends so we can have fun like this. I mean, why did you come here?"

Brian hadn't raised his head throughout the conversation, but I got the impression he was knitting his brow beneath the tangled hair as he confronted a topic. It wasn't as if we hadn't chewed it over before. But no matter how many times we posed it to each other, I myself could only ever answer it by way of an evasive thought process.

"Man, I came here for the same reason lots of other Americans got the hell out after we had that damn president visited on us for another four years. I wasn't going to stay around and watch the US go down the toilet with that jackass in charge, so I made up my mind I was leaving. I'm like a political exile, or something."

To either side faces lit with silent mirth.

"Well obviously there was the political aspect," I said, mastering my amusement, "But there must have been something else."

"I guess we could all say we wanted to see a little of the world," chipped in Michael. "But it's something more than that, maybe. I wasn't escaping anything in particular. And it's not like I was searching for something, some kind of better life. Maybe I was just bored…"

He petered out.

"I suppose we're just lucky enough to have the leisure to indulge our safe notions of adventure," I said. "Most of us probably got on the plane over here for very little reason… other than we could, and we had nothing better to do. We're a generation of over-educated children with nothing to aim at or aspire to. I don't know – maybe I'm just speaking for myself, but I never had any real idea about what I would be doing in my mid-twenties. And it's terrifying to realise, but that's where we now are. And if you don't know what you want or what you are doing, you might as well bury this ignorance in unknown soils. At least being clueless in an alien world kind of gives an excuse to your lack of direction."

It was the best I had. I looked at Nadya across the darkness of the table, sat back and tuned out.

***

I came round with Ahab banging about as he wedged his statues back in their box. He didn't speak much normally, but now he was licking his big, red chops in preparation for something. He pulled Yui close to his barrel chest in a bear hug, then pushed her away, just as fast, reflexively.

"You are just kids – you need to learn from an old pro how to have a good time. I came here to study many years ago, and yeah, I never left. You want to know why? I stayed on for the party. I stayed on because I can smell an easy meal ticket a mile off, and this one stank to high heaven."

He nuzzled his nose into Yui, who laughed her twittering laugh, her large earrings dancing against her flawless cheeks, eyes shining, not quite understanding the joke; radiantly oblivious.

"Neil is right – all you have to do is play the game for a couple of years until you find something better, something like a lady who is going to put you on easy street."

He was obviously talking about his wife, even as he sat with an arm around Yui, a quintessentially Japanese piece of doublethink, like it had become so natural for him to practise.

"When I first came out here nigh on 20 years ago I was just a college man like you guys. I came to study the language on a year abroad as part of my course. I didn't understand what was going on any better than you at first, but after that year I knew I had to come back. Do you know why? Not because I was desperate to gain some 'greater insight into the culture', or any shit like that. I could see the lifestyle would be something I could slip right into. I don't mean I played at being a native or anything so worthy – you've got to enjoy the special place you occupy as gaijin, and that means not giving a fuck about the ins and outs, the whys and wherefores, but walking around with your hands quietly held out for whatever you can get. You play the polite beggar long enough and you can maintain this strange position – not wholly accepted, but nevertheless part of society. Because, make no mistake about it – that's what you are to many people here; just someone on the periphery, and you will never get beyond that."

The jaded realism of the ageing ersatz captain, his Ainu statues in a box tucked under one arm, and his bit of fluff dangling off the other, could still be shocking in its blunt philosophy; its cutting grasp of reality. I would have liked to think that in comparison our inarticulacy was charming, but I wasn't so sure. Give us a few years, and any of us could be sitting on the other side of the table.

The usually taciturn sailor was enjoying holding court, and Neil was getting twitchy, unused to sitting back and listening to someone for so long, especially when the words spilled so easily from the lips of someone he did not like. Though Neil himself had swallowed a bitter dose of reality in recent weeks, in his labyrinthine sense of morality he could not accept the pontificating of someone who had given up all respect for the host culture, and fallen into a lazy confederacy with his own cartoon status. Perhaps being a little closer to the captain in age, he must have disliked the patronising attitude the older man was showing.

This wasn't stopping Ahab though.

"I was once in the same position as you boys – kicking my heels, worrying about which dragon was going to burst the bubble on my little world and send me scurrying home. I worked for two years in a language school, teaching whoever came my way, keeping my eyes open the whole time; learning how to spot a chump. Students would take me out, pay for my meals, for days out, little trips here and there. And I wasn't always the old misery you see before you today. I was living in Kobe in the big city and I played the wide eyed foreigner to perfection, going along to every two-bit event people had planned for me. Feigning amazement at the latest visit to a temple, the original of which long ago burned down, and the current shack dating from 1967; pretending to hate natto bean curd; marvelling at the skill of a taiko drummer beating monotonously the same big skin with a couple of wooden truncheons. Because at the turn of the 90s we folk were a lot scarcer than today. You poor boys are ten a penny. Back then it was quite something for people to parade their western puppy dog about."

Ahab stopped talking and drained the last of his beer, tipping up the front of his white hat with the neck of the bottle, exposing a matted, lank lock of blonde hair. He had probably told this story, this weary collection of practical philosophies, to ten sets of people just like us, year in, year out, a fraction fatter, slower and more disillusioned each time it rolled around. His indolence was like a sphere, running up one side of the valley and back across to the other, an executive toy pendulum of ambivalence; a spitball of lazy spite.

He was shipwrecked in his sea of mountains, marooned in the middle of Japan. A castaway who'd evolved his own value system, his own mythology.

Leaning back, a self-satisfied look on his face, Ahab was the epitome of the unattractive westerner made good; transposed and suddenly imbued with a new mystique for the women of a foreign culture. I imagine the countless times he'd held court, neophytes in thrall to his wisdom, as he became the patron saint of the dowdy losers; the charmless bumpkins given another chance, now slyly taking it for all it was worth. And if the whale was his spirit animal, then that hat was his totem.

"After that I had a year on the outskirts of Kyoto and then I made my way up the valley here after a spell in Nagoya. We had some scenes down there, but it was a last fling in the big city and I knew I was going no further. I'd battled my way upstream far enough. You can only push against the tide for so long, and this is where I gave out. A man can only live that buccaneering lifestyle for so long before he feels like he needs something permanent, an address to tie him down and give him ballast. I must have lived in a dozen different apartment blocks those first few years in Japan and you get sick of the mail arriving from home months late because it can't catch up with you, and your family far away can't seem to decode the latest crazy collection of digits you write after your name. You live in a building with 20 other people you never see and have to stake your claim down by the communal mailbox; you loiter on the hallways and the balconies of high rise buildings just to give yourself some tenure.

"But don't worry, you haven't missed the party yet. Five years maybe and it will be over for new intakes. Even the Japanese Government will have to terminate its half-assed subsidised holiday plans for language 'teachers' at some point and make a proper effort following some new avenue. But I will still be here, sitting pretty in my American truck."

He winked at Yui. "And with my girl waiting in the port."

We couldn't help it, but everyone was sitting in rapt attention at the monologue from the old master.

"And your boat docked at the health spa pond, you old bastard?" Michael smirked.

"You bet," smiled Ahab. "You watch – you'll all move on in some way, even those of you who think you've got nowhere else to go. People who come to this godforsaken place first do Japan in reverse. They see the small things, the back street life of laundry and dogs and grandmas. They think 'This isn't what I came to see – I want the skyscrapers and space cadets'. They move on because they are chasing some guidebook, some Sunday supplement, some blog post version of Japan and they hunger for the adventure of the big city. They don't find it here so they try Nagoya, or Osaka. Then they don't get the fix there, so maybe they go north to catch it in Sapporo on Hokkaido. Usually they cut to the chase and go straight for Tokyo. They walk about for a week or two looking at the clouds swimming around the high-rise buildings. But whichever big city they go to, it will never be right, because when they are taking pictures of the panty machines in Kabukicho, in their heads are those back streets of Takada with the family cake shops and car lots where they felt so out of place with the common people.

"*That* was the buzz of the culture shock. And they don't get it when they go to the big city. Leave that to the tourist. And anyway, the tourist's cultural shock is quickly overcome. But when you've landed in small town Japan, what you face is something more insidious. You see the everyday aspects, feel a stranger in the mundane world of Takada and that is what you internalise. It hurts. It's the lotus which once you eat, enraptures you; the *flurrz du mal* which sink you under with a sour taste. And once you've got a whiff of that sickness, there's no further thrill which can purge it.

"But maybe one person per cadre sticks around. Maybe he can't get the smell of the pine trees and the rivers out of his nostrils long enough to clear his head and make a break for it. He can't make it over the brow of the hills and out of the bowl the mountains make around Takada.

"You know what? Right now, I really can't say who it is."

The old seasalt had said his piece. I couldn't help but think of the turtle in the tank, beak slowly opening and closing. We carried on

209

drinking, caught in the bowl of the mountains too. Michael planted a dribblingly drunken kiss on Hanako's cheek.

Brian was in a bad mood, in his wisdom down on the man and the education system; down on the children.

"You know, I'm so close to quitting right now," he said, making eye contact with no-one, but rather addressing his remarks to one of the two bottles of beer in front of him.

"Let's hope you have the chance," said Neil, taking up the baton. "Maybe we'll be cut before we get the chance to stick it to the stuffed shirts at the education board."

"Assholes," was Brian's only reply.

Neil continued: "I would love to see the reverend Okada's face if any of us just walked in there and dumped our resignations on his desk. Come to think of it, we probably wouldn't be dignified by his presence – he would be locked away in some inner chamber. We'd get Oni. He'd come scurrying out at the sign of aliens dirtying the purified atmosphere of the municipal buildings."

Brian snorted with contempt.

"Do you know what shit I've had to do this week?" he asked no-one in particular.

"Don't tell me," I answered. "It wouldn't by any chance be something to do with the essay competition?"

"You got it. I sit around all day doing nothing, and then have to wait for an hour after I should have gone home, just to help out this little pain in the ass with his damn English essay. I sit there waiting for him to do his goddamn baseball practice every night, just so I can help him with his reading. He should pay more goddamn attention in class, that's what I say. Get his work done at the right time."

This was a little unfair, because if Brian's protégé was anything like mine, he was just doing his best and was probably knackered after a long day in class sandwiched between sports sessions at either end of the school day. All the schools were taking part in the city's creative writing competition, whereby a 'nominated egregious representative from each establishment' (the exact words of the competition rules) would produce, with varying levels of autonomy, a piece of writing which they would then read at a showdown. In my own school the essay, a dispiriting call to arms for civic recycling, was clearly written in its totality by Iwabata sensei and her magical electronic dictionary of malapropisms. Despite asking me for help once the piece had been set in stone, it was clear any suggestions for a more natural phrasing would be politely ignored, lest they obscure the central, defined message.

All I was needed for now was the Sisyphean task of correcting diction and accent for poor little Kouta, who clearly wished he was anywhere else than in the English room every evening. And indeed each evening the corrections we had pointlessly toiled over the night before had reasserted themselves in the stubborn mouth of the schoolboy.

The winner of the competition would be crowned 'Takada All-School Creative Writing Champion', and from what I could gather, it was something of a glittering prize for whichever English faculty produced such a linguistic marvel. Alas, it was not viewed with the same importance among our little coterie of cynics.

"Takada all school creative writing champion," enunciated Neil with a pedantic air. "A ridiculous title for these kids with their proscribed and predestined lifestyle."

"It's a bit like being the Bilderberg Group's preeminent Marxist," Michael said, raising his head from Hanako just long enough.

"Or professor of art at the reservation's community college," Ahab lazily chipped in, mixing up his native references as he rattled the box with his Ainu statues.

"You know what?" Brian roused himself once more. "In the end, it all comes down to personal choice. I feel sorry for these little assholes, stuck in the lives their ancestors laid down for them. There's no choice here, no individualism. And they just don't know anything different. Makes you glad for the good 'ol States, with its thousand ways to kill yourself."

Nadya's eyes were drooping, but now her nostrils flared and she spoke up, uncharacteristically, to the whole group.

"You know, American 'choice' isn't everything, Brian. And it isn't what everyone wants – even if you think it's what's best for them. People can be just as happy living among what they know and expect. In fact they can be even more happy without the tiring need to make a choice every minute about what brand of cola resonates with their personality best."

"Oh, is that right, huh?" Brian drawled, with a dumbly sarcastic nod of the head.

"I guess you mean back home, yeah? In Russia?"

"It's Ukraine," Nadya noted, curtly. "And 'yes', that's exactly right."

"Yeah well, you guys can keep your limitations if that's what you think makes you happy. But I think I know better. And I'll tell you why. When I was a ten-year-old kid, Boris Yeltsin came to my backyard. He'd just been 'elected' supreme presidential secretary, or whatever you want to call it. Soviet times, anyhow. He was visiting our space centre. But to show he was just a regular guy, he arranged to go round a grocery store. You should've seen the pictures in the local papers. Looking up and down the aisles like he was from the moon. He'd never seen such choice. Eyes popping out of his head. He didn't need to say anything – it was caught in his expression as he looked around. He was the head of a superpower, but he could only dream of having the same lifestyle as a suburban Houston shopper."

"He's got you, Nadya," I chimed in. "You were just telling me about your mother's perfume, how she longed for that sophisticated life-style. Kind of pathetic, really."

"She wanted a little luxury, a little something to remind her she was a woman. But that's not the same as hungering for some tsunami of personal choice at every turn. And you know what, Brian? You can't force people to have more choice. That's not freedom. If you can't see that, then you are no friends to the Russian people."

It sounded like a joke; a pastiche of a denouncement. She turned to me with a sharp look, rolling her eyes.

"It seems you don't know much about women, either."

30

Later, I tucked her up underneath her kotatsu, Nadya snuggled down while I went out to Lawson to buy a Pocari Sweat, a drink which promised to replace lost nutrients to ward off dehydration. It didn't taste great, but did the job. Anyway, what did you expect given the name?

As I came to the bottom of the staircase on the way back up to Nadya, I stopped for a moment, then felt myself pulled down to the little subterranean passage beneath the building, following the forlorn neon sign for Nick's.

The passageway was dark, but infused with a soft pink from the slowly decaying neon of the sign. It lit the way to the lone door set in the left hand wall. This again bore the name, now in a sober, rather meagre sign set at eye level. The door itself was like the entrance to an antiquated doctor's surgery, its dark mahogany effect inlaid with a luxuriant burgundy leather, like a Chesterfield sofa back; a bizarre effect in this charmless boom-years building.

I listened at the door. Nothing to be heard above the omnipresent whirr of air conditioning units somewhere in the carcass of the block. There certainly seemed no sign of life within. And yet there was the insistence of the sign forever burning its floating message in the dark.

I took a deep breath and tried the door, which gave way with a surprising ease into a room equally gloomy as the corridor outside. As my eyes adjusted, I just made out a long bar, in the American style, with a scattering of tables and chairs further afield in the darkness. An antic trumpet played subliminally in the background.

There was no-one around and yet the place was surely open.

"Well, to what do I owe the pleasure?"

I literally jumped at the sound of the voice in the darkness, straining my eyes at its source. The urbane self-possession of the speech was offset by the heavily accented Japanese pronunciation.

At one end of the bar stood... Nick?

"So, are you new here?" he asked.

As he spoke, Nick leaned forward out of the darkness, his purple crushed velvet jacket swinging into view. Then came the cravat. Finally, Nick's face appeared, plastered with a huge and rather winning smile. There was a manic aspect to his countenance, at odds with the whisky he swilled slowly in his small hand; the whole jazz club vibe his establishment conjured up.

"I'm Nick, by the way," he added. "And this is my place," he gestured expansively. "Many people forget I'm still here. Even 'Ahab', maybe. Know him?"

"Well, sure. Yes."

He spilled forth a syncopated torrent of questions and reminiscences about former language teachers. The energy was remarkable. Quite enough to obscure the agrammatical flourishes and non sequiturs which were starting to erode the studied composure of his opening.

Nick was leaning against the other side of the bar, as if he had spent a long, tiring evening serving, but I doubted this was the case. The immaculate collection of bottles ranged along the wall looked as if they had never been poured, and three perfect bowls of bar snack crisps and mixes stood at intervals along the counter, untouched.

"What you have to understand is that this can be the greatest experience of your life."

"Sure, I've got that already – " I said.

"Indulge an old hand," Nick said, in what seemed once again to be an exquisitely practised turn of phrase, raising an arm to stop me in my tracks.

He set off again; a stream of consciousness gushing over a precipice. I recreate the flavour, if not the precise wording, here.

"If you know Ahab, remember him as a warning of what happens if you spend too long here. A year or two here can be most refreshing." He raised an eyebrow in emphasis.

"You will learn much about yourself and go home a new man. I've seen it so many times. Japan can make everything seem like an instructive, cautionary tale. Take the time to look and consider what you are seeing; how it reflects back on you.

"But if you stay here too long, then all of that passion, those new possibilities just wither away and leave you a pale imitation, a cartoon white ghost of what you thought you were. Just look at Ahab – back home, wherever that may be, he would never act like he does, never get away with playing this sad character. It's just the dream of an adolescent, driving through the mountains, his telescope on the front seat, his girl curled up in the rear. And his wife at home, of course."

Nick shook his head sadly. "But there's no-one to tell him any different. I mean, no-one but me to tell him, of course, and that's why we don't see eye to eye. Believe me, I know well that a man owes it to his wife to go home without the smell of girls' perfume on his shirt. We used to be good friends. James and his wife, Natsuko, and me and Chiemi. They were in school together, you know, our wives. But I suppose we just became too stark a reminder of reality for Ahab to deal with. As I said, take it as a cautionary tale."

He smiled, waved his hand airily to dispel the energy of his address; diffuse the tension.

"He's harmless, of course." Nick leaned his neat body back on a barstool. "By the way, would you like a drink?" he asked.

"I think we've all had too much tonight, thanks. It sometimes seems to be all we do."

Nick nodded thoughtfully and dipped one hand into a bowl of nuts, as he swirled the whisky again in the other.

"You need to get up in the hills and get some of that fresh mountain air on your weekends," Nick suggested, "Do something worthwhile with your time."

I fixed his lounge act attire with a quizzical look. He certainly didn't appear to be the hiking type.

"You may laugh," he said, "But there are some really beautiful walks up there alongside the dams and reservoir, if you follow the Matsugawa upstream. And some beautiful old shrines up on the hillside. Maybe you know something about the Japanese religion, how there is a real feeling for nature. And you'd do well to get out there and experience it, see the way the Japanese show their love and their respect for it.

"There are all sorts of hokora – small shrines – built on the mountainside and by where the old waterfalls were. In the old days, when the Matsugawa was in full flow, there used to be flooding and landslides. The hokora were built there at these places of great beauty to propitiate the powers that be. Great beauty; and danger too.

"Of course, now the dams do a better job of keeping the old gods in line, but there you are. Look out for the tori gateways which will lead you past the shrines hiding in the forest. My tip for a nice, quiet day out."

I did have a little nightcap. I had so many questions, but on the topic of Nick the man, he was strangely quiet. The single malt burned beautifully as it made its way down to my belly.

I left him in his strange, twilit underworld and went back upstairs to Nadya. She was still tucked up underneath the kotatsu, head tilted back and fast asleep, though as I blundered around in the enclosed space, I woke her.

***

When we tumbled into bed just before daybreak I put Bulat Okudzhava on again, so it was barely audible. The clear, keening melody competed with the more precocious of the birds sitting on the flowing musical stave of the overhead powerlines, the changeless feature of the Japanese landscape.

We fell into the single bed. Something was calling from the hills in the distance, up among the jinja and the tori, keeping the peace in the wilderness. Dawn was just around the corner.

In a drowsy voice Nadya told me what the birdsong meant to her. I knew she'd lived in another apartment, further up the hill, under the raised motorway, on towards the wild forest.

"Back then I used to walk to work early in the morning, and the birds were still out and about in numbers," she whispered.

"Something appalling happened with those birds?" I asked with one eye open.

"It did, my sarcastic little reserved *Angleechanin*," she said, mocking the English in the accepted Russian way. "I would pick up my break- fast every morning. I would be walking along happily eating my syrup pancake – these gorgeous, warm pancakes they heat up for you – and my coffee drink, not a care in the world, just slowly coming to."

"That's how you used to start off every day?" I asked. "You must have been a porky little thing."

"I'm just setting the scene," she chided. "I would cross under the raised section of the Chuo Expressway and out the other side. But before I went into the gloom and echo beneath the road I had to run the gauntlet of these big powerlines."

"You really are building this up," I said. "Those bloody powerlines are everywhere. What's the issue with those ones in particular?"

"Loads of these horrible black birds used to settle in tall trees near the road. I think it was to eat the bright red berries which grew in the branches. Later, they would fly from the trees to settle on the power-lines, and the dirty animals would crap everywhere the second they landed on the wires. They would be taking off and landing in forma-tion – I don't know how it worked, but there seemed to be a shock which hit them every time they touched down on the wire. There would be a mist of poo which drizzled down over the pavement. Why they kept on trying it in this place I don't know."

"A kinky bird thrill, or just animal stupidity," I said.

"But for me there was no choice – this was they only way through under the expressway, so you just had to hold your breath, judge when the next flock was going to land and beat them to the punch," Nadya said.

"I got it right most days, but those first few trips were really hit and miss."

"I guess there was a steep learning curve," I said.

"Yep – and there were a few soiled pancakes before I got the hang of it," she yawned.

In a few seconds more she was asleep.

I thought of her lithe body dodging the faecal bombs in the early morning, the quavers and semi-quavers falling off the stave, melting from the living landscape of animal and electricity, the air alive with current and perverse animal processes.

I was learning all the time, settling into a comfortable, contrary routine. But despite the new faces and the characters with their invigorating desperation, I couldn't help but feel something was coming to an end.

31

Big school dragged on all the while. No one was watching me with quite the same critical eye as with Neil and Brian, but still I was feeling the reflected heat of the focus they were attracting.

In the English room Iwabata sensei was her normal bubbly self with no suggestion of embarrassment about her Christmas shenanigans. I too had tried to banish it from my memory, but now, given her immediate, blithe friendliness and levity, I began to wonder if I had drunk too much sake and had made the incident up, or at least misinterpreted it somewhat. I determined simply to play my part in the social amnesia of which the Japanese were so eminently capable when covering up indiscretions. Poof! It's gone; I did not hug the boss a little too tightly or without the correct reverence at the company bash. Poof! I did not break wind in the railway carriage. And, of course: Poof! I did not soil myself under the appalled gaze of the manger scene.

Izumiyama sensei was still bright eyed, displaying the patience of a saint when explaining the travails of the differently-abled to classes of snoring teenagers. Her bright smile survived the coldest spell; the sprig of errant hair around her crown had refused to capitulate and lie down to the snows and winds of the mountain winter.

Then one day, back in the English room after one of Shimoida's lessons, Mrs Masada dropped by. As usual, I could not tell the precise nature of her interactions with other teachers, but she was as direct as ever, quite unlike that of a 'normal' Japanese as she flitted from school to school. Her questions were pointed to the brink of insolence.

"Do you like Mr Shimoida?" she asked. "I don't know if he likes western teachers here."

It was said in such a deadpan way, her comment took me quite by surprise.

"Well, what do you mean?" I spluttered, particularly caught off balance by the fact she had pinpointed my unease.

"Oh don't worry, it's nothing to do with you," she continued, unabashed. "Mr Shimoida does not like you because his parents are hibakusha." She looked at me slyly, testing whether I knew what she was talking about. When she saw I had no idea, Mrs Masada's eyes grew huge and round for the first time.

"You'll have to explain, I'm sorry," I smiled. The eyes narrowed once again, and she gave a small nod of satisfaction.

"Hibakusha is the name we give to people injured in Hiroshima and Nagasaki," she said delicately. "Nuclear bomb victims. His parents were schoolchildren when you attacked them."

"God – that's awful," I said, passing over the bald accusation that I was in some way responsible.

"Yes, they had terrible burns on their bodies. They never go out, not since they were small children. Mr Shimoida looks after them at their home near Nagoya each week. He is a good son."

She let out a slight sigh, but kept a poker face, her high forehead framed with a long straight fringe; the gaze of the Anubis Sphinx.

"Yes," she added, "I don't think he ever forgives your armies."

Well, at least that made sense, now.

32

I received the latest email from Martin McQueen. The ebullient tone of the earlier messages departed now. Though he made no reference to her, it was clear that gone too was his nascent romance. There was a newly imploring tone in his words, coded from across the continents, suggesting his life wasn't quite as exciting as he would have had me believe in the brave new world of post-university Bristol capitalism. After paragraph upon paragraph of ribbing and fibbing he came out with it and jumped straight in.

Did I know of any jobs going begging over here? Could he offer his little frame to fill one of them? It seemed the trade in socialist carpets was not robust. Father had been forced to lay off son. Whether his father then stood on the picket line outside his own business, Martin did not mention. Perhaps he'd simply realised his ideology was all woollen weave, without underlay

I wondered how the donkey jacket would go down in Japan. He'd probably be hailed as some kind of fashion icon in this kingdom of the topsy-turvy. He'd also probably end up finding a job for life.

I replied, telling him I would keep my eyes open. Jeremy and Jay would be leaving in just a few short weeks come the end of March, when the Japanese school year officially ended and a bounteous week-long holiday – so treasured it was named 'Golden Week' – would settle across the nation.

33

A few days later, after a typically indifferent, slightly tense lesson with Mr Shimoida, we arrived back in the English room together, alone. As conversation ran out, we both busied ourselves at our little desks, and the gap in chatter stretched beyond what could be redeemed with a simple remark. Internally, I was still sulking at him after catching him leaving his tête-a-tête with Oni. I wasn't going to break the silence.

To lessen the tension I got up and walked to the window, with its panoramic view of the sports drilling ground, and the mountains running along the south eastern side of the valley beyond. A lone eagle lazily turned on warm air at one corner of that hectare of gravel, rising on currents coming up from beneath the bluff the school stood upon. It revolved endlessly, easily, with an unceasingly casual majesty. It might've been a buzzard. It didn't really matter; I was neither Linnaeus nor Lafcadio Hearn.

"The bird is a symbol in your culture, too?" Shimoida asked, shocking me from the gyre of my reverie.

"Yes, of course," I answered. "Freedom, most obviously, I suppose."

"This one is often here," Shimoida remarked. Then, with a smile: "And I never once saw it move its wings. Maybe it is laughing at us?"

"You think? How?" I was intrigued. (How did he know it was the same bird?)

"It is so relaxed. And we are always so tense and careful."

"Humans, you mean?"

"Well yes," Shimoida chuckled indulgently. "And me and you also."

I was a little taken aback.

"Well, we are both very busy..." I said sheepishly, casting a look at the crates of books on his desk, then contrasting it with the doodled scrap of paper on mine.

"It is not this, I think," he said with a tone of cheery finality. "It is very difficult to know how to speak to other people. You are foreign; we are so different. Of course there is no connection. But with Japanese also. We are difficult people, at times."

He went quiet. I was accustomed to a type of disarming frankness from his compatriots – usually when they were struggling to express precisely what they meant. But with Shimoida this was not the case. These words were the exact ones he intended, chosen for their clarity. I knew this, and I nodded quietly, catching his eye with a slight smile and a shrug.

We continued in this way for a while. Me at the window, him half buried behind his books; the eagle turning on the spot.

"But I don't think this matters," he said at last. "I cannot ever love English, I'm afraid. There is too much... history."

It was a dramatic pause; he wasn't struggling to find the word. While it was a candid remark from the head of the language department, it merely made explicit what I already knew he felt.

"And I cannot truly like Japanese either. It's a strange feeling when you are not part of one side, or the other, despite your pride, or how much you are in... pain. I think you probably can't understand this. I'm sorry."

"No, no. I mean, why would I come here to Japan if I was truly comfortable in my own society, my own little world?"

"Thank you for trying to understand," he said. "This is not the same, as it seems to me. But still, thank you."

And he took off his glasses, lay them on top of the pile of books, wiped the back of his hand across his eyes. A tremor rippled through my own body; was Shimoida just toying with me?

He looked down, inhaled a jagged breath, picked up his pen again. Streaking the back of his hand were tiny wet traces in the perpetual coating of chalk dust, and for the first time I could tell these were tears, like yours or mine.

34

The air had cleared. Then a shogakko day like any other saw me riding the old local train with the high school kids south-west back down the river towards Tenkyobashi to meet Neil. He'd already be poised, I knew, like a malevolent spider over his white Suzuki van as he waited for me in the scruffy tarmac turning circle outside the station, with its banks of drinks machines lined up against the side wall of someone's house.

As ever I tried not to make eye contact with the giggling girls in their sailor suit tops; the tough gangly boys slouchy against doors with their ties yanked down into tight knots. I needn't have bothered; these kids with their outrageous haircuts and uniforms embellished with neon liberties studiously ignored me. Acknowledging a gaijin in the cloistered public space of a train carriage would be a transgression for a regular Japanese – for a cool kid with a rep to protect it could be social suicide.

I sunk into a similar mood of cool indifference as the crowd thinned towards the limits of suburban Takada and I found myself increasingly alone. Once more the tiered rice fields with their concrete buttresses ran past on one side, while the river plodded by on the other. A fine, rich drizzle obscured the mountains all around, while the train ran down a tunnel of the rain's making towards the village where this local service would halt, just out of sight of the suspension footbridge round the headland of the gorge. There the Tenkyo made its steady way onwards to the Tokaido, the eastern coast road of the 53 stages between Tokyo and Kyoto, then on to the Pacific Ocean itself where there would be no stopping before the vast continental bulk of the Americas pulled round with civilisation of a different bent.

When I arrived, indeed Neil was leaning against the roof of his car, his hair slicked back even before the rain had got to it. He was smiling the thin-lipped frog grin while the amphibians belched from the nearest field.

"Why are you waiting outside in the rain?" I asked him.

"Ah, you are looking at the weather from a western perspective," he told me. "You cannot avoid the rain. The oriental mind says: 'it is raining and therefore we will become wet – the only question is to what degree'. And I've made my choice."

It rather struck me that the degree to which one would get wet depended wholly on the amount of time leaning against a car beneath the constant rain, but as he said, I was approaching it from a western perspective. I allowed Neil's fatalistic comment to go unchecked.

As I got in the van, I was sure I recognised a driver waiting across the road from the station in a huge, professionally sober Toyota Crown saloon. My mind flashed back to the fluorescent buzz of a meeting room; the shadows of a school corridor. Was it… Oni? The tint of the windows prevented positive identification, and anyway, rather faceless 40-something men in sober attire weren't exactly uncommon. But wait… was that a short-sleeved suit jacket?

For once we knew where we were headed and climbed through the shanty of house-shops in the centre of the village with a greater purpose than we usually showed. Neil's gear change of the sawdust-dry transmission was a little slicker than normal, I noticed. All the time, I kept one eye on the wing mirror. As we twisted and turned – nothing. But once we hit a stretch of open road, there it was: the big Toyota tailing our nanovan up the mountain.

Still, it was a fair way to Serow-ki shogakko, and by the time we got there, I'd put the vehicle out of my mind. We were greeted with a reserved friendliness; old news already, following our first visit.

The day passed off without mishap. A child poked himself in the eye with chopsticks during the relay race game, but immediately pulled through. In another lesson, a pretty young teacher looked in my direction just long enough for me to idly imagine it was a type of fondness, then broke off to whisk an errant child back into the midst of the action the moment I returned her gaze.

The night before I had stayed at Nadya's. It was close to the station, and perfect for my days travelling to shogakko. We had drifted off together in the early hours, still in each other's arms. I caught her scent on me in the classroom and it seemed suddenly innocuous on the fresh air of the hills.

On the way to lunch, we were walking down a long, grave corridor, giving each other the usual faces of mock apprehension, when I noticed something moving away from us in the shadows. My eyes refocused, catching the distinctive short-sleeved suit jacket, just as the figure rounded a corner and disappeared. I kept it to myself; Neil would think the altitude had got the better of me.

Over lunch itself we went through our usual rigmarole with me cracking open the crisps and coke and Neil pushing aside his platter after the most perfunctory assaults on its pickled riches. As usual the children looked on in wonder, most sporting rice grain adornments to their faces. Neil offered his inevitable lie to them in Japanese – I'm not hungry anymore; I had a big breakfast today.

Following our customary meditation in the relaxation room, our first lesson of the afternoon was interrupted midway through by none other than Mrs Masada. She glided into the back of the classroom

229

and loitered, quietly discussing something with the teacher; asking darting questions, then nodding as the answers came back. Neil and I knew the drill. She was checking up on one of us. Probably here to pass on some message regarding Brian; devolving some micro-management onto Neil's shoulders.

The lesson went better than usual. No injuries, and a little more enthusiasm than the norm. Neil was in his element, interspersing a little Japanese to keep the kids on target if things ever looked like drifting. If he felt anything like I did, Neil was settling into his stride six months in.

Abruptly, though, the classroom emptied, following a few sharp words from the teacher as the bell rang. Then she herself noiselessly disappeared.

Neil and I exchanged a brief glance. We had both noted the oddly muted end to a good lesson. And then we were alone with Mrs Masada.

"Ahh, Willu sensei, could you please go and help with the cleaning." She dismissed me.

I smiled in resignation. It didn't even seem like the normal regimented cleaning time, but sure enough, two kids appeared in the doorway, handed me a rag, and we set to, wiping the floor of the long corridor. This was indeed odd. The door closed on Neil.

The kids scooted up and down the hallway, hands and rags out in front, bums in the air. Dipping my own rag in the bowl of water we used, I gave a quick polish to any patches they'd missed, while circling near to the closed door. What was going on in the room between Neil and Mrs Masada?

As I lingered outside the door, I heard snatches of English and Japanese from both of them, self-righteous annoyance vying with strangulated incredulity, as they sought to understand and be understood in a common language of emotion.

Suddenly, Neil burst out, shaking his head. Mrs Masada followed, ignoring him, and addressing me now.

"Willu sensei, Mr Neil is unwell. You must please take him home to rest. Teaching is finished here today."

With that simple statement, she turned and walked off. Her footprints left traces in the damp corridor, fading slowly after her as the soft afternoon sun shone down its length. This was her style; breeze in from nowhere, upset the applecart, then slink off – a proxy for the faceless city administration and its shadowy motives.

I looked at Neil. He was wearing his defiant smile; the broad grin which suggested he had again anticipated a typically mercurial move, and was simply refusing to be phased by it.

"So – what was that about?" I asked him.

"Well, I have AIDS," he beamed.

"Jesus, Neil, I had no idea."

"No, obviously I don't actually have AIDS…"

"Just HIV at this stage? OK, we still have time." my brain was working overtime.

"Yes, I think HIV was what I negotiated them down to. *Eichee Ai Byee Kansensya desu.* But seriously, I have no terminal illnesses. Touch wood." He bent to knock on a dark floorboard.

I genuinely had no idea what was happening. Instead of trying to unravel it right now, I led the way out to the car, pausing to remind

Neil to remove his green and gold slippers and switch them for his outdoor shoes.

As we got into his ineffectual little van, I turned around. Lined up under the portico, the host of school staff were giving us a grave send off.

"Are you OK to drive?" I asked Neil, trying to gauge if he was any more ashen faced than usual.

"Just get in."

We drove back down through the mountains. Tracks to the side of the road appeared and then petered out into the blanket of trees. We passed an occasional car.

"Want to see where I live?" Neil asked.

35

We pulled up on a patch of muddy earth, by what can only be described as a shack. Neil jumped out in a surprisingly sprightly manner, straightened his tie, twirled the keys on the long chain which hung from his belt, and we were in.

I almost wondered why he bothered locking it. From the outside, the door seemed barely substantial enough to deter an inquisitive badger; from within, there was scarcely anything worth protecting.

"Would you care for some green tea?" he asked. I didn't, as it went, but graciously accepted anyway, going along with the joke. I looked around his living room. It was hovering somewhere between minimalist, and downright empty. There was a single MDF dining chair in front of a small TV. A grubby mattress in a far corner. The squalor sat oddly with Neil's immaculately drab dress.

He appeared at the door with two cups of tea in plastic beakers.

"Please, to sit down," Neil suggested archly, motioning towards the uncomfortable looking dining chair. Neil put some music on, a mix of swirling classical and techno Japanese video game soundtracks. Typical Neil – more Japanese than the Japanese, and yet something more alien than any of us. He sighed, indulging me and the world with his endlessly forbearing smile, sweeping a lock of his lank hair off his brow.

I waited for him to speak, but Neil just sat there, on the mattress on the floor, awkwardly cross-legged in his corduroy slacks, smiling his singular smile, just taking occasional sips of his unpleasant tea.

"So, are you going to tell me what happened?" I asked, finally.

He raised a long, thin index finger, lifted his beaker to his mouth one final time, and let out a peculiarly contented sigh once more.

"It looks like my brave failures to take on the lunches have finally caught up with me. They are convinced my lack of appetite is sign of something sinister – rather than it being just what it is; me not liking the cuisine. And they put two and two together, and because I don't look exactly like them – taller, skinnier, paler – they are concerned that I may have brought HIV into the country."

"But I was screened for that – weren't you?" I asked. I recalled the barrage of tests, including a bizarre lung x-ray, I was required to take before getting the final nod for my visa.

"Yes, yes," he said, quite unflustered. "But once they get an idea in their heads… the local government is full of cowards. I know what has happened. There were a couple of reports from the schools. The gaijin wasn't playing ball. Setting a bad example, etc. Then someone noticed it at city hall. Someone high up, probably. He mentioned something to an underling; there was an implication, an inference drawn, and a bureaucrat was tasked with preparing a report. And rather than write in black and white that his master was being silly, he will have left a lot of room for doubt. Presented the evidence, left it hanging. Glossed over my glowing medical record, probably, as an inconvenient truth. The simple point is that they would rather alienate and humiliate, than question and confront a directive from above. And why not? They're here for the duration, their whole career. I'll be gone in months."

"Home, you mean – not 'gone' gone…"

"No, quite. Departed from these shores; not from this earthly realm." He tapped at the chipboard chair, a touch more listlessly this time.

36

I left Neil framed in his doorway, a symphonic richness pouring from his speakers to infuse the whole shack; a piece which would have scored the moment a character achieved something satisfyingly great in the video game it came from. There was something else too. Neil said Masada had intimated he could make things easier on himself with the city education board if he worked from the inside to 'observe and prompt changes'. He didn't elaborate much, just added he thought it was probably nothing more than weaning me off the 7-11 lunches. In any case, his first report on the topic was expected following next week's big day out at the little schools. Neil gave me a look of paternal indulgence as he took me into his confidence. I felt sure he could cut some deal on my behalf.

Just as I left his little world, heading out into the forest clearing, something caught my attention. Past his little van, lining a dirt track which led further up the hillside to another, distant hut, I saw the anonymous little groupings of stones; the proto-figures standing together in a shrine, their exact meaning impenetrable as ever. Neil would let me in on their secrets one day, perhaps.

I walked the couple of miles back down to the station. It was an early spring afternoon in the mountains. The famous cherry blossoms were still a few weeks distant, but already the feeling of something about to change was suffusing the air. When Mrs Masada had called in at my own school the other day, along with atomic humiliation, the other point on the menu was my suggestion to bring Martin over to fill one of the empty job posts. Now he would be coming over in time for Golden Week. Pending his acquiring a clean bill of health – increasingly important in the light of the HIV lunch fiasco – of course.

That night I met up with Nadya and we went for a drive. Another string to Mrs Masada's bow was as a broker of long term rental cars, and she had sorted me out with a real humdinger. An off-gold exterior with rich, chocolate brown velour effect seats, my ride was a *Cresta Super Lucent*. And if it sounds like Toyota's marketing department had simply flung a number of cod-Latin phrases at a wall to see which stuck, then that's quite possibly what happened. The style was more 70s sub-American hulk than 21st Century Japanese efficiency mobile, but I loved it. With its considerable bulk, 2.5 litre engine and automatic transmission, it was hardly built for the narrow streets of the old neighbourhoods, but out on the US-style shopping strips, was quite in its element. I loved driving along with the window down, the music up and the sun warming my forearm on the brown plastic sill.

Tonight we cruised up the shopping avenue, ducked under the elevated expressway, and steadily accelerated up the foothills of the mountains. It was becoming dusk, and alien sounds came from the gullies, or echoed out from the dense trees; possibly the *kodama* spirits said to inhabit certain special trees. I insisted on the windows down. The irresistible mountain air flooded into the car, filling my lungs; cool, calming and delicious, it immediately made me feel drowsy.

Nadya was less convinced.

"Please, William; can we put the windows up now?"

She clutched the neck of her cardigan closed with one hand.

"Darling, it's only fresh air – and monkeys, of course" I said, eyes fixed on the road.

"Abezyanni? I mean, monkeys? Bleen," she said, artlessly mixing in Russian in alarm.

"Don't worry. Just hang on, Nadyushka." I used the sweet diminutive.

We went over another narrow bridge which crossed the throat of a waterfall, then I pulled over, parking facing the body of water pent behind it. The lights picked out the ghostly currents.

"It's nice up here, no?" I opened the door and walked the few steps to the edge of the water. I beckoned her to come and sit down on a rock.

Nadya shook her head. "I'm OK here. You do what you need."

It was deserted. Not even an alien sound now. The kodama had departed the clearing, it seemed, unable to walk on water.

I went around the back and took a beer from the boot of the car.

"No, William. You need to concentrate for the drive back down," Nadya implored.

"I'll be fine. Just the one."

I put the CD on in the car, left the door open. Tim Buckley singing River, from Blue Afternoon. The great hollowed-out oak of a voice rang clear over the water.

I live by the river, and I hide my house away

And just like the river, I can change my ways

I sat down on the rock again. The beer went down easily. I felt great: relaxed and in control; the ceaseless sky above, the crisp pines all around, and everything – each sound, feeling and fear – sunk in the water. I went back for another.

"Do not, William, drink another."

"You know I'm going to do it and enjoy it, so don't worry, Nadezhda," I said, grinning, now using her formal name. I turned the music up another notch. If it was too loud, she could come and sit outside on my rock.

Oh, if you come to love me, you'll stay forever...

This went the same way, as I perched there still. I was looking forward to seeing Martin again. Looking forward to being the experienced one, glorying in my munificence of bringing him out into the world. He would see the life I'd created for myself. And just as I was a little ringleader in our student house, influencing from the edges, so he'd see the subtle hold I had developed here; the ease with which I took my position.

I had reason to be proud. Nadya was the first proper girlfriend I'd had. Once, people had known me perhaps as a curious mix of self-possession and shyness. Like a less risible version of Martin, I hoped. Now I'd really come into my own. I shook my head and grabbed one more beer from the car.

"What are you doing, William?"

"Gaijin operate by different rules. Because almost everything we do is a transgression of some sort, we're practically immune to prosecution," I laughed, aping the expository style of Neil; or maybe the world weariness of Ahab. "And besides, police can't be bothered to pull us over."

"I won't drive with you. You'll have to call me a taxi," she said.

I leaned in to kiss her, but she turned away; from me, the river.

The music played on. *Blue Afternoon*; that beautiful, fleeting album. And by the time its blue melody had floated away, my empty third bottle was by my side in the sandy bank. It was all too quick.

"You're right. I'm too drunk to drive now. You do it. Come on, get behind the wheel."

Nadya looked up at me, amazed. "You know my licence doesn't work here."

"Sure, but who's going to check. You can drive, right?"

I think she swore in Russian. But even as she shot me a filthy look like I'd never seen on her face before, Nadya walked around to the driver's seat, altered it awkwardly, then pulled the door shut.

"Ok, just put it in reverse – you've driven an automatic before, yes?"

"I don't want to talk. Just let me concentrate."

The car lurched backwards, spinning its wheels in the dust.

"I bet this feels a whole lot different to your father's Zhiguli, yeah?" Leonid's car was the domestic version of the much-reviled Lada; a tiny, tinny saloon, of which he was hugely proud, having inherited it from his own father two decades before.

"Look, if you can drive that, you can pretty much drive anything." I thought I was being encouraging.

We crept away from the strand, turned left onto the short bridge, wobbling slightly down the centre line. Nadya banked right as the forest rushed up at a corner, skirting the small roadside shrine, and passing the monkey warning road sign. I may have seen a tail disappearing into a thicket.

She settled into her task – and I knew she was enjoying it. We were untouchable, wafting down the mountainside, crossing the river back and forth another couple of times. Then we passed under a towering ceremonial gate, and were out of the country park.

Nadya drove down the gentler slopes, past peach trees in the dark. Their scent, a woody promise, beyond blossom, but not quite fruit, drifted over the car. A few random houses spotted our route as we came to the outskirts of Takada.

Now we were out of the landscape of ravines, I was about to tell Nadya to pull over and let me get behind the wheel. The fresh air had cleared my head and I felt great again. No sooner had I formed this thought, than I noticed up ahead a glowing beacon. As we got closer I realised it was brandished by a lone policeman. Nadya was a split second slower in noticing.

"OK, ok. Just slow down slightly," I said, trying to understand what he was doing here in the darkness at the edge of the town. The road came to a T-junction, and the policeman was standing across from this. Of course, it didn't matter why he was posted here on a country lane. Here he was.

"What do I do?" Nadya asked.

"Just come to a complete stop at the junction, then move off slowly," I answered. "He's not interested in us."

On the other side of the road, one of the monkey signs glowed in the periphery of the headlights.

"Stop, Nadya."

But we were already on top of the junction. Nadya slowed, feeling for the clutch that wasn't there on the automatic car. You had to give the brake a good stab, and ignore the slightly odd feeling of not depressing the clutch as you came to a halt. I'd got used to that already – Nadya hadn't. She slowed to walking pace, then panicked.

"The engine will stop if I slow down too much!" she shouted, then rolled slowly through the junction, turning onto the deserted main road, but running wide into the gutter.

A frenzied shriek cut through the darkness, followed by an angry face flipping up parallel to the passenger window. It rotated fully 360 degrees, pausing as it reached the top of its parabola, perfectly level, eyes looking just as evenly into my own.

"Jesus!" I shouted.

We'd clipped a primate, snoozing in a layby. And he was livid. Then, as the face fell out of view, there was a bump and one of the rear wheels skipped into the air.

As we pulled ourselves together, the policeman calmly decided he'd seen all he needed. He casually overtook us at a jog, then skipped along backwards, still rhythmically pumping his little beacon like a relay runner, flagging us over to the side of the road. This time Nadya stopped perfectly.

The policeman approached the open window, while we looked at each other helplessly. I felt sick. He leaned in, face clouding over as he realised what he'd let himself in for.

We stumbled through the Japanese.

Arimasen.

No, Nadya didn't have her driving license with her. Yes, here was her gaijin foreign ID card. Did we do something wrong? We're very sorry. We made a mistake.

Machigae mashita.

He disappeared to his car for a moment.

"I think we're alright, darling, don't worry," I said, feeling hugely guilty, but still just a little smug.

Nadya looked back at me, sheepish, but furious.

The policeman poked his head back in the window. He was smiling. We were fine. I'd perfectly balanced the level of Japanese needed; making sure he didn't mistake us for genuine speakers of the language – and so probably not worth the hassle of bringing us in.

"Please, come with to station," he said, in English; very pleased with himself. "Please follow. Driving problem. Monkey problem, too." Big smile.

So I was wrong then.

As we followed him to the small police station in the centre of Takada, Nadya was more disgruntled than the disturbed primate.

"How can you humiliate me like this?" she pleaded, eyes downcast to the ground. She was furious, in fact. And ashamed. I could only apologise.

We went inside and thrashed out the story with the policeman, mixing Japanese and English. We were still hopeful we'd get away with it. We promised we understood the point about stopping fully at junctions. Yes, of course Nadya had a licence. (We just didn't let on that it was not valid in this country. Nor that it was sitting at *home* home – in Donetsk.) He called our bluff, and sent me back to Nadya's apartment to fetch the document, which was happily sitting in the top drawer of her parent's dresser – next to an expired Young Pioneer, communist youth card – thousands of kilometres away.

***

Sweating, I walked into the foyer of her building, started up the stairs, then had another thought. I headed down towards Nick's. I hesitated slightly before pushing at the door. Would he be there? Of course he was, standing behind the bar with shining eyes, as if he'd been expecting me at any moment.

"William-san, yes?! Good to see you again. What would you like?"

"Well, a drink will definitely come later, but I need some help first…" I said. "Please, is there any chance you could come and help me out – with the police?"

Nick's ears fell, even as his nose twitched upwards, the aggregate effect setting his glasses dancing in bizarre waves.

I explained to him what had happened, and the need to backtrack from our licence claim. Would he help?

A grave expression settled on his face, then he straightened the lapels on his velvet jacket, harrumphed to himself, and marched out. We walked the five minutes back down Chuo Dori, him slightly in front, proudly and deliberately stalking downhill to the little office. His little legs pumped away in their heavy chinos, and Nick swung his arms. *Was he wearing a cravat again?* I don't remember.

Still without making eye contact, Nick leapt up the three steps to the office and stood to attention at the counter. Looking straight ahead, as if addressing someone in the middle distance, he spoke in rapid fire Japanese to the officer who had pulled us over.

In the background, two other officers whispered to each other, then started an unbecoming cackling. Nick's eyes darted towards them, then he carried on his monologue. The poor officer tried to interject a couple of times, but Nick talked over him. In the background again the guffawing, rising in intensity, competing with Nick, who frowned, screwed up his eyes and rose to the challenge. At one stage, an officer emerged from a back room with the monkey on a lead. It leapt up onto the counter as the policeman made a point, gesturing to the ape's hindquarters as it performed on cue, limping stiffly across the surface.

I thought they were inspecting the gait. Then I noticed more attention was drawn to the configuration of markings on the animal's buttocks.

Nick offered spirited protestations in defence, and eventually turned to us, nodded, and led me and Nadya out of the building, laughter following him out onto the street.

"It's fine. All decided," he said. "No problem for you."

"What on earth was going on there when Diddy Kong made a cameo appearance?" I asked.

"Initially they said your charge was (he deftly consulted a pocket dictionary) 'malicious destruction of protected state primates'. But as you could see, the animal was very much alive, More importantly, they realised he was a common monkey – not the special bathing kind. You know; the ones who enjoy spa onsen, and so on. They downgraded the charge to 'wilful hobbling or paralysing of indigenous fauna'. This is important, because a far less serious charge."

I was delighted the diminutive – but irascible – chap was up and walking, though was slightly disappointed to hear he was not partial to a snowy dip in the natural bubbling outdoor spas, like the monkeys we all know from the nature documentaries.

"But the monkey was fine, really, yes?".

"Yes," Nick agreed. "But as I said, under Japanese penal code, degree of disability is not the important thing, when dealing with apes. It is their classification you have to watch for. So look to the buttocks for the identifying cheek configuration."

"Now, Nadya: they will probably phone your language school to tell them you've been disobedient..."

Nadya's face was bright red. She thanked Nick, as I introduced them for the first time. When I popped her back into her apartment, I knew she'd had enough of me that night. And as the door slammed in my face, I knew it was the perfect time to drop straight back down to Nick's on the way home. Now was the time for a drink; rich dark Japanese whisky, pulling down the curtain on an act, like the falling shade of cloud on Shuetsu-san.

37

The final day before Golden Week came and went. The education board were still watching Neil closely for signs of illness, through the eyes of Mrs Masada, and along with Brian, he had to give his presentation lesson at elementary school. Judging from the coldly unimpressed – but not actively disgusted – attitudes of the assembled teachers, Brian had kept hold of his job. Perhaps in the final estimation, his by-numbers, conservative approach may even have been exactly what they were after.

One highlight was Brian's hilariously cack-handed demonstration of wielding chopsticks during my alphabet relay game. Another was Mrs Masada's spectacularly offhand remark to him during lunch, regarding his refusal to pick up his soup bowl and raise it towards his mouth as he ate. "You eat like a dog, you know. Like a Korean." She barely even turned her head in his direction as she said it, just smiled slightly, pleased with herself for sharing this cultural difference.

Then, on the first day of Golden Week, Martin arrived from the UK. I agreed to put him up for a couple of nights, while his flat was arranged. He was all brisk optimism. Determined, even.

He'd taken my warning about the importance of appearances to heart, turning up at my front door on the anniversary of Emperor Showa's death, wearing a sharp little mod number. Apart from that, he had nothing more than a small carry-on suitcase. Martin travelled light.

Something else that was unexpected: he had totally shaved his head. He looked like a spry little Buddhist monk, wearing the Sunday best that no monk would ever possess, of course. Martin's change of look signalled that he meant business.

"What do you think?" he asked with shining little eyes.

"Remarkable. You look like you're ready to go native at a Kyoto temple. I'll fetch the rake, and you can get to work creating an oasis of calm in the gravel car park out back."

I took him out for a couple of days, acquainting him with the sights of Takada. We got him kitted out with a couple of essentials, like the slip-on shoes he'd need for school. We trawled around the strip malls, and I enjoyed playing the old hand for him, guiding him around the more recherché corners of the 100-yen shop; explaining what the hell pachinko was, though I still didn't know myself quite why it was so ubiquitous.

As we walked through the streets of the town, orientating him, a change was in the air. Buds were out on the trees running through the broad plaza of Peach Avenue.

"I envy you," I told Martin. "You're getting to know Japan at exactly the right time. Forget the skyscrapers of Shinjuku, or the castles of Kyoto – peach blossom in Takada is the quintessential experience."

"Perfect timing, as always," he returned, cocky, good-natured; a spring in his step.

I felt good for him. I was sure that, like any of us, he needed this escape. We went to Sergo's karaoke bar one night, then drove downriver to Tenkyobashi the following afternoon. In the evening, we went for a drink with Michael at the pool hall.

I was surprised at how much Martin had changed. Just that little extra self-possession glossed over the usual defensiveness, and it suited him. He got on well with Michael. I'd been worried how these two parts of my life would come together. Whether Michael's easygoing globetrotting would rub Martin up the wrong way; or if Martin's repressed provinciality would make a bumpkin of us both in Michael's eyes. As it was, each of them screwed up more than a few shots, turning away from the table laughing as the other laid on a skit or a wry observation – sometimes with me as the butt of the joke.

Later, Martin settled into his own place, a comfortable, slightly charmless low-level apartment block right by the Matsugawa as it flowed through the centre of Takada's lowlands. I showed him a few tricks; pointing out which seemingly delicious dumplings were most likely to contain an alarming cube of octopus tentacle, and passing on a couple of utility words which I'd found useful in almost any circumstance which involved reassuring a solicitous Japanese that you are perfectly happy just as you are.

As I went to say goodbye, Martin took a step towards me, reached a hand out as if to pat me on the arm, then stopped short and gave an awkward smile.

"I just want to say cheers mate for getting me this gig," he said; the words unbearably light, the expression in his eyes somewhat more serious. Martin wasn't the kind of person to whom gratitude came easily, so I appreciated this.

"You know, there's been a few problems back home," he confided. "My old man is losing the business, so I've kind of been a spare part. Worried about the future, actually. It's amazing how little an arts degree sets you up for."

"Hey, no problem. It's good to have a trusted wingman in these dangerous latitudes."

"Still, you know – thanks and all. There's only so long you can stick the bloody politics of the local trades union chapters…"

I knew Martin hated feeling beholden to anyone. And I know how much his hopeless old dad with the socialist rhetoric meant to him. Finally he was moving on.

38

At the end of Golden Week, I took Nick up on his promise to lead us on a walk up the hillside. It was the perfect introduction to Japan for Martin. And for the first time I would finally venture out onto the playful Shuetsu-san, whose capricious face looked down on Takada with infinite variations of amused indifference.

Me, Nadya and Martin met the rest of the group at a bus stop just inside the country park. Nick was already leading the party by example, wearing an odd mix of safari-inspired clothing; all muted beige tones, lapels and loose tailoring. Hanako and Yui were with him, while Michael, Neil and Brian made up the party.

"You ready?" Nick said. A circle had formed around him, and he himself was indeed ready to lead us.

"It's almost 10km each way, you know? So we'll have a really hard walk uphill before we rest for lunch." Brian grimaced, while Martin puffed out his little chest.

We set off, running alongside the road at times, then taking a direct route up and over, cutting between thick tree trunks through certain sections, while the tarmac wound around, making work for itself. The path was a loosely defined affair, gently cushioned by the pine needles, with occasional flights of wooden steps when the incline demanded. Soon Nadya's shoes were full of the needles and she shook them out, not quite on board with the experience.

As we made our way higher, the moments of direct sunlight shocked us with their warmth as we came out of the forest to cross a bridge, or inspect a roadside shrine at Nick's bidding. But the canopy of tall trees mostly hid us. The coolness settled on us; little pockets which caught me as we rounded a large rock, or a sudden chill which stopped Nadya's breath in a denser section of shadow. Occasional fragments of light stabbed at my eyes when the strong morning sun penetrated the trees in long, striated shards.

In the middle of the group, Brian grumbled, but kept himself shambolically together; Neil maintained the doughty smile on his face, despite the inappropriate choice of cotton chinos and sports jacket. Michael, Hanako and Yui pushed on happily at the front with Nick.

Nadya and I formed the final group with Martin. He was struggling, though would not show it.

"What's the matter?" I asked. "Isn't this what you expected of the Japanese mountains?"

"It's sound, it's fine. I'm enjoying it. Just working up an appetite for lunch."

He'd brought a still more cravenly western meal than me: a 7-11 special hamburger sandwich and cheesey puff crisps.

"No sushi today, then?" I laughed,

"I bloody love sushi. But, you know, need the calories today to bulk it out," he explained, slightly turning his arm to flex a putative tricep. I was confident that, however hard Martin tried to play catch up on Japanese culture, I would never see him shovelling raw fish into his milksop mouth.

We stopped at the occasional clearing; resting on benches at a small building used by schools for geography field trips, or kneeling down by a tiny running stream which splashed over pebbles. Here I ran my hands through the cold water, cupping them and bringing it back up to splash on my face. I gasped at the sting, then smiled at the shattering sense of reality the motion gave me; my eyes focussing slightly clearer on the trees in front of me; the blood in my limbs suddenly feeling hotter, more pressurised.

"Give it a try!" I encouraged Nadya and Martin. They weren't having it. Nadya shook her round head vigorously; Martin turned on an immediate spurt of pace, pretending he didn't hear.

Higher up in the Japanese Alps the snow was melting and the Matsugawa, tumbling down through the middle of our route, was in full flow. Its continuous crash, muted at a distance by the woods, was a calming white noise, a constant backdrop and a comfort. No-one was talking much as we climbed.

Finally, we crossed the river one last time at a tall concrete road bridge, and found our way to a clearing, just metres from the bank. We spread out on the ground, forming a loose circle, gathered around Nick.

Everyone broke out their picnics. The sun was warm, and we screwed up our eyes against its reflection off the Matsugawa. But at the same time a breeze rumpled its surface; caused Nadya to pull the collar of her jacket around her neck.

"Are you OK, darling?" I whispered to her.

"You know what the Ukrainian people say. If cold wind touches your neck, that's it: you'll have a sore throat the next day when you wake up. I know you don't believe it, but it's true."

Martin struck a pose as he leaned back on one arm, legs crossed and flared jeans legs fluttering gently. Brian eyed him cautiously, while Neil pulled his knees up under his chin, stoically refusing to eat, a succession of self-satisfied expressions slowly running across his face like the changing facets of cloud on Shuetsu-san.

"You know why I know so much about Ahab?" Nick asked me, the brio of his delivery eclipsing any grammatical errors, glossing his narrative into a smooth ride for his listeners.

251

"We used to be friends. He was one of the first teachers who came here. At that time, my former wife and I were very close to him. We had met in the education department in the city. We used to be teachers, you know? James was my assistant in those first couple of years as the education department found its feet with the system. Of course, he really was one of the only western people in the Takada area. I was kind of like a big brother to him. And he was a great kid. My wife introduced him to her best friend. We became a little group. For a time, Ahab went native – he really is very good at Japanese, you know."

It fell into place. How the cabin boy earned his water-wings in such an alien environment.

"He got married. Then a couple of years went by, and things started to change. It was difficult to get the pair of them to come out for meal with us. I heard rumours. You don't have to hear from your friend himself. Takada is a small place. Then it just gets more obvious with each year."

He looked me in the eye. "You know Yui is my niece, right?"

I really didn't. I looked at her. She was pretending not to hear, but we were having the conversation in full earshot of the group. I nodded awkwardly. Yui, however, was chatting very softly to Martin. He knew nothing of Takada's politics, of course. She was looking directly at him and laughing, while Martin gazed bashfully across the water. I almost felt embarrassed for him.

"You know when I came to the police station with you the other week? This was very difficult for me. The people there were rude to me."

I lied. "Yeah? I didn't notice anything."

"Well yes. You see, there was a little incident a few years ago. When I was married to Mrs Masada."

Brian snorted in the background.

"We only know one Mrs Masada," Neil said.

"And she just told me that I eat like a dog," chipped in Brian.

"Yes, that sounds much like Chiemi-chan," Nick said. It was unclear how Nick meant the remark; it was pitched halfway between a tender wistfulness, and straight matter-of-fact. A curiously Japanese delivery.

"Well, she was the woman I was married to. You see, she cheated on me," Nick said simply. This, disarmingly deadpan.

I wasn't the only one who could see where this was going. Brian laughed out loud, uncharitably, almost in triumph.

"So now you know why I don't get on with the sailor. And you have an idea why I'm no longer married. You still don't know about the police though."

On the outer edge of the circle, Yui and Martin were deep in conversation. I noticed how his studiedly sensual reclining pose thrust his breast forward. He was enjoying the attention and the adulation which requires no quid pro quo. I knew what it felt like in this situation. Now Nadya put an arm on my neck, her mood thawing in the sunshine, tousling my hair, while Hanako and Michael kissed. Out on the Matsugawa, still before the mouth of the drop beneath the bridge, something moved under the water, ruffling the surface.

"It was the undergarments," Nick sighed.

Everyone turned to him except Hanako and Yui. Their jaws kept on chewing their daikon radish as they stared at the glow of blossom on trees along the bank.

"I couldn't help taking the panties. It made no sense as I was doing it. But still, I picked them up. I put some down my trousers. Two packs up my jumper. Held one right in my hand. Then I walked out of the superstore. A security guard stopped me immediately. Two of my pupils were there watching by the time the police arrived.

"I think I wanted to be caught, no?"

Nick fell silent. Blinking slowly, deliberately.

"Yep – sounds like a protest to me," Brian nodded.

"A dirty protest," Michael said quietly. "Yui – you didn't tell me about your disreputable old uncle."

Her eyes rounded and she looked hurt. For a moment I felt bad for her; the nuances of understanding that she could not grasp in real time, just like the mysteries of daily life impenetrable to me here.

Hanako slapped him sharply on the arm. Michael just gave her his wide, sharp smile, and she hoisted her moon-like face to him, indulgent; without expression.

On the other side of the circle, Martin stirred slightly from his reverie with Yui. I saw him slowly piecing together the complicated back stories, turning over these histories, lives in the mountains. Yui continued her blandishments, unperturbed, while Martin stiffened slightly at her touch, dabbing lightly on his arm.

The party fell quiet after lunch. Waves on the water settled, and we all lay in the grass, in our pairs or alone, the sun just warm enough at last to enjoy. Yui spoke up, for the first time, to the group.

"The blossoms are a little late this year. They're almost in full flower now, but in one week maybe, they will already be almost gone. That's it. This full bloom stage we call 'mankai'. We should enjoy it now."

"It's a long year until they come again," Hanako chimed in thoughtfully.

"'Mono-no-aware' in action," said Neil. "It's uniquely Japanese to see this ghost of decay even before something beautiful is even mature," He mused.

"Ah, yes, Neil-san," Nick said. "But maybe it's also uniquely Japanese to see this death as something beautiful in itself. To celebrate and codify its impermanence."

Neil's face darkened as he realised he had missed the opportunity to make this point himself.

Time passed, and we needed to head back down. Our group spread out once more as we retraced our steps. Nadya led the way, suddenly peevish once again; her mood disturbed by retracing the uncomfortable journey back down the mountain. She was still not entirely over the incident with the policeman. Martin settled into a semi trot between me and Michael, with Yui and Hanako just behind. I noticed how Martin was now keeping himself carefully apart from the girls.

"You know, you're an honorary Gaijin now," Michael told him, leeringly. "You should get used to taking what you want – whenever you can get it. There's no rules here, man."

"Yeah – it's not like university. Let it go." I joined in, knowing just how to hurt him. "Set yourself free from those embarrassments down the Roxy. Message from mother: No one's going to pat her little boy on the head and smile condescendingly here."

This last bit was uncalled for, I knew. It was certainly how we used to mock Martin. Women tended to see him as a silly little boy. His unproductive attempts to approach them invariably ended in someone tousling his hair, infantalising him in public.

"What's that?" laughed Michael. I performed the patronising gesture with a big smile, walking backwards down the path and looking through Martin to Michael.

The little choirboy usually had a way of directing his attention elsewhere, to pretend it wasn't happening. But here he was caught between us.

"You cheeky bastard!" He shouted, forcing a jaunty edge into his voice.

As per an old tick, he went to run fingers through his spiked hair, then realised there was nothing to tousle.

I knew that Michael could be trusted with this kind of patronising anecdote; that he wouldn't hammer it home. But Martin didn't know that yet. I realised I'd gone too far. He was just trying to make a fresh start, like any of us – and there'd been an unwritten code between us that I would let him get on and do just that. Instead, I'd brought up the ghosts of his past; the insecurities he thought he had left behind in England.

As Yui came up to the front and chirruped to Nadya and me, I saw Martin's face flush. I felt bad, pulling rank like that, but also giddily excited. My replies to Yui rang out a little louder than normal. I snaked my arm around Nadya. I knew she was still angry with me, but for now I didn't care.

We crossed the last bridge, dove down one final bank of trees, skipped through a hollow, and we were out along the flat footpath.

Heads hung, we all went beneath the monumental wooden gateway, as Martin's cheeks burned pinker than the cherry blossoms. Takada lay just a few streets down below us, its peach trees poised, almost on the wane.

39

After Golden Week, the school year started once more. Shimoida maintained his strange relationship with me. Thanks to Mrs Masada, at least now I understood why. Big Hiromi too was becoming more distant, perhaps getting the message at last. That worked nicely for me. I could count, however, on Izumiyama coming back like the reincarnation of the beautiful waning blossoms. Another year to teach the same lessons; turning like a makeshift wheelchair's revolutions.

Following the hike, I was keeping an eye on Martin, helping him to settle in. Masada wangled me a day off to spend with him in his school, helping him understand exactly what was expected of him. As all schools were run in precisely the same manner, the experience was interchangeable from mine to his, and I could guide him through the need to be seated in his faculty room by 8am sharp, how best to navigate the trials of lunch; the specific ways to greet and then bid farewell to the hierarchies of teachers he would encounter each day.

Martin seemed to get it. He was a little slow on the uptake of the Japanese language, but after all that was not what he was here for. It turned out that his claim of 'studying Japanese' in the weeks before he came amounted to stunted ordering of food in a restaurant. But that's fine. Martin was always one of those people for whom speaking a language well amounted to a handful of ill-remembered phrases and a few nouns, unclothed by grammar or context. Given the fact his horizons had never extended beyond a school trip to France, he was doing well.

I accompanied Martin into the formal meeting with his new head-teacher, who looked underwhelmed by the little chap now in front of him, as they stood eye to eye, sizing each other up. If we liked our caricatures, then so did the Japanese; Martin was standing in for the rangy Jay, and he didn't measure up.

When I dropped him back at the English room before leaving early, I noticed the pretty young, slim woman at the desk across from him, and the sporty language teacher who doubled as the school football coach. These two also sized Martin up – and it looked like they too found him wanting.

***

Meanwhile, Nadya was in a state. She was spending more time on the phone to her parents. There were real problems back home. As the protests led to a recounting of the votes and a new, western-leaning government in Ukraine, people in the Donbass took to the streets themselves, armed with whatever they could find. Police in the area were beaten back when they tried to protect regional buildings, and were swiftly becoming unable to keep the peace. Increasingly they didn't try.

"It's very serious there and I'm worried about my parents," she'd told me, concern in her voice, the hint of tears in her eyes.

"Darling, it won't affect your parents. They are quiet people. Your father isn't going to head out into the street with a gun. In any case, they don't believe in all this fuss – they don't need the aggravation."

She looked doubtful.

"Actually, they do believe in standing up to Ukrainian nationalism."

"What does that mean," I asked. "Demonstrating? Storming buildings? Walking the streets with weapons?"

"They wouldn't be violent. But they agree with moving closer to Russia, away from the influence of Europe and America."

"You were very happy to acknowledge the influence of Europe when you studied there. Or when your father's ancestors came from Wales to help prehistoric Russian industry," I pointed out.

"Don't say things like that. It's more complicated," she said, quietly determined, instantly a little riled. "I wouldn't expect you to understand."

"Oh, I know," I jumped in. "The good old days of Soviet communism; jobs for life, free holidays for all and piping hot apartments all winter. Well, I don't think they can go back to it, I'm afraid." What was it I wasn't seeing?

"Maybe you just can't understand the differences between east and west," Nadya said, with a sharp sideways look. "Maybe that's why you engage with Japan on your own terms. Send it up. Talk around the subject, but keep the people at arm's length, like a specimen – "

"Like a pickled bee?" I asked.

"They're all people, you know. Pickled bee eaters, or whatever you think they are. Like my parents are people. Like me and you."

"Sure, but maybe these people like your parents have to recognise when things change," I said. "It's not the Soviet Union. It's not the Second World War. The atom bombs exploded decades ago."

***

Only for Nadya's parents, for her, it almost was the Second World War still. Very quickly, the Ukrainian army rolled east, encircling towns of the Donbas. Cast in the role of murderous fascists by the Russian news which her family watched, the army was met by local militias, bolstered by 'volunteers' from across the Russian world.

Her widowed grandmother, living alone in a forgotten village, and bombarded by rhetoric calling her countrymen Nazis, seemingly became confused about time. Reliving her childhood, she believed Germans were again attacking. Confused even within herself, she forgot how to speak Russian, and ironically defaulted to a Ukrainian mother tongue which went beyond politics.

"It's crazy, darling," I pleaded with Nadya. "Can't you see that a media environment which can actually bend people's minds back sixty years through fear and propaganda just isn't healthy?"

"William, I don't have time for these arguments," she would counter, exhausted.

"I don't care about the rights and wrongs. What I care about is my family. They are everything. And what they believe, I believe. Or at least, I will let them think that I believe it with them, to give them some comfort. This is more important. For god's sake, think about my grandmother's life for one minute."

She'd been born at the peak of the collectivisation famine in the early 30s, and was a young girl as the Germans really did sweep up through Ukraine to strike at the heart of the Soviet Union, at Stalingrad.

"The little stream at the end of her village where she played ran under a bridge where the German tanks and troop transports rolled. Imagine being a child when you witness this."

"Yeah, it's impossible for me to understand, of course," I accepted. "But don't forget that everything you've told me was just the start. She survived the war, along with the Russian people, victorious – only to live through thirty grinding years of poverty. Yes, some years might have been better than others. Maybe there was even a time when it all made sense to her, the whole march to communism. But none of this could've been much consolation when she was left a young widow, ten years into the Stagnation."

"Grandfather died in 1975, yes. But what is this Stagnation?" Nadya asked.

"Right. It's what the rest of the world calls the two decades of the economic cobwebs and ideological malaise which finally ended with Perestroika. And from there, guess what? She just about has time for a quick breather, then you're into Ukrainian independence, and all the crap that went along with that."

"Thing is, William sensei, did you live through those years? No. You didn't struggle to stay in university while your father was paid in coal, your mother in sugar."

"Maybe it's the sins of the father..." I tailed off. She hadn't understood my sarcasm, but Nadya's face showed she got the gist of my attitude. "And back to your grandmother, after that economic collapse, she just had time to squeeze in another quick war before she hit the life expectancy ceiling for Ukrainian women. But she's still soldiering on. Good for her."

We were in my flat. Nadya stood up quietly, and walked out. I didn't blame her. I sat down for five minutes, stared blankly at the *washi* room dividing sliders, a funny taste in my mouth, then did the same as her, walking out and down the hill to Michael's place. We drank a couple of beers, then tumbled into his car, laughing, and he drove us to Strawberry Fields.

40

The next day I woke up with a hangover. I opened my gummed eyes and looked at the same *washi* walls with their mountain scene print; an impressionistic double spike of peaks, a broad wash of blue anchored by the radial spokes of a sunrise. The same taste in my mouth, this time sharper, more putrid.

We'd had a good time at the pool hall, from what I could remember. Me and Michael – well, mostly me – setting the expat world to rights. Laughing about Martin; how hopelessly forlorn he looked on the picnic. I told Michael about the bike lock incident from university. He'd looked more incredulous than amused at my anecdote, I recalled awkwardly.

I jumped in the shower, turned the temperature down a couple of notches from normal and revelled in the cold plastic cocoon of the room, its ceiling barely higher than my scalp. The phone rang and I jumped out. I scooted over the reed matting floor, but it rang off before I got there. The answer machine kicked in, and it was Nadya's colleague from her language school, telling me she had gone home ill and was sleeping through the day.

I thought I'd check in on her later, but would let her rest for now. I didn't know what to do with myself, so I had a swig of whisky from a pocket bottle, then walked up to Music Macaque. It was early afternoon, but Sergo was there already, his loud Hawaiian shirt clashing madly with his bouffant, purple died hair – the look of the 'chimpira' mafia goon. He'd be behind the reception bar area until the place closed at 4am, or the last booth emptied; whichever came first.

I ordered a whisky, the default Suntory brand. This cheap version wasn't the smoothest, but it went down passably well, given the hour. And anyway, I was no expert, unlike Sergo. He poured himself one, and we adjourned to the intimate two-table pool cellar he kept. As I racked up the balls, he put on a near-unlistenably frenetic accordion, fiddle and tambourine mélange. Perfect for dancing a Georgian mountaintop jig with a goat and a gourd of wine; less good for dealing with a sore head in the bowels of a karaoke suite.

Sergo split the pack with a disconcertingly energetic thrust of his hips into the table, pivoting upwards on a shiny black buckled shoe, and – striking a pose – we were off. As we played, we shouted over the music to each other. I told him about the argument with Nadya, how I couldn't understand her parents' attitude, her mercurial take on her homeland.

"You are leaving your country behind – just like me and her," he told me.

"But there is a difference. You come here on level terms. In fact, more than level terms. If you want to return – which you will – you know that your country will have you back. It will welcome you home with open arms. You will find it in more or less the same shape as you left it. Your family will be there, safe. You will hopefully find a good job. For us, it's not such a certain thing. Maybe we can return, maybe not. Maybe our country will be happy to see us; then again, maybe our situation will be much changed and we will face difficulties. We will be on the wrong side of the authorities for no fault of ours. Just imagine that for a minute."

I accepted the general righteousness of the sermon. But it still didn't add up.

I shook my head. "The thing I don't get is the lack of responsibility as an individual to form an opinion; the way you have to hold the same views as everyone else in whatever region you call 'home'.

Always falling back in on your family, and their ways of seeing the world. Surely that's a recipe for nothing ever changing?"

"People think these ways for a reason," he said. "You know why the Japanese characterise themselves as bees, why they say about the sticking out nail that will get hammered back down? Being an individual is not easy in their society. You know the old saying that Japan is a capitalist country run like a communist one. You could say that now about the Russian world too. And you could also notice that being an individual is not too easy there, either. Think about it."

I did. I could appreciate it on a human level, but not as the basis for any kind of social discussion. We stopped talking, beyond acknowledging each others' finer shots, playing six frames. Three-all; stalemate.

"Would you go back?" I asked Sergo, as we headed back up to the bar area. "I mean, did you really have to leave all your family and friends behind for good?"

"You ask me if I had to leave everything? Maybe not. But maybe I would be dead already if I didn't." I wondered if he might be dead from the waist down already, in his viciously skintight black jeans, then downed the last drink and said farewell.

***

At the end of the long Chuo Dori, I turned down the alley, stalked determinedly up Nadya's stairs, and rapped on her door. I was worried about her, and I put on the briskness as an act.

For a long time there was no answer. Then I heard a slight shuffling from within, and the door opened a crack. The shuffling receded. I pushed into the darkened room.

"Are you OK, darling – I can't see you," I said, instantly feeling out of place, but not quite regretting coming. "What's the matter?"

As my eyes adjusted to the gloom, I saw she was turned on her side, facing me, her big beautiful eyes staring through the door behind me. The duvet traced her waist, her haunches and hips.

"William, I think we have to say goodbye soon."

I froze. "Is it a problem with your parents?"

"No. I will have to go home because I will lose my job soon."

"What happened?" I asked.

No reply.

"Did you do something wrong?"

"Yes," she chuckled with a swallowed gurgle. "My language school thinks I'm an embarrassment for them. I caused a problem for its reputation. The thing I did wrong was listening to you and getting into the driver's seat."

"Oh, darling, I don't think it will be such a problem…"

"It is a problem, William. It's a real problem for some of my students, and it's a problem for my manager. And that means it's a problem for me. They told me that there was an issue with my contract which means they are looking for someone to replace me. They were very sorry."

"So you don't know that it is about the police?"

"Of course it is, William. It's their way. They just don't know how to approach the subject. And neither do I."

"What did they actually say? No, this is horseshit; you have to speak to them. Ask for a meeting, look your boss in the eye, and make them explain exactly what the problem is with your 'contract'."

I was out of breath, and slightly angry with Nadya for how she was taking this, actually.

"You don't understand," she said. "I don't want to. I don't want to fight against something I can't see, where a decision's been made. It will only make me angry. And I'm already angry with you. You just don't understand how these things work – you think it's all OK because we are the protected gaijin, and we'll muddle through because everyone's too embarrassed to cause a fuss. Well, maybe I'm not your type of gaijin. I'm not a westerner. I'm used to being treated badly by the powers you can't quite see. And in the real world, embarrassed people are never slow to hide behind the book when it suits them. That's how rules work for many."

"Darling, I'm sorry you feel like this…" I started.

"And you know what? Actually, I'm embarrassed too. Mortified. Because of what you made me do. Now, let me rest – I'm not feeling well."

I didn't want to argue. I felt a little sick too. But I called in on Martin on the way home, walking the long way back down, along the Matsugawa as it ran towards the bottom end of town. As I looped down towards his apartment building, I saw him coming out of his first floor door, and leaning against the broad, rusted balcony, overlooking the road. Below him, pebbles from the patch of barren earth which passed as a car park scattered towards the broad drainage ditch lining the road.

Powerlines ran in all directions, but seemed to converge on Martin as he stood there in the early afternoon. He was all edges; the vertex and the axis of intersection. He leaned over the balcony and smoked, smiling with easy satisfaction, calm. I shouted out to him and he looked up startled, then forced a smile. As he did so, a figure moved in the doorway behind him, drawn out not by the sound of my approach, but by simple momentum. As the figure made it to the threshold of the door, Martin turned to it sharply. The shadow halted, subliminal, then retreated inside.

We held an awkward conversation, me standing in the street below; Martin making no attempt to invite me up. I said goodbye and left them to it, whatever was going on. Looking back as I turned at the crossroads to walk up the gentle hill home, I saw Martin had left the balcony, and a new outline stood in his place, leaning over the rail, motionless.

41

The next evening, I was still feeling a little uncomfortable about the encounter. I decided to go back and pay a visit to Martin. I was toying with the idea of making amends, taking him out and having some fun; lightening him up a little. I called in unannounced, but it didn't cross my mind he wouldn't be home. He wasn't with me; he didn't know anyone else well enough yet. And I was sure he wasn't the type to go randomly exploring on his own, regardless of any claim he would make to be an adventurous spirit.

There was no answer at first as I knocked on his door. Then I heard a noise inside, bustling to and fro. I knocked again. Hefty footfalls approached, moved back, shuffled, then decisively plodded to the door and opened it a crack.

A big brown eye peered at me through the gap, not alarmed, but rather blank.

I introduced myself in English, though there was no response. I started again in my laboured Japanese. Before I managed to get my name out, she turned, pulling the door open after her, lumbering slowly off on heavy bare feet.

Down the short, dark corridor, she moved into what passed for a living room, reemerging through another sliding door into the kitchen. I understood that I could enter. Perhaps Martin was inside?

"Hi – Martin?" I called out.

"A laugh came from the kitchen.

"Hai – Martin!" she parroted. *Yes – Martin, indeed!* she seemed to say.

I craned my head around the corner into the kitchen. She was a plump, rather short woman with a curtain of lank black hair hiding a bad complexion.

"Is he here?" I asked in Japanese.

She smiled slyly, and I saw her bad teeth too, all yellow-streaked canines, just before she raised her hand automatically to cover her mouth. She jerked her head in the direction of a tiny room at the far end of the corridor, Through the open door, I could see wrinkled sheets; the end of a bed.

I looked back at her. She was scrubbing something in the sink, preparing a meal. On the worktop were slices of cabbage and green onions. I peered over. A long octopus tentacle seemed to grip along the length of her arm as she washed it. Slowly our gazes met, mine horrified; hers amusedly blank. She held my eyes, breaking into a smile once again as I walked backwards down the short hall towards the bedroom.

Inside the room, the western-style bed virtually covered the floor. But any space left over was filled with Japanese comics, pages scattered and scribbled with notes in Martin's childish handwriting. Exclamation marks and crude cartoons stood out from the patchwork of paper. In among the comics were a few copies of Girlfriends, a hybrid manga/girlie mag which featured young ladies parading in schoolgirl uniforms with the wrunkled nylon legwarmers. Martin had been trying to make sense of something, but he'd found only a febrile hotchpotch of confusion. Bringing texture to the collage, a single pair of women's underwear.

"Just tell him I came to see how he is," I said in Japanese, before stepping through the front door.

Hai.

270

42

That weekend we were all out. Brian had come out of his slump. Neil was on fine form. Me, Martin – himself now right as rain – and Nadya met them at Elvis, squeezing beneath a grass skirt-fringed table inside a neon booth, and ordering a round of 'pink Caddies'. Brian's loose bonhomie infected the whole group. Even Neil was relaxed, resplendent in a herringbone sports jacket. Martin and Nadya also slipped from the shadows to take centre stage with their stories.

"Just like old times," Brian said, slinging an arm around me. I told him the anecdote about Martin's girl and he loved it. "Ah well, he's getting on better than some of us…"

So, we had perspective to look back on 'old times' already, thought they were only a few months past. In fact, the wonder of those early days only lasted a very few weeks in reality, but I knew what Brian meant. I felt it too. In turn I hugged Nadya, and she didn't pull away from me. She still hadn't heard anything definitive on her job. It seemed the threat – or some nebulous hint of a threat – had been made, and the nuance of this left hanging for someone to push forward. That someone else never appeared. It looked like it had lost momentum. She was in the clear, and finally she had relaxed a little.

We tumbled out into the cool night and walked over to Paradiso, where we found Michael, Ahab and their entourage occupying one of the usual booths. They were well on their way. The girls were cackling – a demure version of a cackle, at least, eyes lowered, hands hovering in front of mouths – at everything their men said. We waved to them from the bar as we ordered our drinks. Michael gave a lacklustre wave, Ahab a sardonic smile. I realised they weren't happy to see us. As we walked over, Hanako whispered something to Yui, and I felt a little uncomfortable.

"Well, you guys look like you're out for some fun," sneered the captain of the good ship condescension.

"We've been sampling the fried peanut butter sandwiches with the King," said Neil, flashing what passed for a winning smile; sublimely unaware of the edge to the atmosphere.

"Yeah, there's only one king," said Ahab, then pulled Yui in close and slobbered a drunken kiss on her pastel cheek. She giggled, looking up for the first time, at Martin.

Michael gave me a look which hovered between helplessness and self-indulgence, as if he was worried about what would happen, but equally relished it as a spectator. I quickly assessed the situation and sat down by him, keeping Martin diagonally opposite Ahab and Yui. The sailor had obviously heard about Martin's opportunistic behaviour at the picnic and was restaking his territory as the premier seafarer in the port of Takada.

At length, the drinks flowed and loosened up the atmosphere. I looked over from time to time at Nadya, deep in conversation with a shaggy browed, sweating Brian, the hard unsympathetic line of his fringe still etched around his face. With Hanako at his other side, Michael was leaning to me, telling a story about a particularly bright eyed 'rabbit' as he called her – his name for the archetype of a uniquely cute, bright eyed Japanese girl he'd taken a shine to.

"She actually brought me an apple this week. Polished and gleaming, put it on my desk with a little curtsey. I might leave a peach in her place and see where it leads. It's OK, she's 18 – I checked on the school records."

"Who is 18?" asked Hanako, suddenly suspicious, snaking an arm into the nape of Michael's neck; surprisingly sharp witted in the echoing darkness of the bar.

"You are, my little rabbit – you look like you could still be in school," he laughed, as Hanako looked a little confused.

"I'm almost in my mid-20s, as you always say," Hanako chirruped querulously. "And still-not-married."

She pulled her hand from Michael's neck and held up a wiggling finger.

"Yeah, you need to join the club," Ahab chimed in, giving Michael first his ring finger, then a condescending waggle of his little finger.

"Yeah, you need one of these, Hanako," Brian shouted, extending his middle digit and guffawing.

"Man, come on," sighed an exasperated Michael.

"I don't know how many more of these evenings I can take, announced Neil with a melodramatic flourish, knocking back the rest of his white Russian.

"You just need a woman, you tired old hen," laughed Ahab, with a rum-sodden rumble. "Start enjoying yourself and you might stop being so judgemental. Maybe I could lend you one of mine for the evening. What do you think, Yui? You seem to have a taste for these skinny Brits."

Through the early stages of an alcoholic haze, I realised that Martin was no longer at the table. I saw Brian sitting next to Ahab, laughing salaciously, perhaps glad it was not about him. I knew they were talking about Martin.

I went to the toilet, knocked on the stall door. Nothing. I knew he had a penchant for disappearing when in a bad mood – one of his old petulant tricks at university – and I was at once both slightly worried and horribly fascinated.

So I jogged down the stairs, looked out onto the street, past the peach trees to the left, then up the road towards the zoo. Had he ducked down into the depths of the building after all, Purgatorio, the quiet port in a storm? The cavernous underground bar had been a refuge more than once when things got a little heated among the alphas of Paradiso.

I stuck my head in the door, walked past the brightly lit alcove with its darts machine, round a scattering of tables in the open plan room. I scanned the scene. Someone was watching me too from a corner. It was the girl from his flat, softened here by the lighting.

She put her hand on a thin, pasty arm, which projected from behind a beam. It could only belong to one man. Our eyes met, and her soft, slight smile faced down my harder twinge of a grin. Gone was her sly look.

This was all I needed. I exultantly turned and jogged back upstairs, shaking my head with a mixture of relief he'd been found, and annoyance that he'd run out in the first place. When I got back, Neil was arguing with Ahab, with Brian improbably playing peacemaker. I didn't care what it was about.

"Guys, it's time to move on. Come down to Purgatory. I think you'll enjoy the scenery downstairs. Come on, drink up!"

Two minutes of protests later, and the whole group was walking downstairs, Hanako and Yui struggling with their high heels, Brian struggling generally.

274

"Why are you so keen to leave?" asked Nadya, perhaps noticing a look in my eye, an uncharitable turn to my mouth she knew.

I led them straight over to a couple of tables next to Martin, who physically started when he saw us approach. Ahab smirked triumphantly but warmly greeted Martin, as if he hadn't seen him in a week. The girls looked Martin's companion up and down, said a curt hello, and then put their heads together, casting supplementary glances in her direction.

We pushed two tables together, me shunting one sharply and vindictively, Michael leaning into another more languidly, effectively blocking the couple in the corner. Martin had no option but to introduce her to the group; Akiko. Her trusting, open look scanned across our faces, and nodded hello respectively to each gaze she met. But as I held Nadya close, and Ahab and Michael pulled their girls into them, Martin inched away from Akiko, as if the more we pressed in upon them, the more he disowned her in the darkness.

"I see you found your own girl then," the captain said to Martin; sneeringly comparing Yui's delicate femininity with the plain young woman in front of him.

I couldn't tell how much Akiko understood. So much nuance of Japanese interaction was far beyond me. Was this sarcasm similarly inaccessible to her?

In any case, the condescension wasn't alien to Martin. He got up, mumbling something, and tried to push past the tables, becoming panicked when they didn't initially give, caught like an animal. His shoe trapped between table and chair, he struggled briefly, intensely, then a moment of clarity radiated from him. All calm consideration, he seemed to weigh up the advantages of sacrificing an appendage to get away, like a lizard shedding its tail. Then the furniture moved,

Martin laughed with a sort of manic relief, and walked over to the bar.

Though there was no one else to serve, the bartender ignored him for a moment, arranging bottles on the shelf and taking a phone call, giving Ahab time to wander over in a bellbottomed swagger. I looked in the mirrored wall at Martin's face as he saw the sailor's approach. The older man, some six inches taller, slung an arm around him, and leaned his fat blonde head in close. From my three-quarter rear view, I saw the length of his heavy jaw moving slowly, as if accentuating some point. In reflection, a break in a section of mirror split a jagged line down their faces, like the two halves of the whole did not fit. Ahab turned his head slightly, cutting across the dividing line again, then patted Martin heavily on the back and took a step away.

I turned to Nadya, raised my eyebrow, and tried to kiss her. She resisted slightly, but I planted a kiss on her broad, soft temple, the closest I could get to the roundness of her cheek.

As I looked up, the bartender was finally laying Martin's drink down in front of him, taking the thousand yen note, and moving his attention to the captain. I caught him in the mirror, his mouth open as he ordered in deft, but defiantly accented Japanese. Michael approached them, put a friendly arm around Martin, a smile of genuine concern and friendship radiating back from the mirror, dissolving into the darkness of the cavern.

This touch was all it took. So fast, it seemed Ahab could not close the round of his mouth to chew off his next word, his head was jerked sideways at a 45-degree angle. Then Martin wheeled sharply in the other direction, something jagged and flashing now in his hand, followed by a sickening noise which cut through the music.

He turned smartly to walk back to his place, blood trickling down his arm and dripping from the goblet he held, leaving a trail on the tiled flooring. The captain stood in silhouette, clutching at a broken nose, whose bone had broke the glass.

Then the music stopped, and our eyes followed the gurgling which filled the underground cavern, our gazes moving away from Ahab. Together we rushed to Michael, who was now grasping desperately at his split face. We saw the deep cut from cheekbone to chin through gaps in his fingers. The bartender pushed a clean tea towel into Ahab's hands and sat him on a chair, then phoned for the police, while Nadya pressed a hoody over Michael's face and put him into the recovery position.

At some point during this elusive minute, Martin had disappeared. By the time the police got there, Akiko was still sitting on her own in the same corner, the tables pushed aside during the commotion, leaving a simple channel for her to escape, if she had wished.

Then blood rushed to my head. The air seemed to smell of blood, even. I sat down with Nadya and held her tight, though she wriggled slightly out of my grasp. I was not thinking at all, but in this absence of thought, had a repellent feeling; like all was now forever beyond my reach, slipping away, on a slick of oily red.

And just as the smells and sounds merged into a singularity, I realised that somehow Nick had found out what was going on and was there before the paramedics. He bent over the downed captain, gently patting him on the back, speaking softly in Japanese, occasionally looking at Yui with a comforting expression.

When he saw the state of Michael, Hanako kneeling by his side, Nick had to steady himself against the bar.

43

Events slowed down, shattered images recombined into one picture; settled. I had to go with Nadya and Nick to show the police where Martin lived. Akiko was mute as she accompanied us, and the officers had given up trying to get through to her. I had no ideas of the address; just communicated where to go with a curt 'left', 'right', or 'straight ahead'.

He was not there. So the police drove us home to Nadya's flat, the smell of peaches filling the summer air through the town, as if carried not just on the wind, but by the old Matsugawa itself as it coursed through Takada.

We collapsed onto Nadya's bed.

"When I was born all of my blood was washed out and new blood put in," she said. She was talking slowly, fixing her gaze on the kotatsu. Even though the night was mild, Nadya had lifted the corners of the duvet tablecloth, allowing the heat to radiate into the room. The element glowed in the dark. It had a hypnotic quality, made me accept her story simply; focused my mind's eye on the slashed cheek, then her small body. The bevelled edge of a mirror.

"My mother had what we call II-negative blood."

"You mean you had a transfusion, I guess," I said.

"Yes. Transfusion."

The word swilled and then spread out as it left her mouth. Nadya breathed heavily.

"She found it hard to have a baby. And when I was born, they couldn't take chances that I would get this condition from her. Do you follow me?"

"I think so. You were lucky."

"I was very special to them. A miracle, my father always reminded me after he drank a bottle of vodka. But, do you know, after those initial minutes of life, babies used to be kept apart from their mothers throughout their first few days in the Soviet Union? Fathers had to be even more patient. They weren't allowed in the hospital at all. My father heard the good news from the hospital bureaucrat on the first day. On the second, my mother smuggled a message out with a cleaner, giving him a little more information about how I was doing. Then on the third, he couldn't wait any more. He climbed up a fire escape just to get closer, and my mother held me up to the window. And that was all he needed."

I considered it for a while. I guessed she was talking about being rhesus negative, but I didn't really know what this meant. I'd never known my blood type my whole life.

"I thought it was pretty crazy how we had to have all those medical tests before we came here. Still couldn't name the blood running through my veins, actually – but at least it's written somewhere on my official documents for Japan. Maybe that's reassuring?"

"Well at least now you see why it's important. And it'll probably be worth it for *that American* and Michael, anyway," Nadya added.

"It still seems like an odd obsession to me. It's like Sergo told me: the similarities he notices in Japan. An arch capitalist country run by socialist forms and etiquette."

"Is that what they say?" she asked. "Well maybe that's right, and maybe it's just something you'll never get."

We said nothing more. The cold, grey dawn filtered down from Shuetsu-san. It seeped through the mountain canopy, ran down the

279

tracks, skirted the drops of the Matsugawa. And as it butted up against the blinds in the room, I awoke, almost catching the snake of dull light inching through the slats, lapping over me, leaving me chilled. In the dark, the kotatsu still burned.

44

A day passed. I called on Martin's place, while Nadya waited in the car, on our way shopping. In the evening I dropped by again, on my own this time. Perhaps more in hope than anything else, I loitered on the balcony, leaning against the railing like Akiko had, before the few brief moments when she'd taken on a name for me. As always in Takada, my gaze drifted upwards, back along the river, over the silhouette of the zoo, vaulting beyond the outcrop where Brian's flat perched, past the station, then the raised expressway, to the mountains.

I waited five, then ten and fifteen minutes. The police had already acquired a key from the landlord. They'd found nothing, I assumed. Now the flat was locked again. I gave up and went home to my own place for the first time in a couple of days, spending a miserable night alone. Strangely, it was only now that the guilt was really setting in. I was the one who was responsible for the whole outcry. Sure, I hadn't been the one glancing at Martin in mockery, leaning in to whisper trickles of humiliation in his ear. But I was the one who had quietly put him in front of the ringleaders. I'd kept Martin in place, positioned him in all his ludicrousness for others to take down. I'd been there at his side, or rather just behind, over his shoulder, but in full view of others, orchestrating his shame.

Just as I'd slyly manoeuvred him around in other people's estimation, when we were still teenagers, or going back further, humbled the child in others, when we all were children. Perhaps because I had always felt a sense of calm, confident in being an influential part of the events in any setting – like the backdrop of the seasons to each scene – I had never quite set myself up for a fall. I'd never given anyone the chance to take me down from a comfortable position perched within time. I'd always been happy to wait patiently and prod at others to abase themselves in their hurry to move on; their need to move beyond the transitory.

Perhaps I despised the ambition – as if any attempt to develop, put on an act, or even genuinely improve oneself, was something to be reviled, and should cause the person to be shunned. I'd done it before, and in demeaning Martin as he tried on this new identity of a mountain man of the world, I was more responsible for Ahab's broken nose than Martin himself. Two men, one experienced, the other just beginning, both carving their new identity from the face of Shuetsu-san.

And then there was Michael, his looks ruined by the great slash running from the edge of his eye to his jawbone. Well, if I enjoyed seeing others get their comeuppance, mine had come at last, and I felt nauseous.

45

The next morning, after phoning in sick to school, I slept in. It was Monday, 9.30am, and I was woken by the telephone. It was Nadya. She had either been crying, or was about to cry.

"William, I've been sent home from work. I'm sitting here with a letter in my hand which tells me I will be moving this week to a branch of the company in Nagoya. They need me to work down there for a few months due to staff shortage. They want me to clear out my flat over the next two days, and a van will drive me and my possessions to the new city. So, I think it is the last time we'll see each other for a while."

"Okay, we'll work this out," I told her. "They can't do this so quickly. Let's speak to them..."

"Will you forget about 'how things should work'," Nadya burst out. "Of course they shouldn't be able to push me around. But we both know it's nothing to do with that. And this is the way they handle it. I can't really complain."

"Nagoya is only a couple of hours away," I said. "We'll see each at the weekend. It'll be fun getting out of this pissy little place, seeing big city Japan. We'll make it work."

"It's too late..."

***

As it turned out, Nadya wasn't going to Nagoya, anyway. She couldn't fly to Kiev, her own capital. But she would be flying to Russia. From there she would catch an overnight train, then a bus to get home to Donetsk. She'd already bought an open return when she went home at Christmas, she explained. She'd had that in her back pocket all along.

And she needed to be home with her parents now, with the situation in Ukraine at a deadlock; a frozen truce, but with mobilised soldiers on both sides, and a ribbon of land separating them, running just kilometres from the edge of the city where she lived. In her 70s tower block she would join her parents watching the frozen conflict on Russian news, inertia repackaged as virile display like the old Cold War marches, now made into a deadly postmodern farce.

There was nothing to say for now. I couldn't believe she was going. In just a few days I'd gone from being closer to the centre of any world I'd lived in, to it spinning and shaking to disintegration, leaving me at its still point, immured in the mountains, somehow immune to the centrifugal force causing others to flee. I lay curled up in a ball on my floor level mattress. It was too painful even to think about where Martin was right now.

46

By evening, a knock at my door. Anyone who knew me also knew it was never locked when I was in. I couldn't be bothered to move. The handle slipped the catch – the door opened just a crack, and the ghastly mountain sun cutting a segment into the tatami flooring.

"Willu-san?"

It was Nick. And he'd brought the police with him. He was jumpy – not because he was in trouble, but because those spectral panties burned a hole in his pocket whenever the law was around.

"Willu-san, the police think that Martin may have gone into the hills. They want me to help them find where he is. I thought you could come to help me remember where we went the other day."

He looked sheepish. I realised he just needed an excuse for some moral support.

"Of course I'll come, Nick. If that's where he's gone, then we'll find him. There's a limit to the places he knows."

We got into the car with the two policemen. One was the quiet, grave officer who had pulled Nadya over. If he recognised me, he didn't betray a mote of this. The other officer was younger, looser, with a sarcastic cock to his eyebrow which suggested he knew exactly who Nick was. As we settled ourselves in the American-style sedan car, he took off his hat, turned in his seat and smiled hello to me.

"Just help," he said, raising his shoulders with a shrug and a little chuckle.

Soft evening sunshine poured in through the windows as we climbed. I let my neck tip back until I rested against the doily covering the headrest. The car twisted and turned, and my stomach along with it. As we crossed each bridge, the car slowed down and the younger policeman craned his head around to look back over his shoulder, a searching blankness in his eyes. No-one spoke between bridges, but as we pulled away each time, a quiet, quick matter-of-fact conversation took place between driver and passenger.

Nick looked at me.

"They keep saying they can't see, they can't see what they expect."

"Now, just what are they expecting to find?" I wondered aloud. We were soon approaching the bank where we'd had food with Nick; where Yui sat down next to Martin.

"It's here, tell them," I said, as we rolled over this one last towering concrete bridge and pulled into a layby. The clearing where we'd had our picnic, where we sat scattered around Nick, was just to our right, trees forming a semi-circle around it.

The policemen got out of the car, and stood outside talking for a moment, then opened our back doors in tandem, letting me and Nick out. I instinctively wandered over to the patch of grass, so lush until recently, now becoming dried out. I sat down in exactly the same place as I had just a few weeks before, the dark forest at my back. Since then it had become much hotter. The river, high until lately, fed by the slow melting snow, had dried to a trickle beneath the intensifying summer.

By the edges of the bank, one policeman was on all fours, while the other crouched down. They were examining something in the dust. Beyond them, rocks like clashes of cuttlefish lay sharply on each other just before the water. The younger man held up what appeared to be a band, dangling it before the calmer officer's eyes. Suddenly sun glinted off the band, and I realised it was a watch. I walked up to them, my steps gaining momentum as my breathing slowed to a stop. An attractive silver case, with a distinctive blue leather strap; now a smashed face. I recognised it as Martin's automatic watch; a gift from his father. I nodded to the police.

As they examined it, I saw the crown was pulled out, as if setting the correct time – stopping the movement, and freezing the timepiece in place. 7.15 on the Sunday, according to the date window.

Nick pointed this out to them, and the police conferred.

"They think it is likely to be 7.15am. Just a few hours after he went missing from the bar," he said. My mouth filled uncontrollably with saliva, then immediately dried out, mid-way through swallowing.

But where was Martin? Had he gone feral; taken off into the woods after abandoning the accessories of civilisation? Nick conferred with the police. A dawn fruit-picking Tex had tipped them off that a lone westerner had been seen walking confidently up the road to the mountains on the weekend. Although he hadn't worried about it at the time – crazy gaijin, he'd thought – he re-evaluated it after seeing a pseudo 'wanted' poster in town. The old guy had remembered more about the man – did he have blood down his t-shirt?.

"What do they think has happened?" I asked Nick. "I mean, is there some kind of implication with the blood, the watch?"

"They just say that he has been missing for two days now. Young men sometimes do this in Japanese society, they say. But with you expats – always so sociable, the schools tell them. It's just not so common."

I nodded slowly, almost enjoying the irony; we writhed next to each other, strange sea creatures without the feel of water on our fins. They called it sociability. I knew it was really a kind of desperation; the lonely inverse of this. It piqued my developing suspicion that Japanese humour had a profoundly dry strain running through it.

287

I thought of the young Japanese man in the news recently who carried the desiccated remains of his mother around in a backpack. What had the police thought of this, then? Sociability too, perhaps; a son and his mummy.

Then I noticed the grouping away to the side before the tree line. The recurrent standing stones of shrines, inscribed with their indecipherable ancient characters, bunched together in reverence, in their own forms of sociability.

I was standing, lost to these sardonic thoughts, when Nick gave a sharp cry, shaking me back to the hardness of the mountainside. I looked up. He was over by the road bridge, one foot on a kerbstone as he looked down, standing motionless. I ran over, arriving by his side just before the police, who had come with a stiff jog from the woodland.

Together, we all looked down. The river was dammed here, forcing the meagre flow through a channel, pressuring a shimmering curtain of waterfall to plunge down parallel to the wall of concrete, splashing at the base. We looked through the spray, then followed the course of the water, as it then flowed towards a gentle bend.

And as Nick pointed to the right side of the river, we saw it together: blood on the nearby rocks – a trace on the bleach-bone of the river bank, before the bounce had settled back in time. Then, bobbing like an apple, out of the alien branches; a body floated like a peach on the Pine.

47

The next morning I lay in bed. I was thinking of the Buddhist poem, written by a monk on the verge of death:

When you contemplate the waters

at day break, you can hear

the lotus blossom.

I had strained my ear, and had heard something of this petal settling on the water. I was in no mood for school, but Mrs Masada had called to say she would pick me up and take me to a special meeting I must attend. I wasn't sure what she knew of the weekend's events, but in the end I thought it easier not to battle. In any case, it would take my mind off things.

We arrived at 8 on the dot, and she walked me in to the deputy principal's office, where a tray of green tea was waiting. After couple of minutes Kocho sensei (he may or may not have been bestowed with a name at birth) came in, exuding an air of quiet calm, thankfully interrupting the excruciating small talk between myself and Masada. In any case, she needed to save her breath for the translation.

It turn out to be a mini performance hearing. Perfect. The lesson content was fine – I'd learned not to deviate fairly early on, so this was not a problem, at least. But rather, my attitude. The reserved Japanese were having problems with my own reserve. I needed to be more animated. More like Neil and Brian, Mrs Masada said. This last bit hurt. Neil the stiff in the suit and Brian a bipedal faux pas? I really must have been doing something wrong.

Did I understand? I was certainly taken aback. Everything I had thought about my ability to get along swimmingly was suddenly undermined. But yes, got it. Thanks.

"Willu sensei," Mrs Masada said as we stood outside the staff room, the darkly reflective wooden floor retreating back down the corridor. "These suggestions come from Mr Oni at the city board. He thought it was better if your Kocho sensei talked about it with you."

Oni again. Damn him.

"Very sensible, yes."

"You know, because we want to give children the best impression of learning a language and all its emotions. It needs to be positive only," she said.

"You see, the teachers at all schools have been watching you for a while. Sometimes people just don't understand so well what is necessary…" she tailed off.

All the heat they'd been heaping onto poor Neil, and in fact they really had designs on shaking me up. With the way these things worked, maybe they weren't even that worried about his immune system; it was just a ruse to get him behind a closed door and talk about me. Anything was possible.

There was one more thing.

"I think it's best I take the car back to the dealer today. It's been decided."

Both wings clipped, I'd lost my professional pride and my velour brown interior in one afternoon. The writing was on the wall.

As I left the room, I walked straight past Shimoida, who was standing to attention outside the door. I didn't even look at him, just flashed a bitter smile in his direction. I never really knew how far he was against me, until now.

48

In the end, Nadya left quickly. I caught the bus with her to Tokyo, saw her to the express train to the airport, and said goodbye as she stood by the door while the rows of seats turned about face, perfectly synchronised.

Perhaps because she was going back to a sputtering war in her home country, perhaps because she was guiltless, Nadya had been unaffected by Martin's death. I had spent a few days helping with the messy repatriation; a Byzantine process with a wedge of forms filled by seemingly unconnected questions, divergent lines of thought, unflinching interjections and then sheepish asides.

I wrote Martin's parents a hasty email, explaining there had been a terrible accident, glossing over the context leading up to it. I remembered what Nick had told me, after the night spent in Purgatory, then again when we looked down the river with the police and saw Martin's body. "No-one is to blame," he'd said. I wanted to say this to Martin's parents; even to believe it myself.

I'd met them a couple of times, when they pulled up outside our student house to pick Martin up. But I hardly knew them. I couldn't face the phone conversation with them, so I went with Nick to the police station and sat in a small plasterboard room on a conference call where we tried to explain what had happened, tried to translate the formal routine the police had to run through. The ferocious heat of the Japanese summer seemed to soak through the walls, though I was the only one sweating.

When it was over, when the tears ended, they were setting off on a plane to Tokyo. I would hang around for a miserable day in the great city, then meet them and bring them back to the mountain town.

Now, as Nadya pulled out of Shinjuku, bound for the airport, we waved. I'd never felt more alone, as the thousands of people pushed past in the vast, endlessly claustrophobic station. The armies of smart schoolchildren in navy blazers and the suited salarymen, some in their short sleeved suits; and me, poised between them on the axis of childhood and grim responsibility. I wistfully remembered arriving here just ten months before. Everything seemed just as strange now, but without the same wonder, the same possibility.

We'd promised to call, to email, to write. But for the next few days we both had horrible realities, inescapable situations to deal with; she, arriving to a changed landscape of her youth, and I putting my signature to the death certificate of my own.

***

Before I'd left for Tokyo, I had to rush in to school to collect my laptop, to send some more fate-laden emails. It was early evening, and the children had gone home. Down the far end of one crepuscular corridor a few muted footsteps were moving away from me. The garden in the central courtyard was a perfection of calm, insects buzzing lazily, frogs belching and chirruping from the pond.

I slid aside the grey metal door of the English room, the frosted glass giving no hint of life inside. But there he was, working by the light of the window, which was open to the mountains. The sun had departed, leaving a dull glow behind the peaks. Shimoida sensei was already composed, looking up at me as I entered.

"I heard about your tragedy," he said evenly. "As you say in English: news travels fast. Especially in the mountains."

I slid the door shut and sat down slowly opposite him. I nodded in a way which was intended to affect a certain gravity, but actually felt more like weariness.

"Yes, it's dreadful. I don't know how to even talk about it." I couldn't understand where the conversation was heading. Was he exultant?

"Then you should not talk," he said. "Though you must understand that others will have been discussing it. I am not talking about myself, of course. But this incident will make some people quite suspicious of you."

I smiled a big, wide, tired smile. Japanese sarcasm?

"More suspicious than people are already?"

"I am sorry, but yes," he replied. "Japanese people have long memories, I promise you. Long memories."

I was sure he was thinking of his parents, the hibakusha, abandoned by society for being a scorched walking monument to Japan's defeat. He didn't quite say it, though. His face again struck that agonised expression which would momentarily incapacitate him in English lessons. He hummed a little grunt to himself, and then relaxed once more.

"But I have learned that when you lose something – even if you are reminded of it every day – you can return from the land of the dead. You can come back. People in this area talk of 'exile in the mountains'. It means when you are not popular, or you find yourself outside of the normal lives of people for some reason. Even if you live side by side with them each day.

"When I first arrived in this town, I was welcomed. As a teacher I was respected. Then slowly people began to discover about where I came from, about the 'shame' of my parents. I was already a part of the school, accepted and necessary, but now bit by bit, I was shunned. Nothing major, just the subtlety of those strained daily relationships when you don't know what to say to each other. And so people find it easier to resort to formula, no longer meeting your eye with warmth.

"But I know you can come back from that exile if you find peace within yourself. Even if you did something wrong – even if you did nothing wrong. But you must return to what you know."

As he said this, Shimoida – so often lost in his own world – met my gaze directly. I wasn't sure what he knew, or even if he was referring to me at all. But I found myself paralysed, chilled all over except for the burning in my eyes as he stared into them.

"I actually understand what it is like to be under suspicion. To have to justify yourself to others," he said.

I didn't really need this sudden outpouring of emotion. It was coming about ten months too late. But I couldn't stop Shimoida sensei.

"Do you remember when you saw me and Mr Oni, or indeed just the other day when I was waiting outside Kocho sensei's room?"

I nodded.

"Every month I must meet with my masters, the education board, to explain the situation with my parents. They were badly injured in the atomic bomb blasts, you know. I must go and look after them every weekend. Sometimes I miss a little of a school day, because it is so far to travel; so much care to give helping them bathe, care for their injuries. Of course, they have other help too. But I feel I must go back to be their son each weekend. Now the education board know about this and are worried about the stigma for our school. They have said they will continue to monitor me. Maybe that is why you sometimes see me coming into or out of meetings with them, why I sometimes look a little distracted."

This time it was me silently welling up. I'd misjudged him all along, shaped Shimoida's situation around myself in my mind. It made me feel even worse about Martin.

"I feel guilty about it all," I said, sniffing pathetically. "I brought him here, even though I knew he might not be happy. In fact, I almost hoped he wouldn't be. I was fascinated by how he'd cope, and I wanted him to look up to me. I was the one who even invited him up the river with the bridges. And I definitely laughed at him when he looked so wretched, so bloody pitiful."

"I don't know what you are referring to exactly," Shimoida said. "But I understand anyway. And you should not worry any more. Everything changes, and everything comes back once more with another chance to enjoy, like the peach blossoms."

And he reached across the broad table, placing his hand over mine.

"Now, you must go home."

49

I'd visited Michael in hospital soon after he was taken in. There wasn't much to say. Now, his injury seemed like a strange anti-climax in the context of everything else; a strange footnote to the conception I once had of Michael as the flip side to my circumspection, the forever open personality in a land of gravity and protocol. Feeling this grim sense of duty myself, I decided to check in just before leaving for Tokyo.

When I got to his private room in a hospital right in the heart of Takada's citadel, I looked through the porthole window, and found Ahab there. But it didn't look like the man we knew. Gone was the knotted scarf, the bellbottoms and the white hat. He was dressed soberly. His nose was healing nicely, and his whole manner seemed changed, less affected. No longer the captain, or Ahab, or anything else, plain James looked up, saw me, and smiled, so I poked my head through the door, saying I'd give them a few minutes.

When I came back half an hour later, he was gone. All except for the famous hat, hanging on the end of the bed.

I stayed and talked to Michael just for a short time, checking he was OK. He was in good spirits, despite the cleft running from top to bottom of his face, still weeping a little though his dressing.

"I don't understand it – I didn't do anything to him," he said.

"I know," I replied; "It's the little man, hitting out at the world in general. You weren't to blame."

I apologised again for everything, but Michael seemed strangely calm. He said he'd been looking into a few opportunities for the next year teaching; thought he could go down to Kyoto, see a little more of the country. If Hanako wanted to visit, that was fine. If not, he wouldn't be coming back to the mountain town again.

I shook his hand, told him not to go to the old capital city too soon, that I'd catch up with him after getting back from the new one. As I left, I went to try on the hat for a joke, reaching out to pluck it from the bedstead, but my hand stopped short.

"This yours now?" I asked Michael.

"I guess someone has to wear it," he shrugged, smiling, then wincing beneath the dressing.

50

In Tokyo, our bus didn't leave until early the next morning. I stayed the night in a small guest house near Ueno Park. After a modest lunch of rice and tempura vegetables, I walked out past the makeshift shanty village constructed by the salarymen who had been made redundant. Some of them had been here more than ten years, squatting in the shadows along the path throughout Japan's 'lost decade' of financial stagnation; among the modern museums and the totem of the five tiered Chinese pagoda.

Then I walked south west down through the sprawling city towards the Imperial palace. In Kitanomaru Park, the grave moats and indifferent walls of the old Edo Castle gave a little comfort. Walls which suggested not the riches and fame of empire, but a blessed anonymity of withdrawal. They spoke to me, a respected nobody in this unknowable world, of people who longed for abstraction, but who had worldly duties to perform.

I looked in the still waters, thinking back to Shimoida's confession and understood for the first time something which I'd long struggled to frame properly in my mind. That it didn't really matter, this fact that some people cannot ever be reconciled. Entire cultures and views of life were just another aspect of this. Even these didn't necessarily need to be squared; but could run in parallel, never touching, whether in conflict or in true understanding. But always in a form of symbiosis, when viewed from the right perspective, with the right weight of passing events.

That you could in fact live with this, and flourish, alongside whatever had banished you to the mountains – given enough time, enough patience, enough endurance. It wasn't easy, but in the long run, every exile returns, to himself at least.

***

I would go back to Takada for a last few weeks, and after I had helped Martin's parents, I would go to city hall and tell them I wouldn't be extending my teaching contract. Michael was staying anyway, as were Neil and Brian, improbably. I would never know truly if I had any choice in the matter; but I knew I would be tainted in the mind of the town. I decided to gallantly pull back. I would sit in the teacher's room in the last days at my school and write Nadya a letter, a long letter. At first I would say I was sorry, and ask only about her; her family and life in Ukraine.

And after she replied, when I had a moment of happiness to spare, I would send another one, explaining that I had grown up. That if I went back to the western world, I would be leaving something of myself here, high in the mountains of Takada, an outgrown offering, like at a roadside shrine. A little for her, a little for Martin; perhaps even a little for Ahab.

A little for the childhood I had finally lost, in the water, by the canopy of trees, now the cherry blossoms had waned, and the peaches had started to fall from the branches of the mountain town.

*****

Tom Hughes has worked in journalism, marketing and copywriting. He lives in West Sussex.

Please leave a review on this book's Amazon page.

21293789R00166

Printed in Great Britain
by Amazon